SHADOW OF THE ROCK

THOMAS MOGFORD

BLOOMSBURY

LONDON · NEW DELHI · NEW YORK · SYDNEY

First published in Great Britain 2012

Bloomsbury Publishing Plc
50 Bedford Square
London WC1B 3DP

www.bloomsbury.com

Bloomsbury Publishing, London, New Delhi, New York and Sydney

A CIP catalogue record for this book is available from the British Library

ISBN 978 1 4088 2416 0

10 9 8 7 6 5 4 3 2 1

Typeset by Hewer Text UK Ltd, Edinburgh
Printed in Great Britain by Clays Ltd, St Ives plc

MIX
Paper from
responsible sources
FSC® C018072

For Ali Rea

There is shadow under this red rock,
(Come in under the shadow of this red rock),
And I will show you something different from either
Your shadow at morning striding behind you
Or your shadow at evening rising to meet you;
I will show you fear in a handful of dust.

T. S. Eliot, *The Waste Land*

The girl gasps as his fingernails rake the soft skin of her inner thigh. She reaches for the whisky bottle and takes a long slow drink, clear brown liquid spilling down her lips and chin. She passes the bottle to the man beside her; he screws it back into the corpuscular imprint it has formed in the sand.

Across the Strait of Gibraltar, just a few miles distant, the lights of Europe flicker, losing their strength to the dawn. The girl manoeuvres herself onto all fours, facing out to sea as the man kneels behind to hoist her thin dress to the small of her back. The first glow of the sun starts to redden the Straits; this, and the electricity spreading up the girl's spine, convince her, ever super-stitious, that her decisions must be right, that today's actions will be vindicated.

Warm water laps at the girl's splayed hands. The tide is coming in; she pushes herself back and forth onto the man's strong extended fingers, grinding her knees down into the sand, watch-ing the European shoreline lights vanish as the sun unsticks bloodily from the mire.

The man reaches forward, easing down the straps of her dress, stroking a shoulder blade. Her head lolls, hanks of dark hair hanging over multi-pierced ears. Out to sea, the morning breeze gusts on the water, drowning out the break of the waves.

The girl sucks in a sudden breath. She feels a sharp, chilly sting on the side of her neck, as though more whisky has dripped down, or some insect or jellyfish has been brought in by the tide. She tries to exhale but the breath will not come. Lifting a hand to

I

her neck, she senses the warmth between her thighs matched by a thick, sticky gush, as a high-pitched whine distinguishes itself above the waves, like a mosquito, the girl thinks dreamily, or a punctured lilo held to the ear.

Her elbow collapses, face slapping down hard onto wet sand. Rich red pools in the film of water, turning to pink before it drains away. The girl sees his shadow darken the sky above, then feels something spatter her cheek. The spittle clings to her eye socket, quivering with the last spasms of her body. Somewhere behind, a call to prayer rings out, marking the start of another Tangiers morning.

PART ONE

Gibraltar

I

Spike Sanguinetti stared across the water at the shimmering lights of Africa. A breeze was whipping in off the Straits; he held his cheek to it, testing for the dry heat of a Saharan southerly. Instead came the same moisture-laden levanter. There would be no sun in Gibraltar tomorrow.

He turned back towards Main Street. Cobblestone lanes that a few hours earlier had been jostling with tourists were now deserted – safely back aboard their cruise ships, or cloistered over the Spanish border in the cheaper *pensiones* of La Línea de la Concepción. The grilles of the duty-free shops were down, wooden pub tables tipped on their sides, gleaming in the lamp-light from closing-time scrub-downs but failing to dry in the humidity. Spike pulled his tie free, folding it into his suit pocket. Then he turned off Main Street and entered the steep-rising maze of the Old Town.

The ancient, crumbling houses clung precariously to the skirts of the Rock. Spike climbed past them, lulled by the routine, into backstreets and alleyways too tight to permit traffic. The Church of the Sacred Heart gave a solitary toll, while high on the Upper Rock, mist was muting the floodlights, lending a yellow sodium glow to the residential buildings below.

Spike stopped as he entered Chicardo's Passage, suddenly alert. Twenty metres ahead, silhouetted in the spectral light, stood a figure. Thickset, with a man's broad shoulders, standing directly in front of his house. Spike watched, heart quickening, as the figure took a silent step forward, then tested the door handle.

'Hey!' Spike called out.

Flinching at Spike's voice, the man turned and launched into a heavy-footed sprint. Spike waited until the figure had reached the end of Chicardo's Passage, then doubled back the way he had come in, pacing himself for the climb ahead.

Tank Ramp, Bedlam Court, Devil's Tower Road: Gibraltar street names were the hallmarks of its bloodstained past. After crossing a narrow passageway, Spike ran up a high-walled set of steps. A fig tree had seeded itself in the ruins of an old victualling yard; he caught a hint of mustiness in the scented leaves and raised a hand to the branches, sending a large grey ape bounding away into the darkness.

Tongues of fog licked at Spike's face as he burst onto Castle Road, the last demarcation before the Rock became too sheer to colonise. Cars and scooters were parked tightly on the cramped pavements; he zigzagged between them, stopping at the point where Fraser's Ramp met the road. Head resting against damp concrete, he waited, allowing his breath to steady. The levanter swept through the Rock scrub above. More low cloud drifted past floodlights. It was then that he heard the noise.

A soft scrape of shoes on flagstones, followed by a coarse, asthmatic panting. Spike edged closer, stopping as the squat dark figure appeared on the road, chest heaving, hands on thighs. As soon as the man straightened up, Spike stepped out of the shadows and grabbed his arm.

A dusty old Fiat was parked ahead on the pavement; Spike slammed the man against it, pinning his thick neck down onto the sloping rear window. In the half-light, he made out pouchy cheeks and round, gold-rimmed spectacles. 'Solomon?' he said.

2

Solomon Hassan leaned against the passenger door of the Fiat, arms by his sides, staring down at the pavement. He wore a pinstripe suit, the right trouser leg torn and the white shirt stained. His black hair was wet with grease or sweat, a tuft at the back sticking up.

'Why did you run?'

'It was dark,' Solomon replied, speaking English in the same lilting accent as Spike. 'I wasn't sure I had the right house.'

A light flashed on opposite, and Solomon raised his head. His small, circular glasses were unhooked from one ear; he reached up to straighten them, hands shaking. 'I need your help, Spike.'

The sash window across the road began rattling up, so Spike turned and walked quickly down Fraser's Ramp, Solomon following behind. They came into Chicardo's Passage by the opposite way. After unlocking the front door, Spike ushered Solomon into the hallway, then through the bead curtain into the kitchen. 'Keep the noise down.'

General Ironside gave a low growl as Solomon passed. Spike raised an admonitory finger at the dog basket, then clicked through the bead curtain himself.

Solomon was standing by the pine kitchen table, head bowed, hands clasped behind back. Beneath the hanging bayonet bulb, Spike could see him more clearly. He was still as short as in their schooldays, but his chest was stockier, pectoral muscles bulging as though from assiduous gym time. The stains on his shirt were of a rusty-brown colour, the tear in his pinstripe trousers just

7

below the knee, giving him the air of a smartly dressed postman savaged on his round. Solomon held himself there, letting Spike's eyes range over him, absent-mindedly picking at his left thumb with the sharp nail of a forefinger. The wooden wall clock ticked; Spike spread his jacket over the back of a chair and sat down heavily.

'Got anything to drink?' Solomon whispered.

'Nothing grown-up.'

'*Agua de beber?*' Solomon added, switching to *yanito*, the patois of Spanish, Genoese, English and Hebrew used by native Gibraltarians.

'*Por bashe.*'

Solomon plodded across the buckling cork-tile floor. A tumbler had been upturned by the sink, alongside a pharmacy-shelf windowsill of pills; he filled it and drank, stubbly cheeks puffing. After blinking over at Spike, as though momentarily puzzled as to who he was, he drew out a chair and sat. 'It's all a misunderstanding,' he said, mopping his brow with his suit sleeve. 'I'm in trouble, Spike.'

'Financial problems?'

Behind Solomon's glasses the whites of his eyes were striated with red, like two semi-precious stones. 'Murder.'

Spike shifted forward in his seat, reassessing the dark stains on Solomon's shirt.

'It's just tomato juice, Spike,' Solomon said. '*Los tomates.*' He bunched up his shirt tail, revealing a braille of dried seeds. 'Eight hours in the back of a lorry . . .' His eyes focused on a knot on the pinewood table, as though he were viewing images within. 'There was this girl.'

Spike raised a dark eyebrow.

'It was three days ago,' he said. 'Feels like more.' He straightened up a little, chest puffing. 'I'm based in Tangiers now: I imagine you've heard. She was new in town. We went to a bar on the beach, took our drinks down to the shore, sat for a while, watched the sunset. Then she leans in and kisses me.' Solomon scratched again at his thumb; Spike saw a drop of blood ooze from the pink, porous scar tissue around the nail. 'So I pull away. I'm only meant to be showing her round, plus she's crazy this girl, tattoos, piercings, the lot. She grins at me: "You know," she says, "I only kissed you because you're such" . . . *Empollón* was the word she used.'

'A nerd,' Spike translated, almost suppressing a smile. 'Spanish?'

'My boss's Spanish stepdaughter. You can see why I didn't want to start anything with her.' Solomon sat back, eyes concealed by two suns of light reflecting from his glasses. 'I get to my feet. It's not completely dark, plus she's no kid. So I left her there, Spike. On the beach.'

'Anyone see you go?'

'Even if they did, you'd never find them. No one in Tangiers talks to the police.'

'But someone saw you come home.'

Solomon shook his head.

'CCTV?'

'Unlikely. It's more in rural, isolated areas. So I go up to my flat. Watch a football game . . .'

'Since when do you like football?'

'There's not a lot to do in Tangiers. Next morning I go into work. When I get home there's a police car outside my apartment block.'

'How did they find you?'

'I used my card in the bar.' Solomon worked a finger beneath his spectacles, itching at his left eyeball. 'A policeman gets out: "Are you Solomon Hassan?" et cetera. He can see I'm uneasy so he goes back to his car. On the passenger seat there's an envelope of black-and-white photos. The top one . . .' Solomon withdrew his finger and ran it beneath his nostrils, laying a gleaming snail trail on the hairy knuckle. 'She was lying on her back, head against the sand. Her eyes were all milky . . . like an old fish. And her neck

– the mark was so small, Spike, like a tiny dash in biro. There was no blood. I asked if she was sleeping and the policeman said the tide had come in and washed the blood away.'

'You went with him?'

'Of course. To the station on the Avenue d'Espagne. Full of Moroccans in djellabas, rocking on their hunkers. He took me into a back room. Stacks of papers everywhere. I told him what I told you. The tape wasn't working so I told him again. Then he let me go.'

'What language?'

'English . . . French at the start.'

'You speak French now?'

'Like I said, Spike, there's not much to do in Tangiers. So I lie awake that night. The Tangiers police . . . they're like animals. If they can place you anywhere near a crime, that's it, they make the arrest, get the stats up. Plus for me . . .'

'What?'

Grinning sourly, Solomon rubbed his finger up and down the bridge of his nose. 'Jews are hardly flavour of the month in Morocco. The next morning I look out onto the street. A police jeep. Same guy as before but talking to two meatheads with sub-machine guns. The doorbell starts to ring; I grab my passport and run down the service stairs. I assume there'll be police on that side of the building, but there aren't, so I catch a *petit taxi* to the harbour.'

'Not stopped by immigration?'

'There's a Gibraltarian who works the port. Slip him enough euros and he'll get you over.'

'You mean you crossed illegally?'

'In the back of a lorry. Six hours before the catamaran even left. The waves . . . felt like my belly was being sucked dry. We got to Gib and the lorry rolled off. Let me out at Casemates. Imagine how it felt to see the Rock again.'

'There was too much cloud,' Spike said.

'Sorry?'

'There was too much levanter cloud to see the Rock.' Spike stroked his jaw thoughtfully. 'Why not go to your mother's?'

'You crazy? She'd have a heart attack. No, I think, my old pal, Spike Sanguinetti, he's a lawyer. I remembered where you lived. Or thought I did.'

'I'm a tax specialist, Solomon.'

'You're a friend,' Solomon said, holding out his shaky palms in supplication.

'You shouldn't have run.'

Solomon snapped closed one hand. 'And *you* don't know Tangiers.'

Spike looked over to the wall, at his father's blurry watercolours. All showed the Rock: from below, from the side, from above with HMS *Victory* towing in Nelson's body, pickled in a barrel of cheap Spanish brandy. He got to his feet. 'I'm going upstairs. When I come back down, you may be gone. You may even have crossed the border to Spain. I doubt the Moroccan authorities will have had time yet to alert immigration. Or,' Spike added, turning from the curtain, 'you may still be here. If you are, this is what happens. You'll surrender your passport and I'll make a call to Jessica Navarro. She'll drive you to prison where you'll be remanded overnight. After that, a criminal barrister will come and find you.'

Spike pushed through the beads to find General Ironside asleep in his basket. He creaked upstairs; from outside his father's door he heard erratic, laboured breathing.

The tap in Spike's sink snarled like an ape. He splashed his face and tasted salt. The house's plumbing was so antiquated that seawater still seeped into the mains.

Downstairs, Solomon was standing by the sideboard, examining a silver photo frame. 'My mother always said your father was the most handsome man on the Rock.' He held the picture out; Spike looked down at the tall, laughing man in his elegant waistcoat and sombre tails. Even with the fading of time, Rufus Sanguinetti's piercing blue eyes stared back fearlessly: northern Italian blood, as he still liked to insist. Beside him, Spike's mother – a foot shorter even in heels – gazed up quizzically, as though unsure of what was to come, but guessing it would at least be amusing. Her left hand held a small bouquet of ivory roses, contrasting with the dark, delicate features of her face.

'You look a lot like him,' Solomon said.

Spike replaced the photo on the sideboard. When he looked back, Solomon had the crumpled purple rectangle of a British Gibraltar passport in one hand.

'All right,' Spike said, taking it. 'Let's get this done.'

3

By 7 a.m., Spike was at his desk. The ceiling fan whirred soporifically above as he picked up a remote, switched off the fan, then picked up another and turned on his iPod speakers, feeling the humidity rise as the first arpeggios of Caprice No. 5 filtered through. Spike could do ten minutes of music with no fan, ten minutes of fan with no music, but combining the two created a discord that made work impossible.

The tax statute had downloaded; Spike checked an appendix, fountain pen in hand. Ahead, a pair of high French windows gave onto a paved patio. A date palm had centuries ago cracked through its flagstones to provide shade, not that that were needed today – the levanter breeze had drawn in a blanket of thick, humid cloud, shrouding the entire peninsula of Gibraltar, while out in the Straits, the sunshine blazed.

Spike heard the distant scrape of chair legs on parquet. The offices of Galliano & Sanguinetti had once been a grace-and-favour residence for various Royal Navy sea lords. Spike liked how their conversion reflected Gibraltar's shift from military stronghold to financial centre. Liked that more than the work.

A rap came from the door. 'Keep it on, keep it on,' Peter Galliano said as Spike stretched for a remote control. 'Anything to distract from this *pipando* closeness.' He sank down into the leather armchair opposite Spike's desk. 'Your fellow Genoese?'

Spike nodded.

'Didn't he sell his soul to the Devil?'

'Paganini had Marfan syndrome,' Spike said. 'A rare disorder of the connective tissue.'

'Sounds like the Devil's music to me,' Galliano replied, still arranging his bulky frame in the armchair. 'Anyway, speaking of crafty Devils . . .'

'The Uzbeks?'

'Back in town and meaning business.' Galliano shunted forward in his seat. He was wearing his three-piece houndstooth suit today, a sign of an important lunch. There was even a spotted kerchief in the breast pocket, which he took out to dab at his fleshy brow. '*Jodido* levanter,' he murmured.

Spike switched the music for the ceiling fan, the rush of air making the documents on his desk tremble.

'Why you won't let me buy you an air-conditioning unit,' Galliano said, 'I shall never . . .'

Spike let him finish, waiting for the double blink that signified his mind was focused. 'The key,' Spike began, 'is to impress on them that Gibraltar's ten per cent headline rate is for keeps. Other tax havens may give better short-term deals, but their fiscal future is uncertain. Gib will still be here, same as before. Minor expenditure for major security.'

'Safe as the Rock of Gibraltar?'

'You got it.'

'And the sovereignty issue?'

'There's a new Foreign Office report out. Print it off.'

Galliano waved a pudgy palm. 'Too much detail looks like weakness to your Uzbekistani.'

'Where are you planning to take them?'

'I thought the Eliott.'

'There's always that new vodka bar in Ocean Village.'

'*Ochen horosho.*' Galliano prised himself up using both armrests. With one hand he smoothed down the goatee beard he'd grown in an attempt to reclaim a long-lost jawline. In the three years since he and Spike had started up on their own

– escaping the open-plan uniformity of Ruggles & Mistry, their previous employer – Galliano had had to make numerous adjustments to his wardrobe. Lunching for victory, he called it. 'Still on that e-gaming SPV?' he asked, seeing the statute open on Spike's laptop.

'Yes, but for a different company.'

He gave Spike a sideways bear hug, wafting cologne. 'Goods and services, young Sanguinetti,' he said, wheezing at the effort. 'A few more years of this and think of all the goods and services. Your own palazzo in Genoa. Yo-Yo Ma playing Paganini at your dinner parties . . .' He was still muttering as he picked up his briefcase and huffed into the entrance hall. Spike heard him curse as he met the butterfly-house humidity outside, then pause to light a Silk Cut Ultra as the doors clicked closed behind him.

Spike switched the music back on. On his desk sat a more recent photograph of his mother. He stared at her, embarrassed to be startled yet again by her beauty. He tried to catch her eye, but she was gazing out to sea, dark glossy hair tied back in a ponytail, snapped unawares on a family holiday a lifetime ago.

The intercom buzzed. 'I know,' Spike said, 'goods and services . . .'

Instead of Galliano's jocular tones came a brusque female voice. 'Mr Sanguinetti?'

'*Sí.*'

'It's Margo Hassan. Solomon's mother.'

Spike's finger hovered over the button. He depressed it and switched off the music for good.

4

Spike indicated the leather armchair Galliano had just vacated.

'I'd rather not,' Margo Hassan replied curtly, 'you'll probably bill me.' She stood with her legs apart on the frayed Moroccan rug that covered the office parquet. Above her faded black jeans, a scooped green top revealed a seamed and sun-weathered neck.

Spike leaned against the panelled wall, arms crossed. He remembered Mrs Hassan from his schooldays, waiting for Solomon by the gates. She'd always been a favourite with the older boys – the dyed brown hair was shorter but her sharp eyes and red lipstick remained the same. Spike had seen her around from time to time, in the way the thirty-odd thousand residents of Gibraltar did as they went about their business: a nod here, a smile there; too much courtesy and you'd never make it past your front door.

'I've seen him,' Margo Hassan said.

'I told him to keep it quiet.'

'The warder told a friend and that friend told me.' Her lower lip began to quiver, sending a wave of irritation through Spike. '*Patitu*,' she murmured. 'I'm a bit . . . May I?'

'Of course.'

They both sat down, Margo Hassan neat and bird-like in the armchair. Spike pointed behind him to a shelf of leather-bound spines. 'Tax books, Mrs Hassan. I haven't taken a criminal case in years.'

'He wants you.'

'Drew Stanford-Trench read law at Durham.'

'Solomon says lawyers only practise in Gib if they can't make it elsewhere.'

'I'm here.'

'That's different.'

'How?'

Margo glanced at the portrait on Spike's desk, giving him another stab of irritation.

'He says Stanford-Trench drinks.'

'This is Gibraltar, Mrs Hassan.'

'That he doesn't know about extradition treaties.'

'Nor do I.' Spike stared at her across the desk. He had only the vaguest memories of Mr Hassan, a short, bearded man in a skullcap who used to carry Solomon through the streets on his shoulders. He'd left Gibraltar when Solomon was still young. Just cleared out one morning – the talk was he'd wound up in Tel Aviv with a new family.

'Please,' Mrs Hassan said. 'I know you two weren't the greatest of friends at school. But this is Solomon we're talking about. Solly. He can be pushy, ambitious. But *this*?' Her voice caught as she traced four red nails across a fold of her neck. 'He doesn't even know *how* to lie. As a boy, I'd say, Do the right thing when you go to a friend's house – even if you don't like the food, say you do. But he never could.'

Spike remembered that attitude crucifying Solomon in the playground. 'Mrs Hassan,' he said, 'there are more lawyers per capita in Gibraltar than in any other town on earth. If your son doesn't like Drew Stanford-Trench, I can find him someone else.'

'I want you.' She stalled, casting about. 'You ... won that scholarship.'

The clouds parted behind the French windows, sending a contre-jour sunbeam onto Margo Hassan's face. Spike took in the notches around her mouth, the translucency of her skin as it hung at a slight remove from her skull. The sky reclaimed the sun and her face darkened. 'He won't last five minutes,' she said.

'I'm sorry?'

'As a Sephardi. In a Tangiers jail. Not five minutes.' She rose from her armchair, still staring over at Spike. 'It's always come so easily to you, hasn't it?'

'What has?'

'I mean . . . just *look* at you.'

'I'll walk you out,' Spike said, but she was already in the hall-way, pushing through the doors onto the street.

5

The Union Jack flapped impatiently from the portico of the Convent, the pretty pink building that was home to the governor of Gibraltar. Opposite, the beer garden of the Angry Friar pub was bustling with punters: tax-free shoppers, baffled Japanese, small-time Costa crims leafing through the day's *Sun*. The pub was named after the Brotherhood of Franciscans evicted from their monastery – *convento* in Spanish – to make way for the British gubernatorial household, after Spain had lost Gibraltar in 1704. A group of shirtless youths was marching towards it, tattooed forearms swinging in formation. Their leader – best man, probably – glanced up at the sky, frowning at Gibraltar's curious subtropical microclimate before joining in with his friends' football chant.

Spike shouldered past them, the sharp iron railings of the law courts to his right, a gravel pathway running between beds of orange orchids towards a knot of chain-smoking locals awaiting their turn in the dock. The crowds grew denser; interspersed with the British high-street brands were independent Gibraltarian shops: VAT-free drink and fags, gold, perfume, electrical equipment. One name, Booze & Co., caught the tone nicely. Inside, Spike saw the shopkeeper heaping litres of Gordon's and cartons of Winstons into the greedy arms of expats. They'd be back over the Spanish border by evening, driving their booty down to Sotogrande for a weekend pool party. A leather-faced Brit looked Spike up and down. He stared back and she winked a lazy, turquoise-lidded eye.

Behind the Horseshoe pub, pigeons pecked busily at a heap of carroty vomit. A herring gull waddled over to chase them from their savoury syllabub. As Spike climbed higher, the tourist droves began to thin and the urban beautification so beloved of the Gibraltar government – brass plaques, hanging baskets, ceremonial cannons – ceded to flaking stucco and unionist graffiti. *With Britain till death do us part* was daubed on one block of houses; *We shall fight to the last but never surrender*, a legacy of the constant threat that British sovereignty of Gibraltar be shared with Spain.

Above lay Chicardo's and home; Spike turned left, skirting over Main Street, heading for the easternmost edge of the Old Town. Casemates Square sprawled below, the hub of Gibraltar, formerly a soldiers' barracks and site of public executions, now full of karaoke bars and fish'n'chip stalls. Beyond spread the frontier traffic of Winston Churchill Avenue, queues of overheating cars tooting in frustration as the Spanish border officials deliberately slowed them down: the unnecessary search of the spare-tyre axle, the drawn-out phone call to check a valid EU passport. Gib was like a wart to the Spanish. Pull the noose tight enough and eventually it would drop off.

On the corner of Hospital Hill, Spike saw a group of kids, probable truants from the Sacred Heart Middle School. 'Check it,' the youngest one said, pointing up at the cemetery. '*Macaco.*'

Spike looked up to where a female ape perched on a headstone. Clinging to its underside was a fluffy brown ball with eyes, its fur darker than the light-grey pelt of its mother. Appropriate insulation for the snows of the Atlas Mountains in Morocco, where the apes were said to have originated, less suitable here. The mother gave a hiss, flashing yellow sabre-tooth fangs. Patrolling the unweeded graveyard below was a stocky male, moving on all fours with a swagger that would have impressed the stag parties down on Main Street. Its naked pink face and absence of tail gave it a disconcertingly human quality. It made a lunge for the female, which bounded off the headstone onto a wall – baby still hanging – before thumping down onto the roof of a transit van.

'*Muncho* cool,' the youngest kid said. Time for a cull, Spike thought to himself as he walked away – when the ape colonies grew too large and started encroaching to the Old Town, the government would send in the sharpshooters with silencers.

Ahead rose the Moorish Castle, dominated by the Tower of Homage, built by the Moors when they'd captured Gibraltar in AD 711. They'd held it until the reconquest, seven centuries later, and their leader's name had stuck, *Jebel Tariq* – Mountain of Tariq – had stuck, morphing over time to Gibraltar. Beneath the stone battlements ran dark, sweaty stains where the Moors had poured boiling pitch onto besieging Spaniards. Spike stared up at them, marvelling as ever at their longevity, as he came into Upper Castle Gully. Then he saw Jessica Navarro standing by her Royal Gibraltar Police van.

6

Jessica took off her chequered hat, pinioning it beneath her short-sleeved white shirt as Spike stooped to kiss her cheek. He still had a hand on her shoulder as she drew away; she hesitated, then moved back in for the second peck.

'How's your schedule fixed?' Spike said.

'Pickpocket. Due in the Mags at half two.'

'Looked pretty busy down there.'

'Thought you'd given all that up, Tax Man.'

They both turned, looking up at the Rock, at the gulls circling and squawking as they dipped in and out of a grey discus of cloud. 'Humid one today,' Spike said.

'*Muy mahugin.*'

Spike looked back. The smooth olive skin of Jessica's forehead betrayed no hint of sweat. Her chestnut hair was gathered in a silky knot, the better to fit beneath her police hat. 'So what do you think?' she asked, managing to hold Spike's eye. 'Guilty?'

'Solomon's a chartered accountant, Jess. He's capable of many things but I don't think murder's one of them.'

'People can change.'

'I'm glad you think so.'

She looked away. 'Maybe you're right. He's got that feel about him. Wrong place, wrong time.'

'How do you mean?'

She shrugged, breasts shifting beneath her black stab vest. 'He was hysterical when we brought him in. Freaking out in case he had to share his cell. But when we stuck him in solitary, he just sat there on the bunk and bowed his head. Like he was used to life doing him over. Expected it.'

'What's the commissioner's take?'

'He's waiting to hear from you. Seems we all are.' She stared up again. 'You know,' she said, 'when I saw your number come up, I assumed you actually wanted to talk.'

'I've been busy.'

He watched her beautiful eyes narrow with anger. 'Don't work too hard,' she said. 'All that paper-pushing is ageing you.' She half reached up to touch his face, then let her hand fall as a clank came from above. The portcullis door of Her Majesty's Prison opened to reveal a junior warder accompanied by a sullen, hand-cuffed youth in a tracksuit.

Spike walked Jessica up the slope. She signed a clipboard, escorting the pickpocket back down to her van as Spike and the warder continued on to the entrance, the fifteen-yard passage that represented the thickness of the castle's thousand-year-old walls. There'd been attempts to move the prison wholesale to a shiny new facility on the other side of town. It still hadn't happened.

Before going inside, Spike turned to see Jessica sharing a joke with her ward. Then she slammed the double doors behind him.

7

Alan Gaggero stood up from the front desk. Behind him rose a bank of elderly CCTV monitors. Spread before him was the *Gibraltar Chronicle* crossword.

'Stuck?'

Gaggero grinned. His grey comb-over and kindly eyes were unchanged. 'What's it been now, Spike?' he said. 'Two years?'

'Three.'

'Three years,' Gaggero repeated as he ran Spike's briefcase through the scanner.

'Thought they were shutting this place down,' Spike said.

'Overspill.'

They headed in single file down the side stairs. 'How's your old man doing?' Gaggero asked.

'*Está haleto*. But he can still finish the crossword in ten minutes flat.'

'I'll have to up my game then.'

Gaggero jangled his key fob and unbolted the steel door. 'Back in a mo,' he said, leaving the door ajar.

Spike listened as Gaggero's rubber soles squeaked away down the corridor. The off-white walls of the interview room were windowless and the strip lights hummed. The air smelled of disinfectant and was as dank as might be expected in the deepest reaches of a medieval castle. A table was nailed to the lino, carved like a school desk with initials and incomplete slogans of protest. In the corner, a black CCTV camera peered from its bracket like an alien eye.

Once Gaggero's footsteps had faded, Spike walked over to the far wall. Leaning back against it, he took a tissue from his pocket and worked the two leaves of the material apart. He tore off a fingertip-sized piece, which he moistened with his tongue. After checking the door, he reached up and stuck the tissue to the CCTV lens. Then he returned to the table.

Tipping one of the chairs onto its side, he brought a brogue crashing down on the pivotal leg. With a few more kicks, the wood splintered. He propped the chair back up in front of the table, then went round to the other side and sat down.

His briefcase held a single-deck tape recorder, which he took out and positioned on the table. Moments later, the door opened fully and Solomon Hassan appeared, Alan Gaggero behind. 'You remember the form,' Gaggero said, gesturing at the wall buzzer beneath the camera.

Spike nodded.

'*Vale*,' Gaggero said. 'Enjoy.' He withdrew, sliding the bolt into place.

Solomon was back in his supplicatory position, head bowed, hands behind back. He wore prison denims now – belt-free trousers, coarse button shirt – and tatty flip-flops with, for some reason, a minute Brazilian flag on the straps. His skin was paler and his plump cheeks stubblier, like wintry copses seen from the air.

'Have a seat,' Spike said.

The chair leg gave way at once. Solomon let out a yelp, making a lunge for the table but toppling sideways onto the lino.

Spike moved round to his side. 'You all right there, Solly?'

Solomon lay on the floor in the foetal position, snapped chair beside him.

'Here, let me help. Have mine.' Spike hauled him up and brought his own chair round. Solomon sat down carefully, shaking his head.

'I'll perch,' Spike said, sitting on the table. 'So are they treating you OK?'

'I have a slop bucket in my cell.'

'Ouch.'

'And the guy next door keeps praying. I can't sleep.'

'It is called the Moorish Castle, Solomon. You didn't care for Drew Stanford-Trench, they tell me?'

'He was vague on extradition treaties.'

'Well, I'm briefed on those. Want to hear?'

'Yes.'

'There's good and bad news. The good is that you won't have to see Drew Stanford-Trench again.'

Solomon gave a nod.

'Nor me for that matter.'

Solomon wrinkled his nose as though confronted by a sudden stench.

'Because the bad news is that there's a new Order-in-Council, extending the Extradition Act 1870. Only passed at the start of the year, part of a broader deal made by the Gibraltar government. Trying to seem squeaky-clean to the EU – any fraudsters skip across the Straits, we get them back. But it cuts both ways. So if the Kingdom of Morocco requests the company of Mr Solomon Hassan, they need only say the word.'

'But I haven't done anything.'

'They just need a prima facie case.'

'They don't even have a proper justice system.'

'Oh, I hear Moroccan public defenders can be pretty good. Some of them even speak English.'

Solomon laid both hands on the table. His thumbs were criss-crossed with dark-flecked scabs. 'Why are you –'

'They've still got the death penalty in Morocco, you know that, Solly? Not used much, but in your case, a defenceless girl, a foreigner –'

'I'm innocent, Spike.'

'You ran.'

'I told you, as a Jew –'

'Where are the witnesses who saw you leave? Where's your alibi?' Spike dismounted and came round to Solomon's side. 'Let me tell you what I think,' he said. 'Stop me if I veer off track.' He crouched down to Solomon's level. 'You're on the beach, right? The sun is setting; it's romantic, almost.'

Solomon stared into the middle distance, picking at his thumbs. Spike leaned in closer. 'This girl's new in town, and she likes you, you can tell. You've had a few drinks, you're sitting on the sand, and then suddenly you realise. This is it. This is why you left Gibraltar. This is what you've been pumping iron for all those nights alone in your flat. So you lean across and kiss her. And it was that way round, wasn't it, Solly? But she just laughs. She doesn't say "Sorry" or "Can't we just be friends?" She just laughs in your face. And it all starts to come back. Solly the Wally. Simple Solly. Shoved around the playground by the younger boys. You thought you'd left all that behind, the big shot who went to Africa to make his fortune, but now you see that's how it's always going to be, and something inside you snaps. You smash your bottle of beer, or maybe you use something on the beach. You jab forward and suddenly she's not laughing any more. Stop me if I'm wrong, Solly.'

Solomon blinked behind his spectacles; Spike reached to the floor and picked up the broken chair leg. 'Take it,' he said, wrapping Solomon's thick fingers around the shaft. 'How does it feel? That weight in your hand. Is that how the knife felt?' Solomon's right fist gripped the chair leg, veins rising on the back like worm casts. 'She was laughing at you, Solly, and she's Spanish, and God knows, we Gibbos have all had enough of that. So you lunge at her, and now you're staring at a corpse, and something takes over, an instinct, and you're rolling her into the water, but she's heavy, you can't get her far, but the tide will come in, won't it, so you're running from the beach, slowing as you reach the coast road, then it's home safe to a football match, just to say you've

27

done something, and in the morning even you can't believe it, *did* you do it? Except the police turn up. They're all corrupt in Tangiers, who wouldn't run? And here we are.'

Solomon was trying to speak.

'Sorry?'

He shook his head, blinking.

'When did your father leave?' Spike said, moving in closer. There were flakes of dandruff in Solomon's hair, dazzling against the greasy blackness. 'Twenty years ago, was it? Left you and old Mother Hassan behind. She came to see me, Solly.'

Solomon's head turned a fraction. The red lines in the whites of his eyes were back.

'That's right,' Spike went on. 'Came to my office this morning, low-cut top, legs akimbo.'

Solomon's fist clenched more tightly around the chair leg.

'After your dad left, *ima* kept you close, didn't she? No one good enough for her boy. But you got away. Made it over the Straits, promised to send her money, got to Tangiers where no one was watching. Somewhere you could make a move on a girl. Somewhere you could punish a girl.'

Solomon's teeth gritted. The chair leg rose, angling towards Spike.

'Away from old *ima* nothing counts as much, so when a girl laughs at you, the one girl you thought might actually like you, you can shut her up and it won't matter at all.' At the periphery of his vision, Spike checked the dimensions of the room. 'Murders happen all the time in Tangiers, who's going to notice some Spanish *chochi* who drank too much and –'

There was a clatter as Solomon's grip slackened and the chair leg dropped to the ground. His head slumped down, two oily lines exuding from behind his spectacles. 'No,' he said. '*No.*'

Spike moved behind him, laying a hand on his shoulder, feeling the surprising tautness of the muscles. 'It's OK,' he said. 'I just had to check.'

As soon as Solomon's sobs subsided, Spike sat down on the table and hit 'record' on the tape recorder. 'Twenty-first of August, fifteen twenty hours,' he said into the speaker. 'Room 2, Moorish Castle Prison. First client interview.'

Solomon glanced up.

'Mr Hassan, why, in your opinion, is it unsafe for a Jew to be held in prison in Tangiers?'

'Is this –'

Spike nodded.

'But you –'

'Answer the question, please, Mr Hassan.'

Solomon took off his glasses, dabbing at the teardrops with his denim shirt. 'There was a home-made bomb. Six months ago. At a synagogue in Casablanca.' He sniffed moistly. 'The King rounded up all the Islamists. There've been reprisals in the prisons.'

'Presumably Jewish inmates are held in separate wings.'

'The attacks happen in the yard. In the canteen.'

'Is this documented?'

Solomon slid his glasses back on. The lenses were still mottled. 'The media still gets censored. But people know.'

'And you're a Sephardic Jew?'

Solomon nodded.

'Speak up, Mr Hassan. The machine doesn't register gestures.'

'Yes-I-am-a-Jew.'

Spike clicked off the tape as Solomon's lips peeled back. 'What the hell was *that*?'

'My peace of mind.'

'Your what?'

'If I'm going to represent you.'

There was fresh blood on Solomon's thumbs. He continued to pick at them, oblivious. Spike reached over to stop him and he snatched both his hands away, hiding them beneath the tabletop. 'So I won't have to go back to Tangiers?'

'We can try and stall them on the Jewish angle,' Spike said as he walked over to the wall buzzer, 'but no promises.'

After counting to ten, Spike peeled the flake of tissue from the camera lens. Thirty seconds later, the metal bolt began to slide.

'Find out the time of death,' Solomon said hurriedly as the door creaked open.

Spike looked round.

'The precise hour. Someone from that bar must have –'

'Twelve and a half minutes,' Gaggero said as he came in. 'You'll tell your old man that, won't –' Gaggero broke off, seeing the carcass of the chair on the ground.

'One too many halal burgers for Mr Hassan, I'm afraid,' Spike said, giving the chair back a prod with his shoe. 'It just went.'

Gaggero frowned, then tapped Solomon on the back. As Solomon rose, Spike thought he saw the ghost of a smile on his mouth. Maybe it was a grimace. 'The girl's name,' he said. 'It was Esperanza.'

Spike nodded, then put away the tape recorder and returned to the office.

Galliano was still out to lunch. Spike sat motionless at his desk until the harsh staccato notes of Caprice No. 9 reached their climax. Then he picked up the phone and placed a call to the court of assizes in Tangiers.

8

Spike watched the paintbrush swish back and forth: the cyan sea, the outline of a boat. A moment later, the Rock of Gibraltar began to loom from the centre of the canvas as Rufus's long thin fingers worked the brush, each tapering down to a dainty nail.

'It comes to eight pills a day,' Spike said, looking back down at his list. 'Four lots of two.'

Rufus began smudging the area beneath the Rock with his thumb, creating the impression of a dark, foreboding shadow cast over the Straits.

'Dad?'

Rufus winched up his head, frowning like a hermit disturbed.

'I've written down all the times.'

'Pills, pills, pills,' Rufus said. 'Pure buggery quackery.'

'The fridge is fully stocked, Dad. Any problems, just give me a call. Day or night.'

Rufus peered from behind his bifocals, blue eyes freakishly magnified. Silver hair curled onto his shoulders like the tendrils of the spider plants that grew upstairs in his study. 'It's you we should be worrying about, son.'

'Why's that?'

'Tangiers. Easy place to get entangled.'

'I'm just gathering evidence for an extradition hearing. Three nights, max.'

'City of Perfidy, Jean Genet called it.'

'I'll bet he did.'

Rufus laid down his paintbrush. 'I used to go there every month in the seventies. When the generalissimo had closed the border with Spain. Ferry to Tangiers, transfer, wait, ferry to Algeciras. Ten-hour round trip to go the best part of a mile. A man needs to watch his step. Could run into trouble like the Hassan boy.'

'I really wouldn't worry about it.'

'There's always baksheesh, of course. Financial inducement. Foul and filthy lucre.' Rufus combed his fingers through his hair. 'Maybe I'll pay a visit to Mrs Hassan. Damned handsome woman.'

'You just take it easy, Dad.' Spike stood to help him tidy away the watercolours. He slipped an arm beneath Rufus's shoulder but he shrugged it away. 'I'm fine, son. *Entro en pala.*'

Beneath the table, General Ironside's tail tapped out a steady tattoo before he appeared with a scratch of unclipped claws on cork. Spike fell in behind both man and Jack Russell as they creaked upstairs.

'Get some sun in Morocco,' Rufus said, turning once they reached the landing. 'You look worn out.'

'I'll bring you up a cup of tea, Dad.'

9

Spike stood in front of the mirror, pushing his dark hair back from his forehead and forcing a smile. Jessica was right. Crow's feet crinkled the corners of his eyes. He let the smile fall. The resemblance to Rufus was there in his height and blue irises, but his full mouth and dark Latin skin were his mother's. He rotated his shoulder blades, searching for traces of pain. Fifty-fifty, the Spanish doctor had said, that Marfan syndrome passed from father to son.

Setting the music to low, Spike stretched out on his bed, watching the curtains swirl as the violin strings hit an uncomfortable pinnacle. He'd always been more of a Mozart man, much to Rufus's disapproval, but now that he'd reached Caprice No. 10, he had to admit there was something haunting in those shrill, tremulous notes.

Through the open window, the terracotta roofs of the Old Town concertinaed down to cranes and high-rise apartments. Luxury tax-exile accommodation built on land reclaimed from the sea. On the far side of the Straits, the lights of Africa pulsed, as though flashing out signals that Spike was supposed to decipher.

He tucked his hands behind his head, thinking back to the doctor's lame attempts at reassurance. The list of famous people who'd managed to thrive with Marfan's had not been long. Initially the name of Niccolò Paganini had not stood out; indeed, it was only when Spike had learned that Paganini had originated in Genoa that he'd taken an interest, ordering a collection of the caprices online, twenty-four solo pieces designed, so far as Spike could tell, to showcase the composer's unnatural capabilities. According to the CD sleeve, he could play up to twelve notes a second, handspan stretching over three octaves.

No. 11 was a caprice too far; Spike reached over to kill the music. A cacophony of karaoke drifted up from Casemates on the levanter. Folding his hands across his chest, Spike pushed the image of Solomon's bespectacled face to the back of his mind, then willed himself to sleep.

PART TWO

Tangiers

IO

Spike Sanguinetti stood on the wooden deck of the catamaran, watching the Bay of Tangiers emerge from the heat haze. He'd been here once before, perhaps a decade ago, accompanying an English girlfriend on a quest to buy some authentic Moroccan saffron. They'd arrived in the morning and left by the afternoon. Spike hadn't stuck around long enough to find out if the mother had liked her present.

Much of the city resembled a wasps' nest – box-shaped, paper-white houses clustered on a hillside. The steepest and brightest part was the Medina, a walled zone that still followed the contours of the ancient Roman settlement, stone towers and minarets jutting towards a blurry skyline. Stretching around the bay were the more modern tenement buildings and broader boulevards of the Ville Nouvelle. Curving in front of both was a dark yellow scimitar of sand.

The breeze fell as the catamaran slowed. The crossing had been calm, belying the dangers Spike knew lurked beneath. British sailors nicknamed this stretch of water 'The Gut', due to its hidden, churning currents. The rivers flowing into the Mediterranean replaced only a third of the water lost through evaporation – as a result, extra water was needed from the Atlantic, so speeding up the movement on the surface of the Straits. The denser, more saline waters of the Med, meanwhile, sank down to the seabed and spilled out into the Atlantic, causing the currents at the top and bottom of the Straits to flow in opposite directions. It was what one couldn't see that needed to be feared.

An announcement crackled through in English on the tannoy. By the time it had been repeated in Spanish, French and Arabic, its information was outdated. They were already at their destination.

Grizzled Moroccans in Western dress began filing onto the deck, yawning as they shielded their eyes from the glare – manual workers who'd spent most of the crossing asleep on the bench seats inside. Gibraltar had opened her borders to them in the 1970s, when Franco had shut the frontier with Spain, and labour had been needed in the commercial dockyard. The younger ones were still employed, and this Friday afternoon catamaran brought them home to their families, bundles of Gibraltar pounds sewn into their trousers, plastic tartan holdalls zipped at their feet.

After passing an industrial mole – cranes, bunkering equipment – the catamaran eased into a buoy-marked lane. From the lower deck, ropes weighted by miniature cannonballs were flung onto a jetty by unseen hands, collected by dark-skinned men in white djellabas, who lashed them to iron ringbolts, creating a creak as the hull battled its restraints.

The air smelled of diesel and woodsmoke. Spike leaned his fore-arms on the railings and looked down into the murky water. Just below the surface, a large grey mullet was swimming in a circle. It kept stopping and flipping onto its side, white belly glinting in the sun. After sinking down a foot or so, it would right itself and swim back up to continue its circle. Its spine was kinked, Spike saw, injured by a boat propeller or malformed through pollution.

The jaws of the catamaran began to gape as the vans and lorries rolled out. Painted on the side of one, Spike saw a cartoon tomato in sunglasses. As he waited for the passenger gangplank to lower, he took a notebook from his leather overnight bag. Below, the kinked fish still described its circle.

11

On the far side of customs, families were gathered, women in head-scarves trying to sneak a look past each other's shoulders, toddlers pincering their legs like stag beetles. Spike slid over his passport. The immigration officer had a mongrel look, oily dark hair hanging over a pallid, sunken-eyed face. A Gibraltarian kind of look, Spike thought. '*Nulli expugnabilis hosti,*' he said as he stamped Spike's passport.

No enemy shall expel us – the Rock's official motto. 'I'm surprised you left then, *compa*,' Spike replied in a thick Gibraltarian accent.

The officer gave a smile, rubbing his thumb on his first two fingers in the universal gesture of money. Spike pushed on through to arrivals.

The moment Spike entered the hall, a crowd of hawkers surrounded him like a celebrity lawyer leaving a courthouse. The swiftest on their feet wore knock-off Levi's and trainers, those behind more traditional white tunics and sandals. 'Hey, Jimmy,' called one. 'Hotel? Lovely price.'

'*Amigo!*' cried another, scrumming over his rival. 'Guide for the Kasbah?'

'DVD film, *mein Herr?*'

A tangle of arms extended. '*Uzbek,*' Spike said firmly.

The hawkers stared up in puzzlement as a teenager with a downy moustache tugged at the sleeve of Spike's suit. '*Du kif, monsieur?*' he whispered.

'*Uzbekistan,*' Spike repeated, and the hawkers switched their attention to an American backpacker who'd just come in through the gate.

By the main exit, Spike saw a European holding up a placard. He wore a seersucker jacket and mirrored Oakley shades. As Spike approached, he pushed his sunglasses up onto his high freckly forehead. His eyes were watery blue with sandy lashes, the thinning blond hair side-parted.

'That'll be me,' Spike said, indicating his misspelt name. Above it was a logo, 'DUNETECH', the 'N' stylised to look like a desert sand dune.

The man held out a signet-ringed hand. 'Toby Riddell.'

'Spike Sanguinetti.'

'Crossing OK?'

'Incident-free.'

Riddell smiled slightly as he walked down the steps. Out in the sunshine, a queue of lorries was waiting to exit the port complex, harbour guards in Aviators checking documentation. Gulls circled above, cackling as though some stale old joke had set them off.

They headed towards a silver Mercedes saloon. A hunched, toothless man emerged from the shadows, fingering a necklace of tasselled fez hats. 'Special price –' he began, but Riddell interrupted him with a palm to the forehead, handing him off like a rugby player. The man clattered back against the barbed-wire fence that ran along the pavement.

'They're like dogs,' Riddell said without breaking stride. His shiny black shoes ticked on the flagstones like a metronome.

With a satisfying bleep, Riddell unlocked the Mercedes. As soon as Spike got in, they accelerated away beneath an archway dedicated to private cars. The guard waved them through at once, and they came out onto the coast road, the Medina rising above, various official-looking port buildings to the left. The roadway was divided by a central reservation of dried yellow grass, on which clusters of men in prayer robes sat eyeing the traffic as though plucking up courage to leap before it.

Riddell drove with a single, freckled finger on the wheel. 'So how is old Solly-man?' he said.

'Bearing up.'

'At least he's back among his own –' Riddell broke off to hoot at the moped in front, on which two men in tunics were perched, one clamped to the other. A container lorry was blocking the right-hand lane; Riddell drew up so close to the moped that his bumper was almost touching its back wheel. The driver glanced right before wobbling sideways, wing mirror inches from the lorry's rusty steel slats. Spike saw wide, terrified eyes as they passed.

'Give this mob half an inch,' Riddell said, 'and they'll half-inch a mile.' He adjusted the wheel with a fingertip to avoid a *petit taxi*. 'So how's business in Gib? Economy booming?'

'Ticking over.'

'I suppose there are enough Solomons and Abrahams to keep it that way. Angry Friar still open?'

'Was yesterday.'

'Quite a boozer.'

Spike didn't need to ask how Riddell knew the Rock. Gibraltarians had sensitive antennae when it came to spotting the British military. The sun reflecting in Riddell's over-polished black shoes had spoken eloquently.

Spike looked out at the beach below the coast road. Hand-painted signs protruded from the sand. Before Spike could read them, Riddell had veered right and they started to climb a cross street up the hillside. An entire block of buildings had collapsed here, leaving a landslip of rubble and weeds. Some entrepreneurial opportunist had taken advantage of the unexpected exposure to the coast road by scrawling '*Garage mécanique: 933317*' on the wall of the house behind.

They turned onto a broader, French-style boulevard. Rather than plane trees, date palms lined the pavements. The windows were barred with wrought-iron balconies, while interspersed with the apartment blocks were *pâtisseries, épiceries, pharmacies*. On the roof of one, a billboard proclaimed 'DUNETECH'.

Beneath its logo was a phrase: *Powering a Greener Future*. The next hoarding advertised a failed bid for Tangiers to host the international Expo. Spike checked the date: four years ago.

Riddell drove the Mercedes into a large commercial square. A fountain trickled in its centre, a bare-chested old man washing his prayer robes in its stone dish. 'This is us,' Riddell said, breaking sharply. 'You get out and I'll park the steer.' His accent was a carefully neutral English, as though a posher edge had been planed off.

As Riddell sped away, Spike realised why he'd been dropped in this position. Distance was needed to take in the scale of the Dunetech building. It dominated the entire south-facing end of the square, rising at least ten storeys higher than the shabby concrete office blocks on either side. Blue-tinted mirror glass burnished all four walls, gleaming in the mid-afternoon sun as though God had just finished buffing it with His own chamois leather.

Spike watched his reflection elongate as he approached. The revolving doors were mirrored, the Dunetech logo etched above them in a tastefully discreet font. It didn't need to be any larger; the point had been made.

12

Spike sat on a cream-coloured sofa at the edge of a cavernous atrium. The Dunetech headquarters had a hollow centre, offices rising up around the sides, fewer than might have been expected from outside. Three potted palm trees stretched towards a skylight roof, newly arrived, judging by their greenness. The floor was of black polished limestone, the desk manned by a deeply tanned girl sporting excessive lipgloss. Behind her, an electronic turnstile protected a bank of glass-fronted lifts.

The receptionist shot Spike a smile. He'd been sitting for ten minutes and not a phone had rung nor a person come or gone. From the far wall issued a hi-tech whirr: one of the lifts had started to descend. A moment later the glass doors opened to a tall man in an immaculately cut pinstripe suit.

Spike rose.

'So sorry,' the man called out, rotating the turnstile with a clip of his hip. 'Nothing worse than being kept waiting after a long journey. I'm Nadeer Ziyad. How do you do?'

Spike shook a dark, slender hand.

'So very pleased to meet you,' the man said. He looked mid-thirties, Spike's age. His face was long and angular, his nose hooked like a hawk's and his eyes sparkling with the green and yellow glints that were the hereditary mark of the Berbers, the original inhabitants of North Africa. 'Let's go upstairs,' he said. 'You all right with your case?'

Spike swung his leather bag onto his shoulder and followed Nadeer towards the desk. As Nadeer passed, he whispered something in Arabic to the receptionist, who lowered her head before opening a drawer and taking out a remote. A rich air-con whoosh came from on high as they moved through the turnstile.

Nadeer adjusted his carefully crafted Windsor knot as he stepped into the lift. 'These country girls,' he said with a smile. 'They rate forty degrees as mild.'

The speakers were piping out an instrumental version of 'Candle in the Wind'. As the lift began to climb, Spike saw the receptionist stand from her desk. Her black pencil skirt rucked up her thighs as she crossed the marble to a cabinet beyond the palms. 'So Tobes picked you up OK?' Nadeer said.

'Seemed most efficient.'

The lift stopped and Nadeer extended an arm for Spike to exit. A row of doors ran along one side of a white-carpeted corridor, with a waist-high Perspex screen giving onto the atrium below. Cream-cushioned chairs with plastic covers still on seats had been placed between each doorway. 'Developers are the same the world over,' Nadeer said as he strolled away. 'Take the estimate, double it and add a year. Don't you find?'

At the end of the corridor, Nadeer held open the door to an enormous corner office. Two of the walls consisted of floor-to-ceiling glass, the others solid and decorated with Rothkoesque sunscapes: burning reds, yellows, tangerines. In front of the tinted glass stood a heavy mahogany desk, to one side of which, propped against the skirting board, leaned a framed photograph of the King of Morocco.

'On a clear day we can see your homeland from here,' Nadeer said, striding over to the glass. 'Like God reaching out for Adam's fingertip, as my father likes to say. The continent of the past giving its blessing to the continent of the future.' All Spike could see through the haze was a parasailor being towed around the bay, motionless in his harness like a hanged man. 'Does the mirror glass power the building?' he asked.

'It will do,' Nadeer said, pressing his palms together. He smiled, eyes glittering like a tiger. 'Have a seat, Mr Sanguinetti. Please.'

Spike sat down on a stool opposite the desk, as Nadeer settled into a high-backed swivel chair. Spike caught a monogrammed flash of 'NaZ' on the lower left side of Nadeer's shirt. He checked the cuffs of Nadeer's blazer: the last button was undone, a subtle signal that the suit was bespoke.

Nadeer clicked down an Apple laptop, planting his elbows on the desk and resting his narrow chin on interlaced knuckles. 'So,' he said, 'how is he?'

'Still in a state of shock.'

He closed his eyes, breathing deeply. 'It's unbelievable. If there's anything we can do. Anything.' He opened them again, watching.

'We're going to fight extradition on human rights grounds,' Spike said. 'Article 5, Security of Person. We'll argue it's unsafe for a Jew to be held in custody in Tangiers.'

'Would that my country were a signatory to the Convention.'

'Gibraltar is. And so long as Solomon remains on Gibraltarian soil it applies.'

Nadeer tapped a nail against a pearly front tooth. 'You'd need proof of a genuine threat, of course.'

'That's why I'm here.'

He canted his head. 'Morocco is not Gibraltar, Mr Sanguinetti. It is perhaps a little less about what you can prove than who you know.'

Spike glanced over to the picture of the King of Morocco; Nadeer followed his gaze. 'Cup of tea?'

'Not for me, thanks.'

'No, no. I insist.' He lifted the phone without pressing a button and murmured in Arabic. 'All this sunshine,' he said, cupping the receiver, 'and I still miss England.' He smiled and hung up. 'The grey skies. The theatre. Annabel's. Do you get to London much?'

'Enough.'

'And Gibraltar's always been home?'

'University and law school in London. Since then, yes.'

'Doesn't it get . . . claustrophobic? Same size as Hyde Park, I seem to recall.'

'Minus the Rock.'

'Ah yes, the Rock, the great symbol of –'

A tap at the door mercy-killed the small talk as the receptionist teetered in with a silver tray. Nadeer remained seated as she lowered it onto his desk; he reached forward, raising the teapot lid, then dropping it with an icy clatter. Within the faint, rasping Arabic Spike recognised the words 'Earl Grey'. The girl began to slide the tray backwards.

'Mint tea's fine.'

'Sorry?'

'I've come all this way so it's a shame not to drink it.'

Nadeer nodded and the girl crept away. Smiling flatly, he arced a caramel spout of liquid through the strainer into Spike's cup. 'Human rights grounds,' he repeated as he poured a cup for himself. 'I suppose I could have a word with our local governor. Though he might not welcome accusations of anti-Semitism.'

'Nor global media coverage of a murdered Spanish girl on the beach.'

Nadeer puffed on his tea.

'Has there been much coverage of the death?' Spike said.

'Not thus far.'

'Of course,' Spike went on, blowing on his tea as well, 'one good thing about the size of Gibraltar is there's only one proper newspaper. The editor's a close friend.' He took a sip: sickly sweet, sugared in advance in the pot.

'Too sweet for you?'

'I like it that way.'

'Have you got a business card, Mr Sanguinetti?'

Spike put down his cup and reached for his wallet.

' "Somerset J. Sanguinetti",' Nadeer read aloud. ' "Barrister at Law". Your people Italian?'

'Genoese, originally.'

'Escaping Napoleon?'

'In 1798.'

Nadeer turned the card over where the same information was written in Spanish. 'You know,' he said, tucking it beneath his phone, 'we're like blood brothers, Moroccans and Gibraltarians. Colonised. Oppressed. How many wars have you had against the Spanish?'

'Ten sieges and counting.'

'Ten sieges ... I used to talk to Solomon about it. Ours are more recent – 1860 and 1926. Then there's the Spanish Civil War. Franco press-ganged 100,000 Moroccans to fight for him. Wiped out half my family.'

'But you work for a Spaniard, don't you? Esperanza's father.'

'Stepfather. We work together. But we can forgive him that. He's a phenomenal engineer. A visionary.'

'Is he in town?'

'Still in Madrid. Mourning.'

Spike sipped at his dark brown tea. 'Did you know Esperanza well?'

'She came by the office once or twice. Something of a wild child, I believe. Hardly Solomon's type.'

'Did you see her the day she died?'

Nadeer narrowed his green eyes. 'Toby and I were at a board meeting in Rabat with my father. Why?'

'Trying to piece together her final movements. Is Solomon's office in here?'

'Yes.'

'May I take a look around?'

Nadeer put down his cup. 'The police have already been through it with their usual grace but ... I don't see why not. I can trust you not to remove anything?'

'I'm a lawyer, Mr Ziyad. Trust is our watchword.'

The frown translated into a smile.

'I couldn't use your . . .?' Spike stood, motioning to his teacup.
'Of course. Through there.'

Spike crossed the white shagpile carpet to a doorway. The cubicle had a porcelain sink at one end and a wooden-seated lavatory at the other. The walls were papered with red-and-green stripes; propped on the gleaming cistern was another picture still to be hung, a house photograph from Eton College, dating from twenty years ago. The names of the tail-coated boys were given in italics at the bottom. Spike scanned for 'Nadeer Ziyad' and found him at the back, small and shy with a neat centre-parted haircut. As he replaced the photograph, his eye was caught by the face of a boy in the bottom row, seated beside the housemaster. He had thick blond hair and a cool gaze levelled at the camera. His arms were folded across a polka-dot waistcoat, its garish design in contrast to the dull, uniform black worn by all the other pupils. Spike looked down at the list of names: 'The Hon. Tobias Riddell, Capt. of House'. He flushed the cistern and left.

13

The next-door office was marked with a shiny brass plaque: 'Toby Riddell, Head of Corporate Security'. Spike tried the handle: locked. The adjacent door had two empty boreholes in the wood. Spike opened it and stepped inside.

A flat-pack desk faced a bare wall, the only window covered by a venetian blind with dusty blades, which Spike tugged up to a view of the neighbouring building's featureless concrete. There was an empty space on the desk where a laptop might once have sat, a number of tiny yellow Post-it notes dotted around it: 'NB future oil crunch for presentation'; 'Mamma's birthday – card *and* flowers'. Solomon's precise, careful handwriting looked unchanged since their schooldays. Already it had the quality of a relic.

Spike tried the desk drawer. Alongside a tray of golden paper clips was a plastic cylinder, 'CALIFORNIA MUSCLES' emblazoned on the front above an image of a bronzed he-man giving it the flex. Spike undid the taped-down foil, sniffed the powder, then put it back in the drawer.

Behind the desk stood a metal filing cabinet, a 'Gibraltar Rocks!' coffee mug on its top, encrusted with the same vanilla-scented powder. Five green suspension folders hung inside. Spike ran a fingertip over the tabs: 'DUNETECH Phase 1', 'DUNETECH Phase 2', 'Q1 Budget Review', 'Zagora Zween', 'Legal'. He drew out the last and opened it. Most of the correspondence was with Ruggles & Mistry, Spike's former employers. A cursory scan of the documentation revealed that Dunetech were looking to expand

operations, keen to use Gibraltar's competitive tax rates to mini-
mise their liability. So far so sensible, but if Solomon were already
instructing Ruggles, why not ask them to represent him now?
They had the best criminal practice on the Rock. Professional
embarrassment, presumably.

Footsteps outside; Spike quickly replaced the file, knocking
a Post-it to the floor. As he crouched to pick it up, he noticed
something behind the back of the desk. He strained forward to a
stiff card invitation: 'Dunetech Investor Roadshow'. Voices now;
Spike folded the invitation into his inside pocket and walked out.

Nadeer's door was wedged open on the carpet. Ahead, Spike
saw the crumpled back of Toby Riddell's seersucker jacket. Nadeer
had his elbows on the desk, talking in an undertone. He broke off
when he saw Spike. 'Find any lead piping? A candlestick?'

Riddell turned. The mirror shades were off, exposing a pink V
on the bridge of his nose. In his right hand he cupped an olive-
green squash ball, which he compressed back and forth like a
miniature heart.

'I'll have Tobes run you back to your hotel,' Nadeer said.
'Where did you say you were staying?'

'I didn't. Hotel Continental.'

Nadeer waved a hand like the choppy sea. 'Traditional, I
suppose. How long are you with us?'

'Three nights. Maybe less.'

'Well, I've got your card. In the meantime, enjoy our fine city.
It's still Ramadan, so everyone's a bit grouchy, but it'll liven up
after sundown.' Nadeer stood, running his fingers through his
wavy black hair before limply shaking Spike's hand.

Spike turned at the door. 'Either of you know the Sundowner
Club?'

Riddell pumped at his squash ball.

'What's that?' Nadeer said.

'Some kind of beach bar, I think. Esperanza went there the
night of her death.'

'Oh, that place,' Nadeer said as he sat back down. 'Those cathouses change their name by the week. Go there by all means, but if you're thinking of late-night entertainment, I'd advise you to tread carefully. Tobes?'

Riddell escorted Spike down the corridor. 'Give 'em half an inch,' he muttered.

'I'll walk from here,' Spike said as the lift arrived. 'Get my bearings.'

14

The tight, whitewashed streets of the Medina were a hotchpotch of religious dress. Men wore beige hooded cloaks, or candy-striped djellabas, or immaculate white robes with perforated *kufi* caps; the few women wore black veils with eye slits, or embroidered kaftans, or jeans with bandannas over mouths and chunky black Ray-Bans perched on noses. Sub-Saharan Africans strode among them, broad-nosed Nigerians in tribal dress, gangly Masai with tartan blankets draped over shoulders. It was as though the continent of Africa had been tipped upside down and shaken like a pepper pot.

Schoolboys in tunics poured from a side door of the Grand Mosque. Seeing a shadow beneath a scooter trailer, one of them jabbed in a sandal. A kitten darted away as the boy high-fived his friend.

Rugs had been laid out on the road, heaped with pyramids of prickly pears, baskets of star anise, packets of crispy sunflower seeds. The rugs were for sale as well, judging by a merchant thumbing the weave at Spike. A barefoot man in rag trousers staggered by with a tray of samosas on his head, brown chair hooked over a browner arm.

Spike continued up the concentric circles towards the Kasbah, the fortified complex at the top of the hill that had once been the Sultan's palace. When he saw the white, crenulated walls, he knew he'd gone too far. He tried a different route down, passing an American woman of a certain age arm in arm with a handsome Moroccan youth. The irresistible pheromones of the green card.

Just around the corner was an alley lined with beggars. Spike dropped all his coins into the lap of a cowl-draped amputee. As he rounded the next corner, he found a woman with glaucous eyes, rocking on her hunkers.

Hawkers appeared, the first tapping at a bongo. Offers were made in a babel of languages but Spike strode away, dragging the more persistent in his slipstream. He was closer to the sea now, the air fresh and saline, blending with the fragrant smoke of joss sticks that were wedged in the shutter hinges of leather shops. The owners sat on stools outside, fiddling with prayer beads, watching the sky, waiting.

A cross-eyed man crawled by on his knees, scouring for cigarette ends. Spike watched him stop and pick up a twig, then jam it upright in a drain as though it were the centrepiece of some elegant flower arrangement. Two boys in fake Barcelona football shirts crunched it down as they passed by hand in hand, chatting.

At last Spike saw the sign, painted on a stucco archway. *Hotel Continental*. Rufus had made the recommendation. 'An institution, son,' he'd promised, 'good enough for Winston Churchill.' Spike entered the courtyard, where a uniformed security guard sat in a fogged-up hut watching football. He glanced over at Spike, then returned to his black-and-white TV.

Two men stood together at the reception desk. On the counter in front of them sat a triangular cardboard sign: *Together Against Terrorism*. The floor was of chequerboard marble, with a grand piano with the lid down and a smoked-glass art deco chandelier hanging from the wooden latticework ceiling. The curved staircase looked like it hadn't been dusted since Churchill's last visit.

The receptionist was jotting down directions on a free map. The guests said '*Shukran*' in a Spanish accent, then walked away. One had a shaven head with sideburns like drips of dried blood, the other peroxide hair and sugary aftershave. Both made a moue at Spike as they left.

'Single, please,' Spike said. Though old and grey, the receptionist had a chubby, beatific face. He wore the standard white djellaba and sandals but with silver stubble rather than full beard.

'Is the restaurant open?' Spike asked once he'd checked in.

The receptionist handed over the key. 'Hunger is housed in the body, satisfaction in the soul.'

Spike waited for further enlightenment, but the receptionist returned to his seat to pick up a book.

The third-floor landing was decorated with framed maps of Tangiers through the ages: as a Roman provincial capital, a Portuguese colony, an English naval base, and more recently as a hedonistic international freeport, independent of the French and Spanish protectorates that ruled the rest of the country until 1956. Tangier, Tanjah, Tanger, Tangiers – even the present-day name seemed hard to pin down. As Spike passed a doorway, he heard a film blaring within. The adjoining room was his; groaning slightly, he slid his key into the lock.

Wooden-framed bed, cracked dressing-table mirror, en-suite bathroom with inevitable dripping tap. Spike took off his suit, feeling the office lift away as he stripped down to his boxers to unpack his overnight bag: fresh white T-shirts, loose cargo trousers, crisp linen shirt. He'd forgotten his sunglasses, he realised as he stowed the empty bag inside the cupboard. The shutters were closed; he pushed them open to a rooftop vista of water tanks, aerials and washing lines. Doves cooed. The sky was pink, the sun finally gone.

Sitting at the foot of the bed, he picked up the TV remote and found it mummified with yellowing Sellotape. He took out his phone instead as the film soundtrack throbbed through the walls.

'Been to prison yet?' said Peter Galliano.

'Tomorrow.'

'Is that your squeaky fiddler playing?'

'It's the next-door room.'

'Good hotel?'

'Charming. Listen, Peter . . .'

Spike told Galliano about his meeting with Nadeer Ziyad. 'He was talking about getting me an audience with the governor of Tangiers. I promised him a media blackout as long as the trial takes place in Gib.'

'What does he care?'

'There's been nothing so far in the Moroccan papers. Dunetech won't want any bad publicity, particularly as an eco company.'

'So what's he like, this Nadeer Ziyad?'

'Not short on confidence.'

'To those who have, Spike, shall be given. And you really feel we can keep the media at bay?'

'All that matters is they think we can.'

'I've already had the Moroccan authorities on to me. They want a DNA swab.'

'Do it. Keep 'em sweet on the small stuff.'

'Still no bail though. Flight risk.'

'Ask Alan Gaggero to schedule me a phone call with Solomon. If Alan's off duty, try Jessica Navarro. Just don't say it's for me. Anything from the Uzbeks?'

'They liked the vodka bar.'

'*Grevi.* I'll call you later then.'

'Careful, Spike. I know that tone.'

'*Non me voy de weeken.*'

The soundtrack next door had taken on a pornographic slant: moaning, panting. Spike hoisted the shower head to the top of its mast, washed, changed, then descended into the Tangerine dusk.

The sand felt warm between Spike's toes. Seeing a discarded syringe ahead, he dropped his espadrilles back to the ground and kicked them on. The breadth of the beach had been a surprise, more than half a kilometre wide, continuing all along the inlet of the bay, port to the left, hills to the right, bright wasps'-nest city rising behind.

Waves lapped at Spike's feet, propelled by their cross-mix of currents. A shelf of sand rose at the tidemark: if someone had wanted to sit by the sea they could lean on the sandbank and be out of sight of anyone walking behind. Washed up against it was a mêlée of debris: punctured lilo, toothbrush, a plastic doll with a melted face.

Spike took a bite of sandwich. The flat, semolina-dusted bread was spread with a sour and rather delicious goat's cheese. He looked out at the late sun, spray-painting the crests of the wavelets blood orange. It was a still evening, the beach a biscuity colour in the fading light. In its hard-packed centre, street kids were playing football – the ball spilled to Spike and he side-footed it firmly back. Beyond, the lights of Spain gave a watered-down glow. There was something tantalising about that view, Spike thought, close by yet out of reach.

He walked past the footballers towards the road. The row of beach bars was set beneath it, most of them little more than concrete bunkers. Some had gone for a Miami deckchair look, others fenced-off dance floors. Spike took in the plagiarised names: 'Snob', 'Pasha', 'Ritzys'. Most looked defunct – boarded-up windows, trussed parasols, tubs of dead hydrangeas with fag butts jammed into soil.

Spike was about to climb back up to the road when he stopped. Thirty metres ahead, a whitewashed customs depot marked the end of the beach. Just in front, sunk into the sand at an angle, was a wooden sign. Half a setting sun surmounted by a curving word, 'Sundowner'.

The terrace was enclosed by screens of palm fronds and gated by a plywood panel. Spike gave it a shove. It swung open and he crouched through past crates of empty beer bottles and a teetering stack of plastic chairs.

The back door was of salt-corroded steel; Spike put his shoulder to it. Ahead, a corridor led to a screen of velvet. A muffled throb came from behind; Spike felt his way along the cool concrete, then separated the curtains.

Through rotating disco lights, Spike made out the long pale back of a woman. She wore a thong and black, knee-length PVC boots. Her hands cupped her breasts, crimson bra straps dangling as she perched on a small round stage, hip against a pole. Facing her in the middle of a cushioned, seraglio-style set of bench seats sat a suited man. It was too gloomy to see features beyond a pair of large black-rimmed glasses.

Opposite the stripper was another, unoccupied stage, while along the back wall ran a bar with five or six stools. A Moroccan in a leather waistcoat manned it, standing by the sink, topping up a vodka bottle from the tap. The air smelled of perspiration and essential oils.

Spike sat down, and the barman straightened up, replacing the bottle on the mirror-backed shelf behind. '*Vous connaissez cette boîte, monsieur?*' he snapped.

'Vodka. No ice. And no water.'

The barman was bald on top but had contrived to scrape together a ponytail from the lank crop on the sides. He reached behind for a different bottle as Spike swivelled his stool. The stripper was facing him now, hands still teasingly over breasts. She had Eastern European hair and a body so thin the ribs stuck out like the timbers of a shipwreck. She bent down, twitching the T-strap of her thong in her client's bespectacled face. A smack rang out; Spike saw the stripper flinch, then reaffix her come-hither smile.

Spike listened as a techno version of an old Police number started playing, 'Tea in the Sahara'. A thumb-smeared tumbler slid his way. He took out his wallet and let the barman drink in the notes. 'Keep the change.'

A hundred-dirham note disappeared into the leather waistcoat with card-sharp dexterity. 'You like a dance?' the barman said. 'Some . . . private room?'

Spike sniffed his vodka.

'Karim, he dancing later.' The barman flicked his flaccid double chin at the empty stage. 'Two hundred dirham.'

Another slap from the podium, as the barman reached below the counter. Lifting out a crate of limes, he started cutting them into quarters with unnerving speed and skill. Spike looked beyond him to a pinboard of photographs: men hugging women, men hugging men, women hugging women. The blade of the kitchen knife ticked back and forth. The sliced limes rolled into a chrome bucket and the crate returned beneath the bar.

'You know Esperanza?' Spike said.

The barman smoothed back his ponytail.

'Esperanza,' Spike repeated loudly, eyes on the stripper, who tensed up her thighs, thumbs hooked beneath her G-string. The barman lowered his chin into a neck brace of fat. 'So many girls.'

'This one's dead. Found on the beach last week.'

'You from the Sûreté?'

'No.'

'Is like I say before – I never working that night.'

Another slap: Spike glared at the businessman, who was stand-ing to get a better purchase. The stripper was naked now apart from her boots, crouching with one arm linked around the pole. Her face was still turned to Spike.

Spike laid three hundred dirham on the bar top. When it had disappeared, he stepped off his stool and moved to the end of the bar.

'She come in often time,' the barman said as he sidled over. Spike caught something sour on his breath that reminded him of the junkies he'd defended while working at the criminal bar in Gibraltar.

'Western slut,' he went on. 'She go with man, woman. Drugs and drink. Oh yeah.' He sucked in air through his widely spaced teeth. A gold molar glinted.

'What about the night she died? Did you see who she was with then?' Spike reached again for his wallet, laying down another hundred dirham.

'Oh, the little Jew,' the barman replied as he took the money. 'He follow her to the beach. Then? Who knows.'

Spike made a feint at the barman's waistcoat; he skipped back with the certainty of a creature which knows the dimensions of its cage. His hand moved upwards to adjust a spotted dicky bow.

'You can do better than that,' Spike said.

'I never see the Jew.'

'So someone told you. Who?'

'No one.'

'Did they argue?'

'He quiet man. Good money.'

'Did she argue with someone else?'

Spike caught an infinitesimal flicker of the eyelid. He laid down another two hundred dirham. The stripper was on her front now, boots apart as the businessman crouched forensically behind. The barman made a grab for the money but Spike got there first, slamming his palm down. 'Who?'

'One girl,' the barman said, backing away.

'Her?'

'Different. Maybe two week ago. This one, she throw a drink at Esperanza. They shout so I pull them apart, like two dogs fucking. Few days later Esperanza dead. Throat open like a baby lamb at the Eid. Yessir.'

'Which girl threw the drink?'

'She gone now. Owes me money.'

'Her name?'

Spike crammed the note into the barman's hand, folding his clammy fingers around the paper. With a smile and surprising grace, the barman pirouetted to swipe a photograph from the pinboard. Two shiny-faced jocks had their arms around a dark-skinned girl. Spike could see only part of her face: high cheekbones, serious expression, black hair tied back with a single strand over one eye. 'Her name?'

'Zahra.'

'Zahra who?'

'Bedouin bitch. No family name.'

'Dancer?'

'Waitress.'

Another slap; the stripper was trying to stand but the businessman had a fist on the small of her back. The barman gazed on, polishing an earhole with a twisting index finger.

'Second thoughts,' Spike said. 'I will have that dance.'

The barman's pink gecko tongue flapped up and down. 'Five minute.'

'Now.'

'Mo' money.'

Spike gave a nod and the barman reached below to stab a button beneath the bar top. The businessman glanced up as the music stopped. The stripper drew in her bony knees.

'What's your name?' Spike said.

'Marouane.'

'Did you tell the police, Marouane?'

The barman shook his ponytail.

'When Zahra comes back,' Spike said, taking out his business card, 'you give me a call. Understand?' He picked up the photograph and walked towards the stripper.

16

The girl was climbing onto a tiny plywood podium. There was barely room for the pole.

'Sit with me,' Spike said.

'Cost extra.' Her accent was French with a rough-grained Arabic underlay.

'Just to talk.'

The girl stepped down, stilettos scraping the porcelain. Spike glanced around. The 'private' room appeared to be no more than a converted lavatory: red drapery on the walls, two plastic chairs by the stage, floor-to-ceiling tiles exuding an ammoniac tang of a thousand drinkers' pit stops.

The girl took one of the chairs, spun it and pleated her long, smooth legs around. Close up, Spike could see the dark roots of her platinum hair. 'What's your name?'

'Tatiana.'

'Real name?'

'Tatiana,' the girl replied with a smile.

'Don't hear that one so much in Morocco.'

The girl arched an over-plucked eyebrow. Spike held out a note which she rolled and slid into her boot. 'From Algeria. Annaba City. Ten year ago.'

'How much do you make a night, Tatiana?'

'You like to take me home?' She stroked her chin. There was a short, deep scar at its base which no amount of foundation could mask. 'Five hundred dirham, maybe I –'

'I'll give you five hundred just to talk.'

Tatiana started to stand, but Spike caught her wrist. 'It's OK,' he said. 'I'm a friend of Esperanza's.'

She glared down, then draped herself uncertainly back over her chair. 'You from Spain?'

'Nearby. You knew her?'

'I dance for her.'

'She liked women?'

'She liked . . . everyone.'

'Did you see who she was with that night?'

'I no working.'

'It seems the club was running itself.'

She smiled again. 'You friend for Marouane?'

'No.'

'Marouane here . . . all times.' She reached over and ran a long, fake fingernail up and down Spike's inner forearm.

'Marouane sells drugs?'

'If you like, I can –'

'He sold drugs to Esperanza?'

She folded her arms over the chair back, hiding her chin on top.

'Do you know who killed Esperanza?'

The coquettish expression slipped. In repose, her face looked very young. 'Esperanza go to the beach,' she said. 'There, *avec les sans-papiers –*'

'*Sans-papiers?*'

'They coming into Tanger. *Pour passer le détroit.* All of Africa, waiting. No place for sleep. Sleep in park, cemetery, beach. Dangerous *abid* man. Eating cats and dogs.'

'And Zahra is a *sans-papier?*'

'You know Zahra also?'

'She argued with Esperanza, right?'

'One time.'

Spike held out another note which Tatiana tucked into a different boot. 'Esperanza come into the club,' she said. 'She see Zahra, and when Esperanza see . . .' Suddenly she climbed to her feet, enjoying the pantomime now. Through her lace bra Spike made out large, dark areolae. 'Zahra shout at Esperanza. Then . . .' She stabbed forward with an arm.

'She cut her?'

'Champagne wine. In her face. Then Esperanza stand and leave.'

'Why did Zahra throw the drink?'

'Maybe Esperanza touch her wrong. Or . . .'

'What?'

Another hundred dirham gone.

'Two days later,' Tatiana said, 'I see Esperanza's jeep. Zahra inside.'

'Are you sure?'

'I *see*.'

'Where does Zahra live?'

'In Chinatown. Like all the girls.'

'Where's Chinatown?'

'In the hills.'

'Address?'

Tatiana smiled. 'No address for Chinatown, *estúpido*.'

'Does she have a mobile number?'

Tatiana hovered above Spike. 'You strong tall man,' she said. 'But gentle eyes.' She reached out a hand. 'You put contact lens for the colour, no?'

Spike caught a hint of sugar almonds on her skin. He'd known a girl once who smelled like that. She hoisted a leg over Spike's lap. 'Sometimes I like to know a man,' she said, lowering herself down, 'before I give him secret . . . informations.'

Spike raised his hands to her sides, feeling the jutting prominence of her ribs as he eased her down onto his own chair. She edged her thighs apart; the gusset of her thong was dark-stained. Spike reached again for his wallet. 'Here's two hundred more. Now go home. And be careful who you dance for.'

The girl snapped closed her thighs. 'I prefer a man who *fuck*,' she said, fluffing out her crisp white hair. 'Maybe you only talk because you cannot fuck. Spanish *zamel*.'

Spike held open the door back into the club. A new song blared: 'Rock the Casbah' by The Clash. The girl pushed past, the top of each buttock embossed with a cherry-red welt.

Marouane was standing behind the bar, hunting for scurf in his hair. On the previously empty podium, an Arab boy in cut-off shorts and Cleopatra eyeliner was humping a pole. Beneath, Spike recognised the two Spaniards from the reception of the Hotel Continental.

The bespectacled businessman drank alone, scouring the room, legs folded daintily among the cushions. Spike walked over, leaned in close and whispered a few words in his ear. Then he left.

17

Spike crossed the waiting hall of the Sûreté Nationale on Avenue d'Espagne. The fissured marble floor was covered by men reclining in traditional dress. The air smelled like a classroom in midsummer.

At the desk, a duty sergeant was reading the *Journal de Tanger*. Spike asked for Inspector Eldrassi; without looking up, the duty sergeant waved a benedictory hand across the silent, waiting congregation. Spike saw they formed a sort of queue. He asked when Eldrassi would be available. '*Demain*,' the sergeant replied, flipping to the sports section.

Outside, dusk clung on, as though afraid to surrender to night. The restaurant terraces were bustling with men eating sweetmeats. Spike realised Tatiana was the only woman he'd exchanged words with since arriving.

There was a bank opposite; Spike went to the cashpoint. A heavily armed security guard stood by as he made the withdrawal. On the other side of the avenue, three young black men looked on. *Sans-papiers* probably, awaiting their chance to steal across the Straits. Spike had read countless articles on the risks involved – bloated, cracked bodies washing up each month on Spanish beaches, victims of unscrupulous boat runners, victims of the Gut.

A *petit taxi* swerved to a halt, responding to Spike's European height and clothes. The driver had a package of greaseproof paper on the passenger side; he drew it onto his lap as Spike got in and shunted back the seat. 'Chinatown.'

'*Comment?*'

Spike pointed up the hill to where the city rose. The driver shrugged. '*On va à Chinatown, donc.*'

18

Spike forced down the stiff window to let the curried air circulate. Once they'd passed through the Ville Nouvelle, with its ornate, Parisian-style apartment blocks, they crested the hill and rolled down the other side. Vandalised, half-finished buildings – breeze blocks and rusting girders – protruded from a cacti-studded wasteland. The road began to dispense with pavements, then markings, then traffic altogether until a jeep drew up behind. Once it had grasped that the taxi couldn't speed up, it overtook on a blind corner.

The driver braked suddenly as a tall man with a long white beard emerged from the wayside, guiding some goats over the road. Kids crossed behind, bleating. Somewhere a dog barked.

They drove on, turning left down a potholed track. The food parcel bounced on the driver's lap. He stopped the car. '*C'est Chinatown.*'

Spike stared down the slope to a line of low-slung brick buildings clustered at the bottom of the track. The light was poor but they appeared to have sprung up in a dip between two hills, like fungus on a moist enclosed part of the body.

'It's a shanty town?'

'*Bidonville.*'

'Can you get any closer?'

The taxi driver crunched on his samosa. He was a small, bug-eyed man with pictures of small, bug-eyed children gummed to his glove compartment. Spike took out his wallet and removed a hundred-dirham note.

The driver shook his head. 'Bad place for taxi.'

Spike looked again down the slope. A few lights were visible. It clearly had electricity. 'Why's it called Chinatown?'

'No laws for building.'

'Seems quiet.'

'People working. In the city.'

'Bedouins?'

The driver coughed a flake of samosa onto his beaming children. '*Tu parles des bédouins?*'

'Do Bedouins live in Chinatown?'

'Desert peoples . . . *C'est bien possible.*'

Spike put away the note and held up a two hundred. The driver restarted the engine and they continued another fifty metres up the road before turning left. This time they drove further down the rough, unsurfaced track. Reeds sprouted by a stream; a patch of dusty scrubland revealed two burnt-out cars, kissing bumper-to-bumper like some untitled art installation. More brick buildings ahead; the driver switched off the engine.

'Twenty minutes,' Spike said, signalling the number with his fingers. As Spike opened the door, he felt a tap on the shoulder. '*Attention, uh?*'

Outside, the air smelled sulphurous. Spike removed some low-denomination notes from his wallet and stuffed them in the top pouch of his cargo trousers. The driver watched on in silence, chewing his samosa.

19

The ground consisted of layer upon layer of trodden rubbish: flattened cans, shredded sackcloth, powdered glass. A stream snaked between the brick shacks. Its stench – eggs and rotten meat – suggested open sewer. The tall, nuclear-green reeds grew on one side only, giving Spike a glimpse of a brownish sludge oozing through the centre.

Covering his mouth and nose, he followed the stream between the buildings. The walls, he saw, had plywood embedded in the brickwork. Sticking from the top of one was an incongruously modern satellite dish.

Spike gagged as he neared the water. Beneath the surface lay an eyeless mongrel puppy, its chest swollen, guts flapping in the current like pink pondweed. He put a hand to his neck as he passed, folding a soft mosquito beneath.

The stream continued on through the settlement, forming a muddy half-moon-shaped bank. A few plastic tables had been pushed together, at which a group of men sat smoking clay pipes and playing cards. All wore thick black moustaches, their faces darker than the other Moroccans Spike had seen, Indian almost. Paired with white djellabas were coiled, light-blue turbans.

Candles guttered on tables, an electric light fizzing behind, dive-bombed by suicidal, shiny-backed beetles. A woman in a headscarf sat cross-legged on the mud, shelling pods with a knife as a child played nearby with a food wrapper. The cables feeding the naked bulb looped away over corrugated roofs – illegally siphoned electricity, Spike supposed. '*Zahra, por favor?*' he called, holding out the photograph of the girl.

The child stared up, open-mouthed, as her mother continued shelling. One of the card-players crooked a fingertip to the left. Spike gave a nod, hearing urgent, whispered rasps as he walked away.

Of the twenty minutes Spike had asked the driver to wait, five had elapsed. A thicker, more faecal smell began to coat the back of his throat as he turned into a gap between the huts. Through an open door he saw the flicker of a TV, a rag-draped figure prostrate before it on a camp bed.

Despite the condition of the buildings, Chinatown appeared to follow a grid system of sorts: parallel roads intersected by narrow alleyways. Spike continued left. Scrawled on a door was a painting of some rapt children with the words *École Primaire Mohammad VI.* The dark, plastic-sheeted windows were too murky to see through. Spike glanced up to the sky: the last of the sunlight had gone.

On the opposite side of the road, a bulb gleamed from an open-fronted shack. A youth appeared by Spike as he crossed over, cycling tight against him, aligning his wheels in the tyre tracks scored in the dried mud. He was staring so fixedly at Spike that his front axle caught in the furrow and he almost fell.

The facade of the shack was made of sliced-up plastic pallets. A man was sitting inside, eating with his fingers as a TV blared out Al-Jazeera news. A balding parrot clattered above him in a cage.

'*Hola?*'

The man suspended his fingers by his lips as Spike drew closer. '*Zahra la beduina?*' he said. '*Dónde?*'

'*À gauche,*' the man said. '*Gauche, gauche.*' He crammed his fingers to his mouth. The parrot chewed at the bars of its cage.

The moon was visible, just a nail clip of white in the hazy, blue-black sky. Ahead in the street, Spike saw the boy on the bicycle joined by four other youths. They were all watching him too.

He turned into the next alley. Some sort of shop, a rack of exhausted-looking vegetables outside and an old, aproned woman hunched on a stool, serving a girl. As Spike drew closer, the girl glanced round. Then she picked up her plastic bag and walked quickly away.

20

Spike kept ten metres behind the girl. Her black kaftan flowed outwards, a sequinned headscarf concealing her face as she glanced around, increasing her speed. They were one behind the other now, following the raised, mud-packed ridge between the tyre tracks.

'I'm a friend of Esperanza's,' Spike called out.

The girl crossed the road beside a half-built breeze-block wall.

'I've spoken to Tatiana.'

She dropped a handle of the plastic bag. Tomatoes and aubergines bounced to the ground. She cursed, crouching as Spike loomed above. Behind, a vehicle began to glide silently along the road. Spike turned to look: a jeep. He took a step closer to the girl. 'I've been to the Sundowner Club.'

She continued gathering groceries.

'You're Zahra, aren't you?'

'Why don't you fuck off back to Ángel?'

'I'm sorry?'

'Or I'll scream,' she added in surprisingly clear English.

A tin can had rolled into the tyre tracks; as Spike bent down for it, he glimpsed the girl's tight denim jeans stretch beneath her kaftan. The sequins on her headscarf began to glitter in a beam of light; the jeep had performed a U-turn and was peeling back towards them. It traversed the road until it was facing the girl, stopping twenty metres shy, engine on, headlights blazing through a bull-bar bumper.

Spike picked up the tin can, then heard the engine rev. 'Zahra!'

The girl snapped up her head as the jeep roared towards her. Sprinting over the road, Spike launched himself into the air. He smelled her sharp, citrus perfume as he pressed himself against her clothing, bruising his shoulder as they thudded down together onto the hard ground. She elbowed him in one kidney, then scrambled to her feet.

The lights of the jeep glowed red. Hubcaps scraped against ridges of crisp mud. Zahra crouched again, gathering her shopping.

'What are you *doing*?'

The reverse lights of the jeep had been replaced by sharp yellow beams. Spike gave Zahra a shove; she took a step forward, dropping her bag before starting to run. Spike followed her into a narrow side street. Headlights tickled its mouth, disappearing before returning more strongly. 'Down here,' Spike said.

The walls on either side of the alley were made of cemented, blue-grey breeze blocks. Glassless windows above revealed dark figures silently watching. Rats scuttled in front, shifting one behind the other like a relay team. A pothole of stinking softness slurped at Spike's foot as Zahra streaked ahead with long strides – she seemed focused, unsurprised.

Spike heard the engine rev behind them. 'Stop,' he called, catching her up. She spun round, fist emerging as though to strike him.

'We can't outrun it.'

The headlights gleamed into Zahra's almond eyes; she glanced back, then dashed towards the side wall.

The breeze blocks were piled seven feet high. Zahra leapt up and got her hands on the top, holding herself in position before slipping back.

Spike dropped to his knees like a sprinter. 'Stand on my back.'

'What?'

'Go on!'

Spike felt pressure on his spine as Zahra's feet pressed downwards. He forced his neck up, her weight finally lifting as she got a hold on the wall above.

The headlights were almost on him. In a single fluid motion, Spike got to his feet and threw himself at the wall. His fingers gripped the top edge and he held himself there, lungs burning, espadrilles paddling against rough breeze blocks.

He hauled his legs into the air as the jeep sped beneath him. Further along, it stopped. There was a sharp double click of doors opening.

Spike felt a touch on a sinew-twisted shoulder. He pulled himself higher, scraping his stomach muscles until he came to rest face down in a flat, asphalted space. Feet pounded the mud below. A flashlight raked up and down the wall.

Spike's shoulder joints sang in a hot and not unpleasant way. The girl grabbed his hand; he'd cut himself, he saw as he stood. They edged for a while along the platform until Spike felt his neck jerk back, the top of his head slamming into a low-hanging pole. He put a hand to his hair, testing for blood, then felt Zahra touch his arm, steadying him. They crouched together in the darkness, the only sound now the pitch and fall of their chests. From below came the slam of car doors. An engine restarted.

Spike sat down, leaning dizzily against the surrounding wall. He felt her breath warm his face. 'Thank you,' he heard her say. Then he closed his eyes.

21

The back of Spike's head was leaning against a rough surface, sandpaper or pebble-dash. The air smelled of hot cat piss. He groped in his pocket for his phone, then manoeuvred it over his eyes. He'd only been out for five minutes. And she was gone.

He hauled himself up. His head throbbed; he explored with his fingers, finding a large bump above the hairline. The skin of his forehead felt taut, uneven with mosquito bites. Balance regained, he edged along the platform, waiting for his eyes to adjust. A makeshift frame of bamboo scaffolding seemed to be holding the structure up, a dusty back road three metres below.

After testing the bamboo, Spike started to climb down. His shoulders ached. There were more bites on his ankles, slick blood on the back of his wrist. He licked it and tasted ferrous grit.

Once on the ground, he saw stars spangling the night sky like the sequins on Zahra's headscarf. At the end of the street, a bonfire crackled, three or four silhouettes gathered round, turning some kind of meat on a spit. Woodsmoke and burnt flesh carried in the air. Beyond, Spike made out the jagged shape of a bicycle.

Fresh tyre tracks scored the mud; Spike kept to the shadows until he caught the first whiff of the stream. The outdoor café appeared, card-players gone, bearded proprietor slowly clearing tables.

Jogging now, Spike followed the bank, dry-retching as the miasma strengthened. Two bristly yellow dogs burst from the rushes and ran at his ankles, thrilled at the speed. Once past the brick buildings, Spike felt his heart lift as he saw the triangular roof panel of the *petit taxi*.

The driver was slumped at the wheel; Spike tapped on the window and his head shot up. Blinking bulbously, he reached over and tugged up the passenger lock.

'Hotel Continental,' Spike said, and the driver twisted on the headlights.

As they reversed, Spike saw a figure appear between the buildings. They rumbled away, pursued by the barking pack of dogs. The figure was gone.

22

The cafés on the Avenue d'Espagne were busy, black-tied waiters shuttling between groups of locals and tourists. Seeing a table of tanned, laughing Europeans, Spike felt a powerful urge to go and join them.

'Slow here,' he said as the police station came into view. A youth with a fishing rod over one shoulder was arguing with a man in chef's whites, their dispute overseen by a harassed-looking sergeant. Spike caught sight of a crowded hallway behind. 'Forget it,' he said. 'Carry on.'

They stopped at the walls of the Medina, the streets above too narrow for cars. The driver hit a button on the meter: '*Bonne continuation,*' he grinned once he'd registered the size of the tip.

A few late-night hawkers ambled over but their hearts weren't in it. As Spike passed the Grand Mosque, he saw a strip-lit room where lines of men chanted, kneeling and bowing in unison. Looked like good exercise.

Outside the hotel, the guard was watching football in his cabin, devouring couscous from a paper plate. Spike strode past him to reception. The lighting from the chandelier created a soothing atmosphere as the receptionist perched contemplatively at his desk. 'A good night, *monsieur*?' he said.

'Eventful.'

'The variety of the rainbow creates its appeal.'

'If you say so,' Spike replied as he went upstairs.

Nearing his room, he heard screeching tyres and machine-gun spray. He stopped, rapping at the door. He thumped harder until it was opened by a tall, well-built black man with shoulder-length dreadlocks. '*Ouai?*' The air behind him stank sweetly of hashish.

'Can you turn that down?' Spike shouted. '*Menos ruido?*'

The man shook his head, dreadlocks held in place by multicoloured beads.

'I'm in the next-door room,' Spike said, feeling fatigue drape him like an oppressive cowl. He tucked his hands pillow-like behind an ear.

The man's face brightened. '*Ah. Mes excuses.*' As he turned away, Spike made out a glowing bank of TV monitors. The noise quietened and he reappeared, smiling. 'Jean-Baptiste,' he said, proffering a pink-palmed hand. The skin was rough yet soft, like the bottom of a dog's paw.

'Spike.'

Jean-Baptiste's eyes fell to Spike's cut. '*Tu veux du . . .*'

Spike shook his head, then went next door, collapsing on his bed as the fan wheeled above. He shut his eyes, trying to think of the name Zahra had used when he'd approached her. What had it been? Sleep tugged at his brain like a crafty hand on the corner of a blanket.

23

After bandaging the cut on his wrist, Spike stared at himself in the bathroom mirror. The pink domes of mosquito bites spotted his forehead. He threw cold water over his face, remembering a story he'd read about Paganini. In the winter of 1786, when Paganini had been four years old, his parents had thought he'd died of measles. They'd laid him to rest in a chilly pauper's grave until the undertaker had seen a wisp of condensed breath emerge from his shroud. The boy had been removed from the coffin and nursed back to health, and the next year his father, a mediocre mandolin player, had pressed a violin into his bony hands. The ghoulish rumours had started when the boy had begun composing sonatas aged seven. They'd stepped up a level when he'd played his first solo concert at nine. Look closely, the people of Genoa whispered, and you will see the Devil guiding his elbow.

The receptionist was still at the desk.

'Don't you ever sleep?'

The receptionist looked up from his book. 'How short is the night for those who sleep well.'

'What are you reading there?'

He held up a front cover marked by curly Arabic script.

'Quotations?'

'A man must take his wisdom even from the side of the road.'

'I'll remember that,' Spike said as he handed over his room key.

The dining terrace of the Continental overlooked an apron of shipping containers. A female dog was lying in their shade as a male sniffed her rear. The female kept her tail down, head firmly on forepaws.

The Arabs were fasting, the Europeans breakfasting. Spike sensed the Spanish couple observing him from behind. The man with the sideburns now had a split lip. Spike wondered what adventure they ascribed to the wound on his wrist.

He drank his coffee – warm and milky, better than the reconstituted orange juice that had preceded it – and stared out at the Straits, where a succession of freight and cruise liners was coming and going from the quayside. On the furthest coastline, his father Rufus would be eating his breakfast egg, slippered, dressing gown gaping as he fed the occasional buttered soldier to General Ironside. Routine: the doomed attempt to defeat the march of time. The past wasn't truly past if it could be repeated.

Spike stood and headed for the coast road.

24

The duty sergeant was reading the next day's *Journal de Tanger*, but the rest of the waiting room had emptied out. Spike walked past him to a side door, where a man at a desk was scowling at a large computer monitor, as though not quite sure what it was, still less how it had come to be there. He wore a brown corduroy suit rather than the sky-blue shirt and peaked cap of the sergeant outside. Beside one hand lay an overflowing ashtray.

'Inspector Eldrassi?'

The man raised his eyes, face long and grey, like a lolly sucked dry of flavour. Contrasting with the sallow skin was a suspiciously dark moustache.

'Jessica Navarro gave me your name. *Hablas inglés?*'

His expression animated, as though he'd been flicking through a mental file of e-fits and come across a match. 'The beauty from Gibraltar,' he said, laying his cigarette in the crematorium of its predecessors. 'They send me there for trafficking conferences. I speak the best English.'

'Spike Sanguinetti.'

The man stood up properly. 'Inspector Hakim Eldrassi. You are also a policeman from Gibraltar? Here on holiday?'

'Lawyer. Here on business.'

Hakim withdrew his hand and rubbed it on his brown corduroy trousers. He motioned with his chin to a chair opposite the desk. 'Five minutes.'

Spike sat down. 'I represent Solomon Hassan.'

Hakim shook a cigarette from his pack even though the previous one was still smouldering. 'He is on his way back to Tangiers, I hope?'

'We're seeking to prevent extradition.'

Hakim's eyes closed in weary disbelief. 'There is an arrest warrant, Mr Sanguinetti. He has a case to answer.'

'We consider Tangiers Prison to be unsafe for a Sephardic Jew. Even if my client were only in custody overnight, that would still represent a breach of his human rights.'

A smoke ring hung in the air, stretching to a Munch-like skull before disappearing. 'Why are you here?' Hakim said.

'Seeking evidence of anti-Semitism within your penal system.'

'But here,' Hakim went on, 'in front of me. Now.'

'Have you been to the Sundowner Club?'

'In this room,' Hakim said, 'we do not care for it when people answer a question with a question.' He threw some ash into the tray with a practised flick. On his desk Spike saw the same triangular card he'd seen in the hotel: *Together Against Terrorism*.

'It's a clip joint,' Spike continued, 'on the beach. The murder victim, Esperanza Castillo, was there the night of her death.'

'With your client, no?'

'Did you know Esperanza was involved in a fight at the Sundowner a few days before she died? With a waitress.'

Hakim sucked hard on his cigarette, as though it were somehow to blame. 'We are considering no other suspects until your client comes back to answer the charges against him.'

'You're not following other leads?'

'Guilty men run, Mr Sanguinetti. Your police friend, Miss Jessica, will tell you that. In fact, she is the only reason I am still talking to you.'

'And I'm the only person doing your job.'

Hakim frowned.

'Last night I went to see this waitress. A jeep tried to run us over.'

'Where?'

'Chinatown.'

Smoke flowed simultaneously from Hakim's mouth and nose. The laugh changed to a cough, which racked his wiry chest until he covered his mouth with a fist, spitting then swallowing. 'Chinatown,' he gasped. 'Normally they just beat you to death with a baseball bat then try to sell your organs. Did you see the number plate?'

'Too dark. But it was a black jeep with tinted windows. Bull-bar bumper.'

'You should not go to Chinatown, Mr Sanguinetti. Especially at night.'

'Like I say, I'm being forced to do your job for you.'

Hakim's face settled into a glare. At the end of his office sat a plywood cabinet, a plastic-framed photo of the King on the wall above, so standardised that Spike realised the one in the Dunetech office must have been a personal gift. Hakim rose, walking over and rattling open a drawer. Ash crumbled down as he drew out a Manila folder.

Back at his desk, he shoved a bulldog-clipped sheaf of forensic photographs into Spike's hand. The top one was a black-and-white head shot. Esperanza's dark shoulder-length hair was washed back from her forehead. Her face was paler than the sand around her and her upper lip shadowed by a faint moustache, like a self-portrait by that Mexican artist. She wore a bolt through one eyebrow and a metal stud beneath her lip. Her cheeks were plump and her eyes open, milky-white, as Solomon had said, with a vacant upward stare that chimed somehow with her strange, other-worldly beauty. Spike brought the photo closer: the cut was just a nick to the left-hand side of her neck, no bigger than a comma. The only indication of depth was the blackness and bruising around.

He turned to the next photo, in colour this time, taken from further back. A juvenile crab was entwined with her armpit hair. Bangles racked up her right forearm.

'So,' he heard Hakim say as he fired up another cigarette, 'the victim and your client are having a drink on the beach. Your client removes the victim's underwear – still missing, if she had any – and they engage in sexual activity. Digital penetration, say forensics; finger-fucking, you might call it.'

Spike reached for the last photo, a full body shot. Esperanza's floral dress sheathed her thighs, revealing a dark raised triangle beneath the cotton. The straps were a rusty brown.

'Your client is carrying a knife,' Hakim went on. 'He leans into the girl, who trusts him, and slits her external jugular with a flick of the wrist. Then he drags her body into the sea – which destroys any traces of DNA – and escapes to Gibraltar.'

Spike turned over the last photo: stamped in red on the back was 'Sûreté Régionale de Tanger'.

'And you,' Hakim said as Spike reaffixed the bulldog clip and slid the pictures back, 'wish to free this murderer on a technicality.'

'We just want him tried in Gibraltar.'

'Because it is more likely he will escape conviction.'

'What if he's not your man?' Spike said. 'Have you even entertained that possibility?'

'He has no alibi.'

'Nor motive.'

'A man, a woman – what more motive do you need?'

'Have you checked for CCTV footage?'

'There were no working cameras on his route home.'

'And no witnesses to prove he was even on the beach at the time of death.'

'The time of death is not yet confirmed.'

'How long?'

'A second post-mortem is being done in Madrid.'

'Why?'

'At the request of her stepfather. A powerful man, I am told.' Hakim began tidying up the photographs.

'Inspector Eldrassi,' Spike said, 'I've known Solomon for thirty years. He's not capable of murder.'

'Sometimes the less you know, the more you see.'

'Is that the motto of the Sûreté Régionale?'

Hakim grinned hazelnut teeth. 'You introduce me to someone you know. You are affected by your experiences of them. I *see* the person.'

'Maybe you see a quick prosecution to keep the governor of Tangiers happy.'

'I see you, Mr Sanguinetti,' Hakim said, face shrouded in smoke like a cheap mystic. 'You are familiar with death, for example.'

'Oh?'

'When you looked through those pictures your face was still. No shock, even when you saw the crab. You have known death. A parent perhaps. A sister.'

Spike felt his jaw tighten. 'Maybe I see you, Inspector Eldrassi.'

'Oh?'

'You've lost your religious faith. But it's not that which keeps you awake at night. It's fear. Fear because you can't shake off the thought you'll still go to hell.'

'Why do you say that?'

'Because you look exhausted. And you're smoking in the daytime during Ramadan.'

Hakim smiled and nodded slowly. 'Your five minutes are up, Mr Sanguinetti,' he said as he crossed the room.

'Go back to the Sundowner Club,' Spike called over. 'Have a chat to the barman, Marouane. He's a small-time drug dealer.'

Hakim shut the folder away with a definitive thunk. Moving to the doorway, he stuck an arm into the entrance hall.

'That cut,' Spike said, rising to his feet. 'It looked precise. Stanley knife? Scalpel?'

'The pathologist believes it was done with an Eid knife; just the tip pressed into the vein.'

Spike shrugged.

'You know of Ramadan but not the Eid? Maybe you have no religion either. It is a festival twice a year. Once to mark the end of Ramadan, another a few months later. Sometimes we kill a lamb to celebrate. A symbol of Ibrahim sacrificing his child, Ismail. A small, sharp knife cuts the throat. They sell maybe five thousand a year in Morocco.'

'Solomon Hassan is Jewish.'

'Jews slaughter lambs, do they not, for Passover?' Hakim ushered Spike through. 'I'm a busy man, Mr Sanguinetti. Until your client comes back, the case is on hold.'

'Can I have access to Solomon's flat?'

'No.'

'Will you get me into Tangiers Prison?'

'You do not stop, do you?' He lifted a hand to Spike's shoulder. 'You are intrepid; I respect that. But if your case against extradition depends on information about our prison, I suggest your client will be back here sooner than you think. Two places a foreigner does not go. One is Tangiers Prison. The other is where you went last night.' Hakim patted himself down for more cigarettes. 'Catch the next boat home, Mr Sanguinetti. And send your client back the other way.'

Two beefy policemen were coming through the main door, submachine guns at their sides. They nodded respectfully at Hakim as they passed.

Spike stepped out onto the street, where the late-morning sun was already blistering. A black jeep was parked on the pavement, 'Sûreté Nationale' painted on the side, windows tinted. Spike stood back and snapped a picture on his mobile phone.

25

Shaded beneath a date palm near the police station, Spike dialled Nadeer Ziyad's number. Opposite, on the central reservation, a young black man was asleep in the sunshine. Spike wondered at the thickness of his woollen roll-neck, before realising he must have climbed the Atlas Mountains to get here, trudging through the Sahara. Even summer nights in the desert were said to be bitterly cold. Where had he started his journey? Mali? Cameroon?

No answer from Nadeer; no voicemail facility either. Spike put away his phone and drew out the invitation he'd taken from Solomon's office. 'Dunetech Investor Roadshow, Saturday 24th'. The 24th was today. A business conference was surely improbable on a Saturday, Spike thought, until he recalled that the Muslim day of rest was Friday. Hence yesterday's skeleton staff at Dunetech, perhaps.

There was a map on the back, which he followed into town, thinking as he walked of Zahra, of the close fit of her jeans beneath her kaftan, of her excellent, foul-mouthed English, husky-voiced as though recovering from a bout of karaoke the night before. He checked the photo he'd taken of the police jeep, trying to remember if there'd been any side markings on the vehicle which had rammed them in Chinatown. It had been too dark to be certain.

The El Minzah Hotel was just past the souk, its sparkling glass doors manned by three porters in fezzes. Seeing the stars arching resplendently above the name, Spike wondered, not for the first time, why he'd heeded his father's advice on accommodation.

'*Je peux vous aider, monsieur?*'

'Here for the Roadshow.'

'Start ten minute ago.'

'My driver got lost.'

One of the porters led Spike through the lobby. The front desk was adorned by a vase of white Casablanca lilies and a crystal decanter of brandy. Past a bank of old-fashioned payphones, a side door was guarded by another porter. The A-board outside welcomed investors to 'The Dunetech Roadshow'; Spike flashed his invitation and was shown into murmuring, air-conditioned darkness.

At one end of the room was a stage, above which a film was projected onto a state-of-the-art screen. Rows of folding chairs were set out in front, an aisle in between. Spike spotted an empty seat near the back by the DVD trolley.

Faces turned, European mainly. Symphonic music and a recorded voiceover were emanating from the stage. Spike heard '. . . over two thousand megawatts of energy . . .' spoken by an actor whose tones he vaguely recognised. Most of the audience wore lightweight summer suits. Spike was in espadrilles, cargo trousers and a T-shirt.

'The sands of time are running out,' the actor's voice said, 'so the time is right . . . for Dunetech.'

The rear wall was lined by soft velvet curtains; Spike backed along them before stepping forward into the aisle. A young Moroccan glanced over from the DVD projector, then resumed pressing buttons.

A prospectus gleamed on the chair, which Spike scooped onto his lap as he sat. The film had switched to sweeping silent images, aerial shots of rows of solar-power units, squatting like triffids in the desert. Their numbers began increasing exponentially, demonstrating how much larger the power field could grow. The last shot panned across an army of mirrored machines, massed to the furthest horizon before the screen switched to black and the Dunetech logo faded in.

Enthusiastic applause swept the room. A woman sitting close to Spike – Japanese or Korean – leaned into a male colleague, whispering in his ear before clapping like an apparatchik.

The projectionist began fiddling with a control panel. The lights came on. The applause ramped up further as Nadeer Ziyad stepped onto the platform. He soaked it up, then raised his arms. '*Shukran*,' he said, stepping higher onto the lectern. '*Namaste. Arigato. Sheh-sheh*. Thank you.' He slid on a pair of rimless specs.

'Ladies and gentlemen, the nature of solar power is such that –' Abruptly he glanced up and removed the glasses. 'My country,' he said, smiling as he leaned a forearm on his notes, 'my beautiful, crazy country.' He looked around the room. 'How much of our energy do we import from abroad? Twenty per cent? Thirty?' He shook his head. 'Ninety-six. *Ninety-six* per cent! No oil to speak of, nor natural gas. In order to make our energy affordable, it must be heavily subsidised by the government. Unfortunately, this eats up resources which could otherwise be dedicated to helping wipe out Morocco's most dreadful affliction.'

Spike saw the audience transfixed as Nadeer penetrated them one by one, giving each a taste of those glittering tawny eyes. 'Investing in Dunetech,' he continued, sliding his spectacles back on, 'is not just about buying into the most democratic and politically stable of all North African countries. It is not just about the provision of renewable, environmentally friendly energy as the world's oil and gas supplies run dry. It is about an immediate and urgent need. A need that will only grow more acute as global climate change exacerbates. One last chance to eradicate the scourge of modern Morocco. Poverty.'

Nadeer turned his head as a series of images of rag-doll children and lean-to huts appeared on the screen. Spike thought he recognised the effluent stream of Chinatown.

'What has traditionally constrained our ability to tap into the immense power of solar energy,' Nadeer resumed sadly, 'is what we in the industry call the three Cs. Cabling, cost and collection.

If I may, I will explain to you how Dunetech plans to revolutionise these one by one. First . . . cabling.' The images switched to a diagram as Nadeer began talking about how Dunetech had secured permission to lay cables from the Sahara, over the Atlas Mountains and into the major cities of Tangiers and Rabat. Spike's neighbour began taking conscientious notes.

'. . . using technology designed exclusively by Professor Ángel Castillo . . .' Spike tuned back in. *Fuck off back to Ángel*, Zahra had said. So Ángel was Esperanza's stepfather. How had Zahra known his name?

Spike opened the prospectus. The first pages were dedicated to exploring the science behind a 'heliopod', one of the futuristic triffids he'd seen in the promo. Hourglass-shaped, each unit stood two metres tall, with a smooth metal base leading up to two concave solar panels. The panels seemed capable of movement, opening and closing like a clam shell as the sun passed overhead.

Spike flicked onwards, stopping at the 'Who we are' section. The first photograph showed Nadeer, narrow chin pinched pensively between thumb and forefinger. His bio revealed him as the son of Yusuf Ziyad, a personal adviser to the King of Morocco – educated at Eton College, Cambridge University, Harvard Business School . . . Spike flipped over to the head shot of Ángel Castillo. The eyebrows were bushy, the salt-and-pepper goatee a luxuriant oval. Bags hung like dried apricots beneath his eyes, creases ran between his nostrils and mouth, and the dismissive smile suggested he had better things to do than pose for a publicity shot. The blue cravat under the collar gave a slightly nautical look. 'Educated at the Complutense in Madrid,' the prospectus said, 'and now tenured at the Universidad de Sevilla, Professor Castillo has worked all his life in Africa and lived in Morocco for the last decade, using his expertise to assist the country's poor. Known affectionately in renewable energy circles as the Sun King, his patents in solar technology have . . .'

Spike returned his eyes to the stage, where Nadeer was onto the final C, Collection, explaining how a single concrete storage tower could regulate energy distribution both at night and in the rare event of cloudy weather. The screen faded back to the Dunetech insignia as Nadeer tucked his glasses into the breast pocket of his suit. 'I thank you all for your patience. Now, any questions?'

'Will Professor Castillo be speaking later?' came a Texan drawl.

'Ángel is slightly unwell. Upset stomach. Incidental pleasure of living in Tangiers.'

A ripple of uneasy laughter.

'When will he be back?'

'This afternoon, inshallah.'

Another hand at the front, a Scandinavian lady enquiring after the timeline of 'Phase Two Expansion'. A moment later, the curtains behind Spike opened to reveal trestle tables of champagne and canapés. Nadeer stepped down to another volley of applause. Spike picked up the prospectus and followed him out.

26

Spike declined a smoked salmon blini. Beyond the buffet, a bank of sliding glass doors gave onto the hotel swimming pool. Spike watched a pale, expensive redhead sway across the suntrap terrace, fanning a hand down the back of her bikini before diving neatly into the water. In the main room, the Roadshow guests seemed more interested in networking than refreshments. Spike looked over as the young projectionist struggled to fit the DVD unit back into a cardboard box. 'Need any help?'

The projectionist shrank back as though he'd done something wrong. The rims of his ears broke the sheen of his hair like two dolphins breaching.

'*Ayuda?*'

Understanding now, the projectionist passed Spike one half of the unit, which they lowered into a Japanese-marked box. '*Shukran,*' he said, eyes drifting hungrily to the buffet.

Nadeer was in the centre of the room, trailed by the immaculate Scandinavian, who kept staring into his eyes as though he were imparting religious homilies. Three Asian men lurked behind, prospectuses under arms. Outside, the redhead drew herself sleekly out of the pool.

As Spike closed in, Nadeer appraised him with an impassive glance, before turning the whole of his head. 'We've already secured second-round investment from – Mr Sanguinetti, what a surprise.'

'I was thinking of upgrading hotel. Saw the Dunetech poster outside.'

'Of course. Miss Solness? This is Mr Sanguinetti.'

The Scandinavian held a Mont Blanc in one hand and a reporter's pad in the other. She bestowed a tight, glossy smile on Spike before turning back to Nadeer, who opened his mouth to continue.

'How did you get on with the governor?' Spike interrupted.

'I'm sorry?'

'Have you fixed up a meeting yet?'

'There's a function tomorrow at my villa. I'll have Toby furnish you with the details.' He turned back to the girl, who swept a manicured hand through her ash-blonde bob.

'Is Ángel Castillo in town?'

One of the Asians stepped forward. 'Castillo,' he repeated, nodding approval as his colleagues did the same. The Scandinavian's gaze dipped from Spike's dark stubble to his red espadrilles.

'As I mentioned earlier, he's not been well,' Nadeer replied. 'Though hopefully,' he added with a smile to the Asians, 'he'll be sufficiently recovered to attend this afternoon's session.'

'I wanted to ask him about Esperanza's final movements.'

The Scandinavian frowned at this new name, and Nadeer gave a subtle nod to the middle distance; almost instantaneously, Spike felt a hand on his shoulder. He turned to see Toby Riddell behind him. Riddell's open-necked shirt revealed a sandy patch of chest hair. His Adam's apple was prominent, one or two reddish whiskers missed on the gristle.

'Toby will be delighted to answer any questions you may have,' Nadeer said, turning back to the Asians.

After tossing a nod at the Scandinavian, Spike followed Riddell to the door. In his right hand he was still pumping that squash ball, back and forth.

27

No one accosted Spike in the cooler lanes of the souk. The covered stalls offered meat, fish, herbs and vegetables, their clientele local, no call for the tourist buck. Craggy Berber ladies in straw hats sold mountain cheeses, while high on butchers' shelves, rows of skinned lambs' heads seemed to follow Spike, eyeballs bulging as though still coming to terms with their unexpected deaths.

Stepping out onto street level, Spike jumped as an engine roared by. Just a rusty three-wheeler, belching fumes. He walked on into the Medina.

A hawker was flogging pirated DVDs; Spike showed him the map that Riddell had sketched out on El Minzah notepaper. Once the hawker had adjusted to the role reversal, he pointed up the hill towards a small enclosed square. The Arabic street sign had a French translation beneath: *Petit Socco*.

The stones of the Petit Socco undulated with the ancient, lumpy quality that suggested continuous use throughout the many guises of Tangiers. The proximity of its two main cafés, Tingis and Central, put Spike in mind of other famous rivalries: Florian and Quadri, Flore and Les Deux Magots, Rick's and the Blue Parrot. An elderly man passed by, dragging a wooden cart as he croaked out his wares, three plump silvery fish reclining behind him on crushed ice. Above, on the wooden balcony of a *pensión*, a woman in a diaphanous veil crooked a long, pink finger Spike's way.

A waiter from the Café Central directed Spike to a lane climbing towards the Kasbah. He passed beneath an arch, turning into a narrow alleyway to find a wall tile painted with the words, 'Numéro Seize'.

An Arabic voice crackled from a speaker in the wall; Spike said 'Ángel Castillo' and the voice fell silent. He took a step back: the facade was blue-and-white-tiled, delineating its boundary from less salubrious neighbours. The front door was of thick, carved oak, the louvred shutters closed, as were all the shutters on this side of the alley. Those opposite were open – it seemed that in the Kasbah, where the streets were too narrow for both sides to open their shutters at the same time, the residents divided their use to one half of the day each.

Spike buzzed again. This time he added the word 'Dunetech' and the catch snapped. He pushed into a gloomy hallway. A shuffling came from above; after climbing a few steps he made out a small, shadowy figure.

'*Duna, duna,*' came a voice.

He climbed further to find an old woman in a black shawl standing in the doorway. She waved him into a long reception room with an intricately-carved arabesque ceiling. A garish acrylic of the Kasbah dominated one wall; on another hung a bank of carved African fertility masks, black-stained and with deep, empty holes for the eyes. The marble floor shone like a mirror; Spike saw a stepladder ahead, its bottom rung draped with a cloth.

'*Min fadhlek,*' the woman said, jabbing forward with her broomstick. Spike slid his rope soles over the gleaming floor. To the left was a tiled room of cushioned marble benches with a plasma TV; to the right, a corridor cross-hatched with light. A spiral staircase rose at the end; the woman pointed towards it.

The staircase led to a cramped doorway. As Spike hunched to step outside, the sunlight stung his eyes. Shielding his face, he crossed a roof terrace surrounded by trellises. A hot tub bubbled in the centre like a cauldron. Beyond stretched a wooden bar backed by shelves of dusty glasses. A table stood to one side with four heavy-looking teak chairs. Slumped in one was a man.

'*Hola?*' Spike called out. The hot tub was redolent of chlorine and something worse; as Spike passed he saw a dead chick churning in its filthy froth. In front of the bar was a binful of empties, fizzing with wasps. The man half sat up: a glass was raised to the mouth, then replaced on the table.

Spike recognised Ángel Castillo from the Dunetech prospectus. He wore beige chinos and a navy, horizontally striped polo shirt. His greying hair and goatee were damp with grease or perspiration. Cracked lips moved as though in silent prayer; a whisky bottle stood at his naked, sunburnt feet.

'*Profesor Castillo?*'

The man squinted up. '*Heebralta?*' he said. His voice was croaky, as though it hadn't been used in a while.

'*Sí.*'

'Here to replace the Jew?' he asked, switching to a serviceable English.

'In a sense.'

'Have a drink, then. *Cagana*, I believe you call it in your Gibberish.'

Spike helped himself to a tumbler at the bar. Ángel picked up the bottle, sloshing brown liquid into Spike's glass before topping up his own. His hand shook; Spike waited for him to raise his glass and drink. 'The answer is no,' he said once he'd managed to put the tumbler down.

Something flashed in the sky above, a swallow, dipping down to the hot tub, chattering as it skipped up over the wooden trellis then down across the rooftops of the Kasbah.

'No to what?'

'I will not come. You can tell him that yourself.'

Spike breathed in the fumes of his glass. 'I'm not from Dunetech,' he said, eventually. 'I'm a lawyer from Gibraltar. I represent Solomon Hassan.'

The swallow swept back over. The bubbles stopped and Spike saw that the chick was still paddling in the water with a wing. Ángel's eyes were closed; Spike stood and went to the water's edge. The mother swallow boomeranged past as Spike cupped his hands into the hot froth and scooped out the chick. Black claws scratched feebly at the decking. Spike returned to the chair.

'There is a nest in the eaves,' Ángel said, eyes still shut. 'It was learning to fly but it fell.'

Spike paused. 'I'm sorry about your stepdaughter, Professor Castillo. You have my sympathy.'

Ángel refilled his glass.

'But I do need to ask you some questions.'

He drank deeply, spilling whisky on the thigh of his chinos.

'Do you believe Solomon Hassan killed your stepdaughter?'

He shrugged.

'Do you know who might have?'

He shrugged again, wincing this time; beneath the sweat-soaked collar, his neck was tender from the sun.

'Do you *care* who killed her?'

'Caring does not bring her back.'

'But you do want justice?'

Ángel reached back for the bottle but found it empty. Returning to the bar, Spike found a plywood case in a cupboard, its side plastered with yellow customs stickers. He drew out a fresh bottle of J&B, glancing through the trellis as he walked back – another landslip below, beggar-built shacks in the rubble. One seemed to be constructed from a framework of shopping trolleys.

'*Gracias*,' Ángel muttered, 'you understand drunks.' He refreshed his glass with a steadier hand. 'You know,' he said, 'my work has taken me all over Africa, but never have I seen poverty like Morocco. Supermodels partying in Marrakesh while children rot on the streets. New luxury hotels in Rabat, while the population flocks in from the countryside with nowhere to live. Rising birth rate, falling employment, corrupt politicians, and not a

97

thing done to change it.' He smiled, teeth indecently white among the raw stubble. 'Until now.'

The bubbles came back on in the hot tub.

'Do you know how many lives Dunetech will save?' Ángel said. 'In five years, it can free up more than one hundred million euros for the King to use against poverty. Think how many deaths that can prevent. Millions.'

'I'm afraid my humanitarian work is on a smaller scale,' Spike said. 'My client is facing a potential death penalty, or an extradition order that amounts to the same thing. Did you see Esperanza the day she died?'

'She was staying here; I saw her every day.'

'And that day?'

'We had lunch together at the Café Central. She went for a beauty treatment – hot wax, I believe.' His tone was of bitter irony.

'Then?'

'She saw a fortune-teller about her luck.'

'Who was he?'

'Some street rat. The police picked him up. Esperanza was superstitious, like her mother. They both had to believe in something.'

'And then?'

'She met the Jew. He was showing her round town.'

'She hadn't been here before?'

'Hadn't wanted to.'

'What changed?'

'She got older.'

'Did she like Solomon Hassan?'

'Did anyone?'

'Did you?'

Ángel drank again. 'He was back office; I rarely saw him. When I did, he was always keen . . . to ingratiate himself.'

'Did your stepdaughter have enemies?'

'She was a *child*.'

Spike paused. 'Have you heard of a girl called Zahra?'

'No.'

'A Bedouin?'

'*Qué dices?*'

'*Beduina?*'

Ángel suddenly drew himself up, grabbing the whisky bottle and slamming its base onto the end of the table. Shards of glass skittered across the decking. He held out the dripping, jagged stump, hooded eyes peeling back. 'You use that word,' he said, 'in *my* house?'

Spike edged towards the bar, Ángel jabbing at him with the sawtooth end.

'Get out.'

'Easy, pal.'

'Out!' Ángel's bare soles had found an unexpected nimbleness on the decking. The swallow chick, semi-recovered, flopped back into the hot tub. 'OUT!'

The doorway part-opened to reveal the maid, beckoning as though afraid to emerge fully. Spike looked back at Ángel's now unshaking hand, then ducked beneath the lintel. '*Samt,*' the maid said soothingly, '*la taklak.*'

On his way out, Spike paused at a room off the hallway. The walls and ceiling were tiled like a Turkish hammam; in one corner stood a wooden console table covered in picture frames. All showed Esperanza, alone or with friends. She looked thinner, younger. Innocent.

Outside, the maid was mopping up Spike's footprints. She murmured to herself as she worked; Spike thought he recognised a word. '*Beduina?*' he repeated.

Head down, with a low guttural sound, the maid sliced a broad thumbnail across her throat. She was still mopping as Spike crossed the sparkling marble floor back down to the street.

28

Spike sat beneath the awning of the Café Central, eating an *omelette au fromage*, the cheese just a rubbery orange bookmark between two fluffy folds of egg. He mopped up the sunflower oil with his bread before pouring himself another cup of super-sweet mint tea. The perforated silver pot had a pleasing ability to yield up another cup just when it looked like supplies had run dry.

A bearded Moroccan with a shaven moustache was watching him from across the square. Spike stared back and the man crept furtively away, up the hill towards the Kasbah. Strapped to his back was a small red rucksack.

At the table to Spike's right sat a couple of gap-year girls, German or Austrian. They kept glancing at him before returning to their guidebooks, giggling as he met their gaze. He had a missed call, he saw – number withheld. He took a punt and rang.

'Hello, Tax Man.'

'Hi, Jess. Did you call?'

'Nope. I'm on foot patrol in Irish Town. So how's Tangiers?'

'They don't seem to like me much.'

'That makes a –' Jessica checked herself. 'Where are you staying?'

'Hotel Continental.'

'*Una tanita?*'

'Seen better days.'

'And you hooked up OK with Eldrassi?'

'Yeah. You sure he's straight?'

'As they go.'

'How's Solomon?'

'Still complaining.'

'I need to talk to him.'

'I've scheduled you a call for 4 p.m. tomorrow.'

'*Tenkiu*, Jess. And let's have that drink when I get back.'

'You OK, Spike?'

'Why?'

'You sound . . . different.'

Spike paused. 'What do you know about Bedouins?'

'Bedouins? Come from the desert. Move about a lot. Big on honour codes, like most nomadic people. Not many left in Morocco, I think. Why?'

'What sort of honour codes?'

'Blood feuds, that sort of thing. Why? Have you fallen for one?'

'A whole tribe. So I call the Castle tomorrow at four?

'*Está penene*, Spike.'

The sun was passing above the square, dragging its shadow line over the cobbles like a tarpaulin drawn by invisible ball boys. Spike's phone rang again. 'Yes?' he said irritably. Damp breathing poured down the line. 'Hello?'

'Is Marouane.'

'Who?'

'From the Sundowner. You come now. Alone.'

The breathing was replaced by dead air.

29

Swimmers and sun worshippers disported themselves in the distance. At this end of the beach, clusters of men loitered in full-length robes, cupping illicit Ramadan cigarettes, chatting surreptitiously as they glanced out to sea. A father and son flew a home-made kite, a mongrel gleefully chasing its shadow. Spike skirted around them to follow the perimeter fence of the Sundowner Club.

The gate hatch was open; Spike ducked beneath and slipped through the metal door. The velvet curtain was hooked onto a nail in the concrete; ahead, Spike saw the back of Marouane, bucket at his feet as he slopped down the bar top. He wore pink Hawaiian shorts, Jesus sandals and a hard-rock T-shirt. His hair was loose, lank black locks spilling over narrow shoulders.

Spike gave a sharp enough whistle to be heard above the brutal music. Marouane turned, tossing his cloth into the bucket. 'You happy with your Marouane,' he shouted. 'Yessir.'

'Turn the music off.'

After glancing left and right, as though appealing to an imaginary referee, Marouane moved to the bar top and turned the music down.

'Off. *Apagada.*'

Finally, silence. 'Vodka?' Marouane said, but Spike ignored the offer, drawing up a chair beside the bench seats. As Marouane came over, he paused by the podium to lick a fingertip. A trail of crusty powder ran along the black-painted plywood; Marouane reconstituted it with his saliva, dabbing the ball of a finger onto his tongue. He grinned. 'You like Tatiana, no?'

'You asked to see me.'

Marouane sat down on the sticky bench seat. 'Marouane must eat, you know?'

'Is Zahra back?'

'Fuck that Bedouin bitch. I see her, I cut her. No . . . Better.' He stood and went to a doorway adjacent to the 'private room'. Spike heard two short, crisp sniffs from inside before he reappeared, handbag over shoulder, sauntering towards the bench seats, hips jigging, one wrist cocked as he placed the handbag on the podium. Sitting back down, he pinched both nostrils, eyeballs bulging.

The handbag was made of expensive brown leather with a zip down the middle. 'One *thousand* dirham,' Marouane declared, holding out a hand, then shaking his head in frustration, hair exuding a stale pomade. Picking up the bag, he set it on the bulge in his Hawaiian shorts, unzipping it and drawing out a wallet with a familiarity that suggested lengthy acquaintanceship. He slung the wallet at Spike's chest; it fell into his lap.

Spike picked it up. Spanish driver's licence in the gauze flap: Esperanza Castillo, smiling, neat collar of a white frilly blouse around her neck. 'Did you show this to the police?' Spike said.

Marouane flashed a gold molar. 'Police don't pay.'

Spike opened the opposite flap – Spanish ID, picture more recent, plumper, scowling – as Marouane removed a tampon from the handbag. Using his right hand, he formed a tunnel into which he jabbed the tampon back and forth. 'Uh, uh, uh. Big bitch,' he chuckled.

Spike stuck out an arm. 'The bag.'

As Marouane passed it over by the strap, Spike caught his hand, wrapping his fingers around the knuckles. Marouane frowned; Spike gave a brisk and vicious twist. His free hand grabbed at the source of the pain.

'Drop it.'

'I'm trying to.'

Spike twisted further until Marouane began to screech, clawing at Spike's forearm. Finally he managed to release the strap, huddling back into the bench seat, hand to his stomach, rocking. 'You break my fuckin' *arm* . . .'

Spike reached down for the handbag, then stood.

'Hey!' Marouane called out. 'One thousand dirham.'

He flicked a twenty note on the ground. 'For the coat check.' He was almost out of the door when he heard Marouane call after him: 'You a dead man. You cunt.'

Spike turned. Marouane's left hand held up his business card. The wrist drooped: he transferred it to his right. 'I find you, cunt. Maybe Tangier. Maybe your home. But I find you.'

'I look forward to it,' Spike replied as he headed back out to the sunshine.

Walking along the pavement above the bar, Spike saw blood spreading beneath his bandage. A young woman was closing in; he recognised Tatiana, casually dressed in stonewash jeans and a paisley headscarf. She stopped, eyes on the ground. 'Zahra,' she said, 'she gone.' Her left eye was puffy, flaking with foundation, the scar on her chin unmasked and prominent.

'Gone where?'

She stared across the Straits. 'Sometimes when a person leave, first they make visit to the Café des Étoiles.'

'Here in Tangiers?'

'Ville Nouvelle.'

Spike nodded. There was fear in Tatiana's good eye as it flitted from the cut on his hand to the handbag on his shoulder. 'Listen,' Spike said, 'Marouane's in a bad mood. *Mal humor.* Take the day off.' He gave her a two-hundred note, then continued along the pavement.

30

Stretching out on the unmade bed, ankles dangling, Spike listened to the rapid-fire finale of Caprice No. 13 in B flat major. No wonder they called it 'The Devil's Laughter'. He stared at the handbag, then reached for the central zip. It felt like opening a body bag. Sitting up properly, he emptied out the contents onto the bedclothes.

Condoms, aspirins, golden tube of lipstick. Well-used pack of tarot cards, screwed-up receipts . . . Spike checked for credit cards or cash. Not so much as a coin.

As he refilled the handbag, his hand brushed something solid. He stood and carried the bag to the light of the window. Drawing the two sides apart, he found a concealed zip at the base. He slid in his fingers and worked out a slim mobile phone.

He tried the on button: the screen flashed white then went dead. He pressed it again and nothing happened.

Turning the device over, he found a hole for the charger. He unplugged his own phone and tried it. Too small. He checked the make: Arabic.

The soundtrack of an action film boomed from next door. Picking up Esperanza's phone, he stepped out onto the landing.

31

Jean-Baptiste rolled his eyes, the whites reminding Spike of the skinned lambs' heads in the souk. 'Relax,' Spike said. 'It's not about the noise. I want to take you up on your offer.' He held out his wrist.

Jean-Baptiste glanced down at the bloodied bandage and made a series of clicking noises with his tongue. He stepped inside, leaving the door half open.

Spike followed him in. The shutters were closed, the air sweet and stale, the only light issuing from a line of four TV monitors, side by side at the edge of the room. The same film seemed to be showing on each; Spike recognised a starlet of the moment, doing 'scared' in the hallway of an ultra-modern house.

'Wait here,' Jean-Baptiste said. His accent was French, deep and languid. On the screens, the girl had responded to the danger by slipping off her hot pants and creeping through the house in her underwear. Spike looked about: four DVD players lay interconnected on the floor. A glinting pillar of blank discs stretched halfway to the ceiling. Turning to the bedside table, Spike saw a photograph taped to the wall, a hefty matron beaming beneath a floral headdress.

'You like movies?' Jean-Baptiste said as he upended an iodine bottle onto a cotton-wool ball and swabbed it over Spike's cut. Spike felt a sting then saw yellowness stain the skin. The film soundtrack changed to urgent strings as the killer snuck up. 'She should run away,' Spike said.

'They never do. *Voi ... là.*'

Spike drew back his wrist then took out Esperanza's mobile. 'You wouldn't have a charger for this, would you?'

Jean-Baptiste examined the handset. '*C'est d'ici, uh?*'

'Belongs to a friend.'

With a knowing grin, Jean-Baptiste crouched down to the bedside table, plunging his hand into a vipers' nest of cables. He seemed able to navigate expertly in the half-light. Spike watched him try various pins until at last he saw the blue-white glow of a phone screen. Jean-Baptiste looked up. '*Tu veux du kif?*'

Spike suddenly felt very tired. 'Why not?'

Jean-Baptiste's teeth flashed like bone as he reached for a drawer and took out a toffee-sized lump of hashish. Sitting back on the bed, he burnt a large crumb onto a DVD case, mixing it with sprigs of tobacco which he stuffed into the mouth of a clay pipe. The cop launched into a showdown with the killer as the girl lay unconscious, breasts straining against her bra.

Spike caught the familiar sweet herbal smell as Jean-Baptiste puffed on the pipe then handed it over. He sucked on the end, hot ash catching at the back of his throat. The iodine on his cut began to throb.

'*Oro negro*,' Jean-Baptiste said. 'Black gold from the Rif Mountain. *Le kif est dans le Rif, uh?*'

'Mercy,' Spike replied, finally letting the smoke out.

'*Tu parles français?*'

'*Pas un word.*'

Jean-Baptiste took a few more puffs. A new sound from the TV, like two men in the distance sawing a tree in half. Spike felt the mattress vibrate then realised Jean-Baptiste was laughing. 'What?' Spike said.

'*Pas un word . . .*'

Spike found he was laughing too. He took another puff, feeling tears prick the corners of his eyes. Jean-Baptiste sat back, sighing.

'So how did you get into all this?'

'Into what?'

Spike forgot what he was going to say. They smoked some more until he remembered. 'The technology. *Technologie*,' he added in a Clouseau accent.

Jean-Baptiste cleared his throat, suddenly serious. 'In the Côte d'Ivoire. Abidjan. I work for the radio. *Producteur de radio*. One day I make a programme the police do not like. My mother' – his eyes flicked to the bedside table – 'she give me money for Europe. All her money.' He puffed out slowly as though trying to cool the memory. 'I cross to the north. Burkina, Mali. Into desert. Three thousand kilometre. Bus, lorry, *camionette*. One month in the desert. When I reach here, I think, it is time for Europe. But for Europe you need money and now my money is gone. So I earn' – he gestured at the screens, as the hero cop and the starlet embraced – 'and I wait.'

'DVD sales holding up?'

'Not just DVD,' Jean-Baptiste said defensively. 'I make slide show for tour companies. Business conference for hotels–'

'The El Minzah?'

'Sure. El Minzah, Mövenpick, Intercontinental.'

Spike received another numbing hit of smoke. 'Did you meet many Bedouins in the desert?'

'*Les bédouins?*' Jean-Baptiste nodded vigorously. '*Très costauds*. Tough man, tough woman. Berber, Tuareg, black man – all are the same to *les bédouins*. First, *les bédouins*, then all else. Not like in Tanger. Know what they call me here?'

'What?'

'*Abid.*'

'Abid?'

'Slave.'

Spike passed back the pipe. 'I get that sometimes.'

'*Tu parles de la merde*, white boy,' Jean-Baptiste muttered.

'In Gibraltar,' Spike went on. 'The Spanish. They call us Chingongos.'

Jean-Baptiste paused. '*Chingongo*,' he said, trying to replicate Spike's accent. 'What is that?'

'A remote tribe of people who are interbred.'

Jean-Baptiste looked puzzled.

'*Incestuoso*,' Spike explained. 'Have sex with their family.' He contorted an eye and let his tongue loll. '*Chin-gon-go.*'

Spike saw Jean-Baptiste's face scrutinise him in the glow of the credits. He looked preoccupied, then his eyes creased and he spluttered out a long, hacking laugh. '*Abid*,' he sighed, '*et Chingongo.*' He pointed at Spike; this set him off again until he wiped his eyes and crouched down to the nearest DVD player. Spike felt his inner thighs squeak as he adjusted his position on the bed. For a moment he envied the flowing cotton lightness of Jean-Baptiste's djellaba. 'Do you know the Café des Étoiles?' he said.

Still on all fours, Jean-Baptiste worked himself round. 'Is like my *salon*. You want to go there, *Chingongo*?'

'*Mais oui, mon ami.*'

Jean-Baptiste gave another serious look. Then he burst out laughing again as he pressed a DVD into its plastic case.

32

The sun was setting, the cafés and takeaway stalls abuzz. Spike and Jean-Baptiste wove through the labyrinth of lanes, towering over the locals. Every third step Jean-Baptiste seemed to stop to greet a vendor or glad-hand a shopkeeper. As he chatted to two weary-looking men with Afros, Spike asked him to wait and went down to the coast road.

The police station was starting to fill up. Spike handed over Esperanza's handbag wrapped in a hotel laundry bag, a letter taped to the front. 'For Inspector Eldrassi,' he said to the duty sergeant. 'Tell him it's to do with the Solomon Hassan case. Solomon Hassan, you got that?'

'Hassan. *Wakha*.'

Jean-Baptiste was waiting outside the police station. He carried his bulky canvas duffel bag with ease. 'You go in there for your friend?' he said.

'*Oui*.'

He nodded, satisfied, and they continued up the coast road. The wind was picking up, billowing out the burka of a lady coming the other way like some funereal ghost. A set of three-footers broke on the beach, the Gut doing its hidden work, roiling and churning beneath the surface.

33

The Café des Étoiles occupied the tongue-shaped end of a shabby block of the Ville Nouvelle. Two boulevards crossed at its facade; a black bin bag had been kicked into one, clipped by cars, spilling its guts. A cedar tree grew outside the main door, gnarled after a lifetime of being kicked by passers-by and urinated on by dogs, one of which cocked its leg as Spike and Jean-Baptiste passed, observing them with pink discomfited eyes.

The brown-stained interior was a fug of malodorous smoke. 'I visit to maître d',' Jean-Baptiste called over the din. 'Ski-Coca for later?'

'Ski?'

'Whi-ski.'

Spike watched him edge through the crowd, somehow avoiding the cul-de-sacs as he moved to a doorway in the back wall. In front, the low tables were crammed together, the spaces between filled by punters talking over the heads of those seated. At one end stood a platform where a trio of rictus-grin musicians were struggling to make themselves heard. The two men on double bass and drums were North African, the keyboard player white. A fellow European, Spike assumed, until he passed and saw he was a freckled, albino black.

Spike sensed eyes on the back of his head. Someone hissed up, 'Change money, friend?' but he continued on by to an empty bar stool, where a white-haired barman was crushing mint with a pestle. Spike shouted out his order; a minute inclination of the head suggested the barman had heard.

He sat down. The two men on adjacent stools turned. One wore an ill-fitting suit, the other a hooded beige burnous. Spike took out his wallet; they glanced at one another then resumed their chat. He caught a glimpse of what looked like a European passport beneath the bar.

'*Vingt dirhams, monsieur.*'

Spike paid up as a giant West African entered the postage-stamp-sized space by his stool. Gathering his drinks with a sweep of the arm, Spike withdrew to sit beside a poster advertising last decade's visit of the Cirque du Maghreb.

After pressing his forehead against the tepid Coke bottle, Spike took a swig, then removed Esperanza's mobile phone from his pocket. His fingertips looked large and clumsy on the keys. No more hashish – ever. The screen lit up – 'Maroc Télécom' – showing two bars of battery but a full signal. He checked the call list: nothing. The inbox contained four texts, each from Maroc Télécom offering hearty welcome in English, French, Spanish and Arabic. Three weeks old: evidently a local mobile had been a recent acquisition for Esperanza.

Another gulp of Coke, then Spike moved to 'Sent items'. A single message this time, sent to a contact saved as 'Abd al-Manajah'. Written out in Spanish: '*Vengo mañana como fijado*'. *I will come tomorrow as agreed.* Sent on the 16th, the day before Esperanza died.

Spike checked 'Contacts'. One name again: 'Abd al-Manajah'. He looked over at the bar: the two men on stools had been replaced by newcomers. Pressing the phone to one ear and cupping the other with his hand, Spike hit call back. Five rings, ten. . . He thought about Ángel Castillo's account of Esperanza's last movements. Tarot cards from a fortune-teller. A trip to the beautician. Fifteen rings, twenty . . . In the dark, uneven mirror on the wall, he saw Jean-Baptiste's head bobbing towards him over the customers.

Spike hung up and reached beneath the bar stool. '*Merci mec,*' Jean-Baptiste said as he accepted his drink. After downing it in one, he did a jig on the spot, dreadlocks clacking. 'Now I buy for you,' he said, turning to the bar. 'Happy hour for *Chingongo et Abid.*' His duffel bag wilted emptily on his shoulder.

As soon as Jean-Baptiste left his sightline, Spike saw something glitter at a table ahead. He crouched down, trying to catch a view through the tangle of limbs. A girl in a sparkly headscarf was passing something to a man with a bushy beard and shaven upper lip. The girl received a package in return, which she tucked into the pocket of her kaftan. As she drew back her hand, she met Spike's eye, then looked hurriedly away, reaching over to touch the arm of her companion before turning for the exit. 'Got to go,' Spike said to Jean-Baptiste.

'*Comment?*'

'See you back at the hotel.'

Spike launched into the crowd as Zahra gracefully circum-navigated the table. He collided with a youth with gaps shaved into his eyebrows, who shoved him back, spitting out insults in French.

A channel opened up; Spike plunged into it. Zahra was almost at the door. 'Wait!' Spike called out.

A hush swept through the bar, broken only by the tuneless rendition of 'Summertime'.

'I'm a friend,' Spike said. 'I've seen Ángel.'

The bar hum began to reassert itself as Zahra exited. Through the misty window, Spike saw her hesitate on the pavement outside, then beckon with a hand.

34

Spike had forgotten how tall she was. 'Come,' she said in her husky voice, 'not too close.' He kept a few metres behind her, breaking into an occasional jog. Most of her face was hidden by her headscarf, the only clear features her flashing eyes and a loose strand of black hair, swaying in the breeze.

They entered the café-clogged Place de France. On the roof of a medium-rise building, backlit so as to be visible at night, Spike saw a Dunetech billboard. *Powering a Greener Future* . . . Beside it was a panel advertising '33 Export' beer. Alcohol was banned within the Medina and Kasbah; outside, most things seemed to go.

Zahra exited the square along an avenue of palm trees, stopping as the pavement widened out to provide a viewing platform over the Straits. Four black ceremonial cannons were pointed out to sea, primed as though to repel intruders. Moored in the bay was a green-lit cruise ship, dull Europop throbbing from its deck.

Zahra sat down on the retaining wall, folding her kaftan beneath. Some Moroccan teenagers gathered further along glanced over. When Spike appeared, they resumed their kif smoking, inured to courting couples. Spike's legs hung beside hers above a shadowy bed of bougainvilleas.

'You know this place?' Zahra said.

'No.'

'It is the Terrasse des Paresseux. The Terrace of the Idle.' She stared out to sea. 'Who are you?'

'A lawyer.'

'You don't look like a lawyer. Where are you from?'

Spike pointed over the Straits to the lights of Gibraltar; Zahra inclined her eyes to see. 'The magical island for the idle English.'

'English speakers. And it's not an island. It's attached to mainland Spain.'

She turned her head properly. Her dark, almond-shaped eyes held Spike's own, causing him a momentary, unfamiliar slide in his stomach. 'Why are you following me?' she said.

'I want to talk to you about Esperanza.'

'Why should I listen?'

'I represent a man called Solomon Hassan. He's the chief suspect in Esperanza's murder.'

'So this is about money for you. Tax-free, I assume.'

'Do you know him?'

She shook her head.

'You argued with Esperanza. Why?'

She turned back to sea.

'Why did you throw a drink in Esperanza's face?'

She pulled up the sleeves of her kaftan, giving Spike a glimpse of smooth, coffee-coloured skin beneath. 'Esperanza used to come into the club,' she said. 'She was friendly at first. Then I processed her card and saw she was a Castillo.' A muezzin began to wail from a distant minaret; Zahra waited for him to finish. 'My father was head of the Bedouin council in my village. Eight years ago, some men from Ángel Castillo's company came to see him. They wanted to buy some land. A Bedouin burial site. Two weeks later my father disappeared.'

'Where?'

'Nobody knows. The elders say he took a bribe. That he's in Rabat, spending the money on women.' Her voice hardened: 'He liked women.'

'And the land?'

'Sold. Most of the Bedouins now have jobs on the site.'

'Did you tell Esperanza about this?'

'At first she just laughed. Then we fought.'

'But you saw her again?'

'She came back to the club. She was upset. We went for a drive and she told me she'd confronted her father. The next day she was dead.'

'Stepfather,' Spike murmured. 'So who killed her?'

Zahra shrugged. 'When I found out what happened I kept away. Then you turned up in Chinatown and we had our fun with the jeep.'

'Do you know who was driving?'

'I thought you might.'

'Why?'

'Because,' she said, turning again, 'it looked like it was trying to hit you.'

Spike paused. 'A police vehicle?'

'Maybe.' Her gaze returned to the European shoreline.

'Where were you the night Esperanza was killed?'

'Fuck you.'

'Could Marouane have killed her?'

'He tried to touch me once. He didn't do it again. He's a parasite, not a killer.'

'What were you buying just now in the café?'

She started to stand, so Spike reached into a pocket for his wallet, stopping only when he saw her look of contempt. Shaking her head, she walked away.

'Wait,' Spike said. 'I've got Esperanza's phone.'

'A lawyer *and* a thief,' Zahra called back. 'How unusual.'

Spike stood and dug into another pocket. 'There's a text on it,' he said. 'From an Abd al-Manajah.' He approached her; she was just a half-head smaller. 'I think Esperanza had arranged to see him the day she died.'

Zahra looked down at the phone. 'It's a Bedouin name. Used for the city. Abd is for Abdallah. Al-Manajah is the name of the tribe.' She passed the phone back.

'Do you know him?'

Before she walked away, Spike thrust a business card in her hand. 'Call me if you remember anything,' he said. 'Especially about Abdallah al-Manajah.'

Zahra turned the card upside down. 'No baksheesh?'

'Do it for Esperanza.'

'Why should I care about her?'

'Because she's dead.'

Zahra strode away into the darkness. Spike checked to see if she'd dumped the card. When he looked back up, she was gone.

35

An empty police jeep was parked on the pavement above the Sundowner Club. Street kids milled around it, kicking the tyres before running away. Spike crossed over and started climbing up to the Medina, where men were streaming out of cafés, plastic carrier bags in hands, chatting as though leaving a sports event.

Stopping at a food stall, Spike bought an avocado milkshake and some dusty unleavened bread. As he paid, he saw a bearded man watching him from beneath a street light.

Spike continued up the hill, chewing on his bread. When he looked back, the man was still following. He turned into an alleyway, then up a wider lane towards the Petit Socco. The man was still behind, his step quick and athletic. Around the next corner, Spike ducked into the first open shop he could see.

The shelves were lined with pots and jars like in an ancient apothecary. The owner creaked up from a stool, as though surprised by the custom. In the back room, Spike saw a shawled woman clipping her toenails as a tajine crock simmered before her.

'*Bon prix pour épices, monsieur?*' the owner said. '*Guter Preis?*'

There was a barrel in the middle of the shop; Spike crouched behind it as his pursuer appeared at the window. His beard was bushy, his upper lip entirely smooth. He carried a red rucksack on his back, which he swung off to remove a slim mobile phone. Still by the window, he made a call, talking animatedly, glancing about before finally moving out of sight.

The owner reappeared with a glass jar. Spike watched him tweezer out a series of fragrant, russet stamens, holding them one by one to the light. Spike bought the bag of saffron for old times' sake, then chose a different route back to the hotel.

36

'An offence by one villain may injure a million.'

'Room 303.'

'You had a visitor.'

'Quotation or fact?'

'A police inspector.'

Spike picked up his key. 'What did he want?'

'To come back tomorrow.'

Spike started walking up the stairs, then stopped. 'Do you have a telephone directory?'

'*Comment?*'

'A big book. With phone numbers.'

The receptionist turned to a shelf behind the computer point. 'A book is a garden you carry in your pocket,' he said as he heaved the directory onto the counter.

'You'd need pretty big pockets for this one. *Merci* and . . . *bonne nuit.*'

'*À vous aussi.*'

Silence from Jean-Baptiste's door, the frosted panel above it dark. Spike unlocked his own room. The bed was as he'd left it: no turndown service at the Continental. He pulled off his T-shirt, opening the shutters to breathe in the warm spiced air. A pale crescent moon hung above the Straits.

After clearing a space on the dressing table, he selected Caprice No. 16 in G minor, composed by Paganini in Lucca in 1805 while he was working as court musician for Napoleon's sister, Elisa Bonaparte. Paganini had conducted an affair with Elisa while also giving private violin lessons to her husband, Felice. The Devil looks after his own ... The cadenzas seemed to clamp Spike's temples like a vice. He forced himself to keep listening, shutting his eyes and seeing Arabic script and musical notes flit interchangeably beneath his lids. The caprice ended; he snapped back to life and picked up the phone directory.

Half the names were in Arabic, half in French. The same names in both languages? No 'al-Manajahs' anyway. He searched for 'Abdallah' as a surname and found two entire pages.

Reaching for his notebook, he began making a list. *Ángel Castillo. Nadeer Ziyad. Toby Riddell. Marouane. Abdallah al-Manajah. Zahra* ... He tore out the sheet, crumpling it into a ball and basketball-pitching it into the bin. He was here with a simple task: delay an extradition demand. And what was he doing? Drawing up a list of suspects like some backwater Poirot. His penultimate night in Tangiers and he'd achieved nothing save for a possible meeting with the local governor. The prison ... He needed to go to the prison, seek out some hard evidence.

Grabbing the phone book again, he flicked through for the most common Jewish surnames: Benunes, Israel, Larache, Levy ... His mobile phone was ringing; he hit 'pause' on the iPod. Number withheld. 'Hello?'

'It's Galliano.'

'*Qué pasa?*'

'I'm afraid there's been some news.'

Spike shot up from his chair. 'Dad?'

'What? No, no. Nothing like that.'

Spike felt his lungs deflate as he sat back down.

'They've done the second post-mortem in Madrid.'

'And?'

'Traces of DNA.'

'I thought they'd been degraded by the salt.'

'Not on the body.'

'The knife?'

'No.'

'Underwear?'

'It seems that no good deed goes unpunished, Spike,' Galliano said. 'The girl was two weeks pregnant. And there's a ninety-nine per cent genetic match with Solomon Hassan.'

37

After a night of disturbing dreams, Spike awoke to find the city back in Ramadan mode. The Mendoubia public park was strewn with *sans-papiers* face down on the grass, as though there'd been a street festival the night before and they hadn't quite made it home. Tethered goats grazed around outstretched limbs.

Once through the commercial zone, the *petit taxi* drove past various small-scale industrial concerns – brickworks, sawmill, bus depot. Spike assumed they'd reached the prison when he saw a gate topped with razor wire; instead, the hand-painted Coca Cola billboard above the walls revealed it as a bottling plant.

The road grew narrower, flanked by scrubland and the occasional caved-in building. Past the next hill, Spike saw Chinatown nestling in its sweaty hollow. The taxi began to slow, stopping at another set of gates. A Moroccan flag dangled from a pole, blood red with a green star in the middle. A metal car barrier was presided over by CCTV cameras.

Spike paid the driver and got out. Two women in burkas were chatting on the pavement, each with a child tugging at a black-cloaked arm. Spike buzzed the door panel. '*Visita*,' he said as a Coca-Cola lorry lumbered behind.

As he reached to buzz again, a jeep with tinted windows turned off the road. The barrier bounced up and the gates began to open. Spike waited, then followed the jeep inside.

The gates clanked closed. The air throbbed with stillness. Somewhere a cicada buzzed.

Passing the entrance the jeep had taken, Spike saw a courtyard of parked cars. He stopped at a wooden hut, occupied by a heavy man sharing a spicy dish with the flies.

'*Visita.*'

The man stashed his carton guiltily out of sight. His face was so fat that the flesh pushed his eyes shut, reducing his vision to a slit of skin.

'*Visite*,' Spike tried, guessing at the French. 'Levy,' he added, handing over a sheet of paper on which the receptionist had written out the surname in Arabic. The guard slimmed his eyes still further, then picked up a Bakelite phone and waited for the connection.

Just past the hut, a two-tiered gate gave onto one of the yards of the prison. The ground was dusty and sun-drenched; in the only shady corner sat a group of men hugging their knees.

Spike moved towards the bars. One of the men shielded his eyes then stood. He took a step forward as another prisoner yanked him back by the tunic. He broke free, loping across the yard. His beard was russet, his forehead pink and flaky. He hurled himself at the bars, one sandal still on, the other left behind in the dirt, shouting in a language Spike did not recognise.

'*Hellas*,' he yelled, just inches from Spike's face. '*Hellas, Hellas . . .*'

One of the other prisoners was striding over, dark tufty beard down to his chest.

'Greece,' the sunburnt man shrieked, '*ambassada, ambassada . . .*'

With a creaking of hinges, the guard emerged from his hut. Drawing his truncheon, he strolled towards the gate, shouting as he swung at the bars. The man gave a bird-like cry as the truncheon crushed his knuckles, and fell to the ground. The prisoner behind him laughed as the guard raised his truncheon again.

'Hey!' Spike called out, stepping between the guard and the gate. '*Visite.*'

Tucking the truncheon under his arm, the guard took Spike's piece of paper out of his pocket and tore it neatly in two. Spike swore at him in English, then turned to the sound of a clank from the opposite end of the walkway. Another jeep was driving in.

The gates were starting to close. Spike set off rapidly towards them, hearing the guard shouting behind him as he slipped between the gap.

The ladies in burkas were still on the pavement. Spike walked past them, waving down a *petit taxi* on the other side of the road. 'Medina,' he said, and the cab performed a U-turn and headed back to town.

38

'Right then, you *charavaca*,' Spike swore down the phone, 'one more lie, one more half-truth, and I throw you to the wolves. Do you understand?'

'Yes.'

'How long do we have?'

Solomon gulped at the other end of the line. 'Twenty minutes.'

'Then get ready to talk. Did you kill her?'

'God, Spike. *No*.'

'But you were sleeping with her.'

'Yes.'

'How many times?'

'Twice . . . once.'

'Which is it?'

'I don't know. The first time didn't . . . work.'

'Didn't work?'

'Couldn't.'

'Where?'

'We went to the Museum of Ethnography. Then to a hotel bar, the El Minzah. She had a few drinks, then went crazy. Pulled me into the toilet but I was too . . . taken aback. So I asked her to dinner at my flat. I'd ordered up some pills online. Things went . . . better. I told her I wanted to see her again. When I asked her if she was sleeping with other people, she just laughed.'

'Which other people?'

'Men she picked up. Women.'

'Their names?'

'I don't know, Spike, I just know there were others. A few days later, we arranged to meet at the club. We watched a woman and a man dance. I didn't like it so we went outside. The rest is as I told you.'

'So who killed her?'

'I don't know. Someone on the beach. Or from the club.'

'The barman?'

'I really don't know.'

'Why did you lie before?'

'I thought you might not take my case.'

'Why?'

'If you knew I was sleeping with her you'd think I had motive.'

'You do have motive, *cortapisha*. Did you know she was pregnant?'

Solomon paused. 'If I'd known . . .'

'You wouldn't have killed her?'

'No! I wouldn't have left her on the beach.'

'Why didn't you use a condom?'

'We did. It broke.'

'Did you use a condom the night she died?'

'It never went that far, Spike. We argued then I left.'

'Argued?'

'About her not wanting to be faithful.'

From next door came a leonine MGM roar. '*Bezims*,' Spike cursed.

'What's that?'

'Who's Zahra?'

'Who?'

'Waitress from the Sundowner Club?'

'Never heard of her.'

'Did Esperanza talk about people trying to hurt her?'

'No.'

'Friends of hers in trouble?'

'She didn't have any friends.'

'Did you hear anything about a Bedouin going missing?'

'Sorry?'

'To do with Dunetech?'

'A Bedouin? No ... I mean, Bedouins are important to Dunetech, we employ them on-site. They're good workers, rank and file.'

'What about Abdallah al-Manajah?'

Solomon went quiet.

'Abdallah al-Manajah!'

'Please,' Solomon said, 'I'm trying to think. Yes ... he came into the office a few times. I remember him, fat guy in his sixties. Dirty clothes.'

'Bedouin?'

'I think so ... He was dark like a Bedouin. He used to work in Zagora Zween in the early days. Before my time. Phase 1 site manager, something like that.'

'What's his connection to Dunetech now?'

'Probably consulting on the expansion programme.'

'You didn't ask?'

'Why should I? People came and went the whole time.'

'Did Esperanza know Abdallah?'

'I doubt it.'

'Could she have done?'

'It's possible. She came to the Dunetech offices. That was how I met her. She could have seen him there, I suppose.'

'Did she talk about meeting him the day she died?'

'I told you, Spike, she never mentioned his name.'

'What else did she do that day?'

'Went to see some crystal-gazer. She was into all that crap.'

'But no mention of Abdallah al-Manajah?'

'No, Spike. Why do you keep asking?'

'What about the stepfather? Castillo. What's his story?'

'They didn't get on. She said he made her flesh creep. That's why she hadn't seen him in years.'

'Why change now?'

'How the hell should I know? Maybe she liked the sound of Dunetech. Wanted to give him a second chance.'

A Hollywood symphony filled the silence. 'What about Toby Riddell?' Spike said.

'What about him?'

'Trustworthy?'

'Decent enough, if a little slow. I think he went to school with Nadeer in England. Couldn't get into university so he tried Sandhurst. Saw some action in Northern Ireland. Then Gib. After that he was decommissioned and got in touch with Nadeer.'

Spike heard Solomon's hoarse, asthmatic breathing.

'Spike?'

'Yes?'

'They're going to send me back to Tangiers, aren't they?'

'Almost certainly, pal.'

39

The *petit taxi* puttered along the brow of the hill. Spike stared out at another flawlessly clipped lawn. A sprinkler clicked and whirred as a green-uniformed gardener tilled the soil. 'What do you call this area?' Spike said.

The driver grinned. His two front teeth were missing and he worked a furry tongue through the gap. 'Is La Montagne. Or Beverly Hills. See here?' He pulled up beside a red all-weather driveway leading to a pair of spiked gates. Two armed soldiers guarded the posts. 'Here is the summer palace for our King.'

'Is he in?'

The taxi returned to the main road as one of the guards stepped forward. 'It is Ramadan – the King is in his castle in Rabat. And here –' they passed a higher set of gates; above, Spike saw the top half of what looked like a replica of the White House – 'here is for Sheikh Ben-Adis, Prince for Saudi Arabia. And here –' the driver pointed to another neo-Palladian Christmas cake – 'is for Mister Forbes.' *Fourbez*, he pronounced it. 'American magazines. *Multi* million.' He sawed his tongue back and forth. 'And here –'

'OK,' Spike said. 'I get it.'

They continued along the ridge, a medley of gardeners and security men sending over heavy, sweaty glances. Below, the Medina and Kasbah were clustered neatly on the hillside. To the right, the Straits glowed tangerine in the setting sun.

At the next corner the taxi pulled up. Two life-size stone lions guarded a pair of iron gates. '*Voilà*,' the driver said. 'La Villa des Lions.'

An open-doored sentry box stood to the right, from which a mustachioed security guard emerged. The driver rolled down his window as the guard peered past him to Spike. 'Name?'

'Sanguinetti.'

'Uh?'

'San-guin-etti.'

Back in his cabin, the guard spoke into a phone; a moment later the gates began to open.

'You like Mister Fourbez,' the driver said, tonguing his teeth.

The driveway was lined on each side by sickly, thin-trunked palms. Between them, Spike caught a glimpse of a concrete helipad on the grass. Thirty metres on, the driveway opened into a turning circle, an umbrella pine spreading in its centre. Parked around the outside like dates in a box were twenty or so executive cars, chauffeurs at the wheels, capped and bored.

A rectangular yellow building blocked the far side of the circle, a smartly dressed flunkey already striding from its central archway.

The taxi driver started to reverse into a space beside a Bentley, leaving Spike room to get out, but squeezing his own door so close to its bodywork that the uniformed chauffeur glared up from a paperback.

The footman wore full livery. For a grim moment Spike thought the function might be fancy dress. He turned to the driver. 'Wait here. OK?'

The footman opened Spike's door as the taxi driver killed the engine.

'Welcome, Mr Sanguinetti, please.'

They crunched over gravel towards the gatehouse, Spike smoothing the creases from his blue linen shirt. After passing through the arch, they emerged into a terrace to the sound of soft music and chatter.

The pool was long and broad, mosaic-tiled and with shallow marble steps at the end. On one edge Spike saw a heliopod solar-power unit, both panels splayed open, crouching like a hothoused carnivorous plant patiently waiting for prey.

The guests were gathered in the last of the sun on the opposite edge of the pool. Moroccan girls in black, sunray-pleated skirts sashayed between them holding trays. A jungle of palms and sunflowers lined the terrace, fed by a serpentine watering system. In front of the main house, a tablecloth-draped bar was staffed by three men, to the right of which a band of traditionally dressed Berbers were knocking on drums and tootling on flutes.

'Most welcome, sir,' the footman concluded, sweeping an arm over the guests. Spike continued onto the bar, recognising faces from the Roadshow. 'Coca-Cola,' he said. 'Cold as you can.' The barman decapitated a bottle with a flair that suggested Spike's order left him seriously underused.

Spike stood with his back to the bar. The pool lights flashed on, sending turquoise sea snakes shimmering through the water. A waitress with hoop earrings offered him a canapé; as he passed up the chance for a second, he made out Nadeer Ziyad among the guests. Eschewing his Savile Row threads, Nadeer sported a full-length burnous, yellow and white striped with a baggy, hanging hood. On his head was a tassel-free fez; on his feet, soft babouche slippers. He raised an arm and started walking over, arching an eyebrow in a manner that suggested he was no fan of this frippery either. 'Hello, mate,' he said. Rather than a handshake, he went for the full body-clasp. 'Thank God you're here. Some sanity at last.'

He joined Spike by the bar. Guests kept shooting looks their way. On the other side of the pool, Toby Riddell was telling a story to a group of Middle Eastern investors, pointing towards the heliopod. He wore a brass-buttoned blazer and high-waisted chinos. His black shoes gleamed.

'There comes a point in a man's life when he must say, No, there shall be no more vol-au-vents.' Nadeer smiled. 'So how's tricks?'

'There's been a development.'

Nadeer pinched his hawk's nose. 'Yes, I heard about the post-mortem. Not good. Not good at all.'

'Is the governor here?'

Nadeer's irises glittered like champagne diamonds. 'The governor is what my father likes to call a dear, dear friend. He doesn't blow out a Ziyad.'

With a firm but gentle grip, Nadeer took hold of Spike's hand. Though Spike had seen men walking this way in the Medina, he still let go after a few paces, and they continued onwards to an urn of sunflowers, where a suited Moroccan was chatting to a blonde girl. Spike recognised Miss Solness, the Scandinavian from the Roadshow, slick in a trouser suit, kitten heels and silver top. Her companion glanced over as they approached. His shaven scalp had a covering of stubble midway up, as though a tide of skin were rising. He whispered something to Miss Solness; she looked on nonchalantly, sipping from a foliage-stuffed tumbler.

When the Moroccan was close enough, Nadeer put an arm around him. 'Spike Sanguinetti,' he said, 'I'd like you to meet His Excellency, the Governor of Tangiers.'

The governor looked barely older than Spike. His smile reconfigured to gruff mistrust. 'Let's go inside,' he grunted, accent tinged with American.

Nadeer turned to walk back across the terrace, Spike and the governor following behind like a couple of international bodyguards. The governor gave Spike a glance, then increased his pace to catch Nadeer up. The band played faster – as they passed through the sliding doors to the main house, the lute player was strumming like a North African Paganini.

The hallway was paved in stone, bisected by a staircase with a curving silver banister. A chandelier hung above a table fanned with copies of *Country Life* and *The Field*. A vase of orchids gave off the fleshy scent of carrion.

On the stairs hung a full-length portrait of Nadeer, leaning on a rifle, foot pressed triumphantly down on the tongue-lolling head of a leopard, the backdrop mountainous and romantic. Neither Nadeer nor the governor looked at the painting, passing instead through a padded doorway.

Spike followed them into an oak-panelled study. Another portrait of Nadeer graced the empty fireplace, his wavy hair slicked back, pastel jumper lightly laid over the shoulders of an open-necked shirt as he perched on a boardroom table.

The governor slumped into a knobbly leather armchair, Nadeer sitting down next to him, Spike opposite.

'You see,' the governor began, as if picking up on an earlier conversation, 'the situation is very delicate.' His voice was deep and slow, as though distorted for a ransom demand. Nadeer kept his eyes on Spike, smiling expectantly like the giver of a present gauging the recipient's reaction.

'It's a mess that just keeps on getting messier,' the governor said. 'And now I hear about some pregnancy?' Flecks of spittle flew from his mouth as he rasped the 'r'. 'And another arrest?' He turned to Nadeer for confirmation. 'A barman?'

'He works in the nightclub where the girl was last seen,' Spike said. 'He had her handbag. I told the police.'

'Ugly,' the governor replied. 'Ugly, ugly, ugly.'

'Have they pressed charges?'

The governor waved a hand as though swatting away a mosquito. 'The issue is as follows. Your client's former employer is about to sign a deal of great importance to the future of this region. It cannot be jeopardised by the death of some Spanish whore.' He stared at Spike, his eyes a nervous brown, ill-suited to the strong, gravelly voice. 'Nadeer tells me you're well connected in Gibraltar?'

'It's a small place.'

'The deal signs sundown Thursday, the last day of Ramadan. The court of assizes will waive extradition on one condition. That you delay the trial until at least three months after the Dunetech deal is concluded. I make that –' the governor glanced down at a chunky sports watch – 'November the 29th. So roll out the red tape. Sit on your hands. Slow-walk the situation. You people do that better than anyone.'

'And any trial will take place in Gibraltar?'

'Agreed.' The governor thrust out a hand. It quaked a little, like a drinker's. Spike reached out and shook it, then followed him and Nadeer out of the study, wondering why he didn't feel quite as elated as he might.

40

The governor strode beneath the gatehouse arch, the liveried footman slipping in behind him. 'He's a cold fish,' Nadeer said. 'But effective. Tourism on the up.'

'How old?'

'Thirty-eight.'

'Your voters like 'em young.'

'Regional governors are still personally appointed by the King.'

'I thought you said Morocco was a democracy.'

'Even with our Arab Spring, there are many ways to define the word.'

The party had hit a pitch that suggested the barmen now had the chance to express themselves. Guests kept trying to catch Nadeer's eye. He reached again for Spike's hand. This time Spike reduced the contact to an elbow-touch.

'He's certainly right about the mess though,' Nadeer said once they were at the bar. 'Best to get it cleaned up. Sorted.'

Spike heard a discreet phut, then saw the barman expertly tip a flute.

'At least it's good news for Solomon,' Nadeer said, turning.

'He faces three months in Gibraltar without bail.'

'Well, hopefully the evidence stacks up against this other suspect. The barman or what have you.' He passed Spike a glass of champagne. 'Of course we'd have Solomon back here like a shot. Exciting times ahead at Dunetech. Need minds like his on board.'

'He was hardly Brain of Britain at school.'

'But you can't teach business acumen, Spike. It's like courage. Or survival instinct. Either you've got it or you don't.' He held up his fizzing flute. 'To Solomon and the future.'

Spike smelled the sour tang of bursting bubbles. 'Fuck it.'

'What's that?'

'It's how we say cheers in Gibraltar.'

Nadeer grinned. 'Fuck it,' he repeated, and they chinked glasses.

Eyes closed, Spike took a deep, sparkling gulp. Then another. When he opened his eyes, Nadeer was watching, drink untouched, smile on his delicate lips.

'Impressive set-up you've got,' Spike said, wiping his mouth.

Nadeer scanned around. 'I suppose so. The firm's based in Tangiers, so there's a certain pressure to appear . . . settled.'

'And your father still lives in Rabat?'

'Yes.'

On the opposite side of the pool, Toby Riddell was pointing a group of Asian investors towards the heliopod. One of the panels moved, making them jump in fright, then laugh nervously at their mistake.

'Ever heard of a man called Abdallah al-Manajah?' Spike said.

Nadeer's champagne flute stopped en route to his mouth. 'Don't think so.'

'One of your employees?'

He lowered his glass. 'That doesn't narrow it down.'

'Solomon seems to think he might work for Dunetech. A Bedouin?'

'The Bedouins are our main source of human capital,' Nadeer replied as though that settled it. 'Our site is close to a Bedouin village so we provide jobs for what's a largely disenfranchised section of society. They're far less numerous than the Berbers, Tuareg or Reguibat, and as such are treated as second-class citizens.' He nodded towards an overweight American-looking man. 'Duty calls,' he sighed. 'Got to press the flesh. And by the look of it, there's a fair old bit of it over there.' He gazed past Spike to the heliopod. 'Christ. What a sunset. Enjoy the party.' Snatching Spike's hand again, he gave it a squeeze.

Spike turned back to the bar. 'Another, please,' he said, putting down his flute, 'this time with some booze in it.' He pointed to a brandy bottle behind.

Drink fortified, he walked over to the far side of the pool. The band were playing the same tune on repeat, some facile flute jig. Ahead loomed the heliopod. At any point it looked as though it might swivel on its stand and blast Spike like some intergalactic droid.

'You like?'

Spike turned into the pale, laughing eyes of Miss Solness.

'Not much.'

'See that mirrored panel? It reflects the sun onto the darker-coloured cells, so they get the natural *and* reflected rays. Doubles the output.'

'The Sun King rules OK.'

Miss Solness smiled. '*And* the panels clean themselves of sand as they move. My name's Regina.' The 'G' of her Christian name was hard, her English as faultless as most Scandinavians'.

'Spike.'

Spike saw that the tip of her nose was peeling. She followed his gaze. 'What can I say? I'm Norwegian. Land of the snow-white tan. You?'

'From Gibraltar.'

'Investor?'

'Not today.'

'You seem pretty close to the money though.' She glanced over to the other side of the pool, where Nadeer was working the crowd. 'You know,' she said, passing her tongue across her pink, chapped lips, 'what the best thing is about Dunetech?'

'What is the best thing about Dunetech?'

She tucked a hank of shiny hair behind her ear. 'Once they get the power into Tangiers, they can start laying cables over the Straits.'

'Underwater?'

'HVDC – high voltage direct current.' She prodded the ground with a diamanté-encrusted sandal: a thin black wire stretched from the base of the heliopod to the side wall of the house. 'Barely any energy-loss. And once you're over the Straits, you can plug into the European grid and sell to the whole of the West. No more worries about Russia dominating the market.'

'Is that part of the official business plan?'

Regina leaned in close to let Spike light her thin cigarette with a tea light. Her scent was sharp and musky, like a man's cologne. 'It's what's exciting investors, I can tell you that much. Why else headquarter the company in Tangiers? It's smaller than Casablanca and Rabat. But closer to Europe. Isn't that what's always made Tangiers special?'

Spike put down the candle and reached over to the shining shaft of the heliopod. He whipped back his hand: felt like he'd just been stabbed with a pin.

'Ouch,' Regina said.

'Not such a friendly source of energy after all,' Spike said, shaking his fingers.

Regina took a step forward. She had a pair of oversize designer sunglasses hooked to her top, their weight tugging down the silk to reveal a smooth arc of breast. 'I'm stuck here with my trade mag till they sign,' she said. 'Want to grab a drink in town?'

'Maybe some other time.'

She tapped at her clutch bag. 'Not tempted by the local specialities?'

Spike shook his head, and Regina shrugged, sliding on her sunglasses and setting off in the direction of the house, a swarm of eyes following her haunch as she swayed across the flagstones. When she was gone, Spike looked down at his hand. A small, greenish burn scored the index nail.

41

High-wattage uplights blazed from the terrace. A cicada in an olive bough duetted with an unseen sprinkler. Spike zoned in on it, amazed as usual that something so small could create such a racket.

Alongside the panel that controlled the pool lights was a doorway. Still facing the terrace, Spike leaned against it, feeling behind for a handle. It twisted and he held it down, kicking backwards with his heel. Another quick glance at the guests, and he stepped inside.

The air had the close, mushroomy smell of an old cellar. Spike felt for the switch and watched the strip lights wink and flicker, eventually revealing a damp concrete stairwell. Downstairs was another switch. A dingy, gaping underground space emerged.

Ranged along one side of the garage was a collection of gardening equipment: rakes, hosepipes, shiny four-pronged forks. Beneath the mouldy ceiling ran a bank of video monitors, each displaying black-and-white images of the terrace, the driveway, the gatehouse, the turning circle, two cars already pulling out . . . Spike located his *petit taxi*, still parked beside the Bentley. A row of numbers updated at the base of the screen. Beneath lay a metal chair flanked by an ashtray and a Moroccan newspaper.

On the other side of the garage, four vehicles were parked, noses pointed towards a ramp which appeared to lead up to the turning circle. A yellow Ferrari, a Hummer with glittering wheel spokes, the silver Mercedes which had picked Spike up. And a jeep with tinted windows and bull-bar bumper.

The jeep was painted electric blue. Putting his champagne flute down on the concrete, Spike delved into his pocket for a ten-dirham coin, then crouched to the mudguard and scraped at the bodywork. Nothing happened so he twisted the coin in a circle. Powdery flakes came away; he brushed them off and saw jet-black paint beneath.

A metallic clank sounded from upstairs. Spike crouched behind the jeep. Footsteps on the concrete, slow then quick; flattening himself, he peered beneath the chassis and caught a flash of diamanté.

Spike rose to his feet. Regina's long legs were tensed in their gleaming heels. Her tuxedo jacket was draped over her forearm like a sommelier's towel. She threw it onto the metal chair and it fell to the floor. Her bra was a similar pale pink to her skin.

'Bit hot up there, is it?' Spike called out, glancing suspiciously over her shoulder. As he stooped to pick up her jacket, he checked her eyes. The pupils were dilated, rolling back and forth in her head as though drawn by a magnet.

Regina smiled lazily as she put down her handbag. A new image was flickering on the monitors above her head: a black-and-white Toby Riddell, striding across the empty side of the terrace. As Riddell reached the heliopod he paused, hand testing for something tucked in the waistband of his chinos. Spike turned to the opposite wall, where a small black CCTV camera was fixed. On one of the monitors, Riddell's arm was extending for the gate-house door.

Spike looked back to Regina. Her bra was unfastened, exposing two neat, coral nipples. She beckoned at Spike, pupils still rolling, and he stepped forward to kiss her. Her saliva had a sharp chemical taste. 'Fuck me,' she hissed in his ear, Scandinavian accent thickening. 'Fuck me on the Ferrari.'

Spike felt her tongue probe forcefully against his. From upstairs came a creak; he slid his hand across her stomach and cupped a breast.

'Squeeze it,' she breathed. 'Harder.'

Taking the stiffening nipple in his fingertips, Spike steered her round until she was facing the stairwell. She'd unclipped her trousers: no underwear, the smooth, pinker skin between her thighs hairless save for a slim strip of blonde. She reached down to his flies: 'Hel-*lo* . . .' she began, before suddenly tensing up and drawing her elbows across her chest.

Spike turned to see Riddell on the bottom stair, hand still tucked beneath his jacket. He drew Regina close, face twisted in disgusted shock. 'Some privacy, maybe?' he shouted.

Riddell continued to stand.

'Piss *off*!' Regina snarled, pressing her half-naked body to Spike's.

Riddell took a hesitant backward step, catching the leather sole of his shoe and stumbling, hand still beneath jacket. He held his watery eyes on Regina, before turning and climbing back up to the door.

'Pervert,' giggled Regina, leaning in and gnawing at Spike's lower lip. He drew away and pointed at the camera. 'Not sure we want to end up online.'

'Oh, I don't know. Behind the Hummer?'

'Probably best not.'

Regina started to blink, as though slowly becoming aware of where she was. She shook her glassy eyes in an attempt to focus, then reached down for her trousers. Spike passed over her bag and jacket, zipping himself up and taking her hand to lead her, dressed, up the car ramp at the other end of the garage. There was a red lever box on the wall; Spike yanked it down and the gates began to open.

They emerged at the edge of the turning circle. Most of the cars were gone but the *petit taxi* was still waiting. Regina laid her head on Spike's shoulder, twining a white lock of hair around one finger. 'Feel a bit sick,' she said in her sing-song accent.

Spike stuck a thumb up at the taxi driver. 'Still time for a loosener?' he asked Regina.

She brightened, lifting her head, and they walked back through the tunnel to the pool terrace. There were fifteen or so guests left, all gathered by the bar. The band had packed up; of Nadeer and Riddell there was no sign. Seeing Nadeer's overweight American friend, Spike led Regina over. 'Do you two . . .?'

'Oh sure,' the Texan drawled. 'Reggie's gonna do a piece on me.'

'Maybe you could give her a lift into town.'

'If she'll wait till this numbskull masters the mint julep.'

Spike turned to Regina. Her jawbone poked in and out as she chewed her teeth.

'Got to go,' Spike said.

'What?'

'Boat to catch.'

'But –'

He squeezed her hand – 'Sorry' – then set off back to the turning circle.

42

The usual traffic hierarchy had been reversed, cars waiting for pedestrians, the road a pavement, choked with people, the majority fighting their way towards a single narrow gateway in a whitewashed wall.

'What's going on?' Spike said.

'Le Jour Sacré,' the taxi driver replied. 'When the Gates of Heaven are open to all.'

'Is there another way through?'

White minivans were parked on the pavements, either having disgorged their passengers or abandoned their journeys altogether. Blankets patchworked the road, women in headscarves selling branches of foliage, slowing progress further as the customers haggled and paid. From behind the walls came the distant sound of chanting.

'Marshan Cemetery,' the taxi driver said. 'Oldest for all Tangiers.'

'I'll walk then,' Spike said. The taxi driver counted his notes, tonguing the gap between his teeth more quickly.

Once through the gate, the cemetery sloped ahead, an uneven rectangle the size of two football pitches, ended by clifftops and the sea beyond. The gravestones were intersected by pathways, the widest running down the centre, lined by beggars, wailing as they held out warty, palsied palms in supplication.

The crowd swept Spike on. The chanting and incense grew heady, intermingled with saline gusts from the sea. Spike turned onto a smaller path: the graves were like concrete bathtubs sunk into the ground, headstones where the taps might have been. Some sprouted with grass, mulched by sprays of decaying flowers.

Spike watched a man and woman approach, escorted by a beggar with a hoe who set to work scraping away the weeds. The woman carried a water bottle; she sluiced it over the headstone, cleaning off the dirt, worrying at the engraving with her fingernails. Her husband beckoned to a holy man, who came over and planted joss sticks in the soil, reciting from the Koran as the woman pressed her face into her husband's chest.

Spike walked to the cliff face, sitting down on a bare patch of dirt. White horses reared in the Straits: the Gut, twisting away with its secret currents. Sickle-shaped swifts screamed above, preparing to migrate south. The murmur of the crowd started blending with the chanting, as though the mourners were singing their own requiem.

Spike took out his phone and texted Galliano: 'Extradition dropped. Taking night boat home.' Then he stood and went to a side exit.

43

'*Ouai?*'

'It's Spike.'

The door opened. Jean-Baptiste's chest was bare above a pair of baggy Aladdin trousers, his brown nipples like tired eyes above the round prurient mouth of his navel. Spike followed him in, bag over shoulder. The air reeked sweetly.

'Where you go last night?' Jean-Baptiste said as he picked up a remote control and sat down on the bed.

'Business.'

'Your friend?'

Spike nodded as the sound of the TV monitors muted. On-screen, an actor with a widow's peak was pinned against a wall, knife point stretching to a nostril.

'I'm going home,' Spike said.

Jean-Baptiste picked up a rubber band and fastened his dread-locks into a ponytail.

'Can I buy you a drink at the port?'

'Have to finish this movie, uh?'

Spike laid a hotel envelope on the mattress.

'No money . . .'

'Good,' Spike said, 'because there isn't any. I've got a friend in Gibraltar called Sebastian Alvarez. He runs cigarettes over the border to Spain. If you can make it into Gib, he'll get you across in his fishing boat. Phone number's in the envelope.'

Jean-Baptiste prodded the envelope with a finger.

'There's a Gibraltarian on the dock who can arrange passage. He takes euros.'

'My Chingongo,' Jean-Baptiste said, smiling. 'Maybe I do come for –'

'Be seeing you, Jean-Baptiste.'

Downstairs, Spike settled up. 'Money is like a rose,' the receptionist said as he handed Spike his receipt. 'Smell it and pass it onto the next person.'

'Did the policeman come back?'

'Not yet.'

Spike reached over the counter. 'It's been a pleasure.'

'Life without friends is like couscous without salt.'

'What *is* that you're reading?'

'Mysteries are the –'

'OK, OK.'

Down by the quayside, Spike purchased a half-bottle of whisky and waited at a café, plugged into his iPod. The lights of the catamaran began to approach, passengers already out on deck. He looked down at his ticket. Gibraltar, *Jebel Tariq* . . . The screen of his mobile illuminated and he swatted out his earphones. 'Yes?'

'It's me.' The voice was husky and low.

'Zahra?'

'I found his address.'

'Whose?'

'Abdallah al-Manajah's.'

'In Tangiers?'

'Terrasse des Paresseux. Half an hour.'

Out in the Straits, the catamaran slotted into the port like the last missing piece of a jigsaw.

44

Zahra was waiting in the shadows on the Terrasse des Paresseux. Her headscarf was tied beneath her chin to reveal a large mobile mouth with dark, cushion lips. She wore a white dress over her kaftan, fastened with a sash. Her smile vanished as quickly as it had arrived. 'You smell like cheap perfume.'

'Whisky.'

'Yesterday kif, today whisky?' She strode away along the line of cannons into the Place de France. The cafés were closing, a seller of individual cigarettes padlocking his wooden cart for the night.

Spike adjusted his overnight bag on his shoulder and caught her up. 'I didn't think you would call.'

'Esperanza wanted to see Abdallah al-Manajah,' Zahra said. 'Maybe he will know something about my father.'

The sky was a dark, denim blue, the moon still too thin to shed light. They crossed over the rue de Belgique. The smaller residential streets had potholes in the macadam and beaten-up cars on the pavements, the apartment blocks seeming to date from an earlier, more optimistic period, acanthus scrolls crumbling above doorways like in old-world Paris.

'How did you find the address?' Spike said.

'I asked a friend.'

'The man with the red rucksack?'

'Who?'

'From the Café des Étoiles?'

Zahra stopped. 'You are spying on me now, Somerset?'

'It's Spike.'

'Why "Spike"?'

'Because it's better than Somerset.'

'Is Somerset a family name?'

'My mother was a fan of the English short story.'

A white, Velcro-strapped trainer emerged from Zahra's dark robes as she picked her way across the rubble. 'It's 13C, rue des Rosiers.'

The bell pushes were unmarked. Zahra pressed the third one down. Nothing happened so she tried the same on the next column.

A light flashed on; someone was coming out. Spike and Zahra drew back like caryatids on either side of the entrance as it opened to an old woman in black. As soon as the woman stepped into the road, Spike moved forward and caught the door. She turned and stared; Spike stared back and she shuffled away into the darkness.

'After you,' Spike said as Zahra came forward, ducking elegantly beneath his arm like an Elizabethan dancer. Inside, envelopes marked with dirty footprints littered the doormat. The ground-floor flat was 13A; they climbed the drab stairwell to 13C.

The doorbell was silent so Zahra knocked instead. 'Why don't you try his phone?' she said, turning to Spike.

'He never answers.'

Zahra stared at him until he took out Esperanza's mobile. From inside they heard a long, distant ringtone. She cast him a querulous glance then rapped again. As she turned to leave, he dropped to his knees and slotted an arm through the letter box.

'What are you *doing*?' she hissed.

'Just watch the stairs.'

He contorted his arm upwards. Blood poured into his head as he strained his fingertips towards cold metal. With one last surge he got hold of the latch and yanked it down. The door shifted, tugging at his shoulder blade. He released the latch and removed his hand.

'You're very flexible.'

'I think it runs in the family.'

The door fell an inch open, releasing a dank putrid aroma. Spike put his shoulder to the frame. Something was blocking it. 'Hello?' he called through the gap. 'Can you try in Arabic?' he said to Zahra.

'You think that makes a difference?'

'Could do.'

'*Salaam?*' she said. '*Billati?*' She withdrew, wrinkling her nose in disgust. Spike barged the door again. It moved a foot this time, allowing him to edge crabwise inside, arm extended for the switch. She followed him in, momentarily throwing them into darkness as she blocked the gleam from outside. Sweeping his hand up and down, he found metal again and the lights crackled on.

The flat was open-plan with a high-beamed ceiling and a mezzanine level accessed by a fixed wooden ladder. A halo of bulbs shone above a motionless fan; there seemed to be a problem with the circuit as they kept flickering on and off.

'*Ya Allah,*' Zahra said.

At first Spike assumed the flat had been ransacked. It looked as though the contents of a skip had been emptied out. The door had been blocked by an armchair, one of three crammed next to each other, springs jabbing one to the other. A racing-green picnic table was heaped with string-bound Arabic newspapers, a tangle of anglepoise lamps beneath.

Zahra shoved the door closed. On top of a stack of microwaves sat a gramophone, vinyl records in a crate alongside. She drew one out, nose still wrinkling: the sleeve showed a Moroccan in a handlebar moustache and seventies string vest. She reached into the gramophone cylinder, emerging with a tangle of round spectacles, most missing a lens. 'Doesn't he throw anything away?'

Spike glanced to his left. Along the far edge of the flat ran a kitch-enette, its floor space covered in empty jars and cans, a knife block on the work surface over-jammed with blades. The aroma of rotting food seemed to issue from there. The lights went out again; Spike heard a clatter as Zahra grabbed his shoulder. 'What was that?'

The lights blinked on to reveal a tabby cat slinking through the detritus. It turned to Spike and Zahra, stripy tail swishing, before hopping onto the arm of a sofa.

Spike squeezed between the furniture towards the only clear space, a nook beneath the mezzanine where a free-standing plasma TV rose like an altar before a canvas director's chair.

'Look,' Zahra said. He turned and saw her spinning a blue plastic globe. The cat reappeared, perching on a heap of step-ladders. It rubbed the side of its head against the metal, clear liquid drizzling from its mouth. Then it sprang down to the floor beneath the mezzanine. 'Maybe no one lives here,' Zahra said, 'and people just use it to dump –'

The bulbs fizzled out. In the silence, Spike heard pulsing purrs. When the light returned he saw the pink rose petal of the cat's tongue rasping up and down the bare floorboards. It slunk away, licking its lips.

Spike looked up at the mezzanine ceiling. A small, dark circle stained the wood. A bead of moisture stretched to a point, then dripped down into Spike's face. He clawed a hand to his eye.

'What?' Zahra called.

Redness smeared his palm. The lights crackled out again. 'Stay there.'

'What?'

Spike felt for the TV, then knocked into it, sending the tabby scurrying for cover.

'*What?*' Zahra said again.

When the lights came back on, Spike found himself in front of the steps that led up to the mezzanine. He glanced back at Zahra, then put a finger to his lips.

45

Light drifted dingily up onto floorboards of stripped pine. Spike made out a single bed in front, a window with the curtains closed, a set of wooden railings protecting from the drop to the main room.

'What's going on?' Zahra called from below.

'Stay where you are.' To his right, Spike saw the silhouette of a floor lamp; feeling forward with a foot, he pressed down. Brightness flooded the mezzanine. As his eyes grew accustomed, he saw that the metal-framed bed was strewn with magazines. Slowly his gaze turned to the floor.

The man lay naked on his back in the space between the bed and the railings. The skin of his soles was cracked. A stubby yellow penis rested on the heaped, distended mound of his belly.

'Don't come up here, Zahra,' Spike called down. He crept forward until he could see past the paunch to the face lying on the wood. The eyes were closed and the lank grey hair oiled back. Stubble pierced wan, sagging cheeks. The neck was visible – skin lacquered bright red – with the hands out in front, clasped together on a hairy pigeon chest as though in prayer. A knife protruded from the right fist, its small curved blade encrusted with blood.

Spike heard a creak. 'I told you not to –'

Zahra put a hand to her mouth. Something twitched on the man's body: a shiny brown cockroach bobbing and weaving over his mountainous belly, clipping the head of his penis before beetling off through the dark red oval that had seeped across the floorboards on either side of his neck.

Zahra spoke between her fingers. 'I recognise him from my village,' she whispered. 'From Zagora Zween.'

At the sound of her voice, the man's lashes flickered. Zahra took a step forward and his eyes flew open, lids stretching wildly.

'Ambulance,' Spike said. 'What number?'

'Fifteen.'

'Are you sure?'

'Fifteen, fifteen!'

Abdallah's eyes bulged as though he were drowning. Pink froth bubbled from the gash in his neck, followed by a high-pitched whistle, like gas escaping. Spike connected to the operator, as Zahra crouched down to Abdallah, who was blinking up at her now, desperate, trapped.

'Don't touch him,' Spike said, cupping the handset.

The whistling deepened to a rasp. Zahra tilted her head towards Abdallah's mouth. His eyeballs looked poised to spray from their sockets.

As Spike hung up, the tip of Abdallah's grey tongue emerged to dab at the canal of Zahra's ear. She recoiled in panic, losing her balance, palms slipping in the ooze that blotted the floor.

Spike helped her up. Her eye was caught by a smear on the front of her white dress. She started rubbing at the blood; Spike grabbed her wrist, loosening his grip when he saw the pallor beneath her natural tan.

'It's OK,' he said. 'Take deep breaths.'

When Zahra's colour began to return, Spike released her. 'What did he say?'

'He was asking for his mother.'

He caught her arm again as she backed away. 'You can't leave a crime scene.'

She wrested herself free. 'You can in Tangiers.'

153

Lowering a trainer onto the ladder, she turned. 'Last night,' she said. 'At the café. I was buying a train ticket home. Tanger Ville Station, 11.30 p.m.'

Spike looked back to Abdallah. His eyes were closing, froth popping on the bristles of his stubble as his breaths grew more shallow. Below, Zahra was creeping through the flotsam. Spike moved to the railings and the lights went out. When they flickered back on, she'd reached the door. The stain on her dress bloomed like a rose. 'Tanger Ville Station,' she repeated. 'Eleven thirty.'

46

'So what you are telling me,' Inspector Hakim Eldrassi said as he drew deeply on his cigarette, 'is that you entered this apartment illegally.' He and Spike sat on the arms of opposing sofas. Upstairs, the floorboards creaked with activity. In front of them, a bearded man in shirtsleeves was perching on a stepladder, tightening light bulbs.

'Esperanza had an appointment to see Abdallah al-Manajah on the day she died,' Spike said. 'It was imperative I talk to him in the interests of my client. When I got here, the door was unlocked. I entered and found Mr al-Manajah upstairs.'

The lights grew steady and the bearded man descended. He picked up a camera from the kitchenette and began snapping photos of the mezzanine ceiling, calling out a question to Hakim, who answered in Arabic, casting about half-heartedly for an ashtray before finally tapping his ash on the floor.

'First,' Hakim resumed, 'you lead me to a barman who you claim was in possession of Esperanza's handbag. Now you bring me here, where a man who supposedly met Esperanza just before she died is killed with a knife on the Jour Sacré, the very day when guilty souls may enter Heaven.' Hakim's sallow eyes managed a twinkle. 'So I ask myself: How far will a lawyer go for his client? Will he seek to incriminate others? Cast seeds of doubt?' He turned, surveying the flat with what looked like sadness. 'Of course, you cannot leave the country now. Not until the coroner has his verdict.'

'I have commitments in Gibraltar.'

'I presume you know the law, Mr Sanguinetti.'

'How long?'

'We bury the dead fast in Tangiers. Two days for the coroner. Another for your statement.'

Spike took out the penultimate business card from his wallet. 'You dropped by my hotel yesterday. Who told you where I was?'

'The Sûreté is capable of a certain degree of efficiency.' Hakim stubbed out his cigarette on the spinning globe. 'So he was alive when you found him?'

'He opened his eyes. We thought it best not to move him.'

'We?'

'Sorry?'

'You said you were alone.'

'The royal "we", Inspector Eldrassi. An English idiom. We did this. We did that.'

Hakim's moustache twitched. 'Not an idiom with which I am familiar.'

'You should spend more time in Gibraltar.'

A creak came from behind as a pair of uniformed legs appeared on the stairs, followed by one end of a black ziplock bag on a stretcher.

'I have circulated your details to the port authorities,' Hakim said, eyeing Spike's suitcase, 'in case you felt the same . . . call for home as your client.'

A policeman passed Hakim a sealed exhibit bag. Inside it was a phone, Esperanza's mobile number displayed on the screen as a recently missed call. Hakim nodded and the policeman began to clear a passageway through the junk for the cortège.

'What makes a man live like this?' Hakim said, shaking his head. 'Burying himself alive.'

Spike picked up his bag. 'May I go?'

'Your prints,' Hakim said, sliding what looked like a cigarette case from his inside pocket. On one side was a spongy black pad, thick white card opposite. Spike pressed five fingers onto one then the other.

'I shall be in touch, Mr Sanguinetti,' Hakim said as he snapped the case closed. 'Until then, I advise you to be careful. The barman from that nightclub had an alibi. We had to release him. He is not your friend.'

On the pavement outside, Spike saw the old lady in black being interviewed by a policeman. She turned to look at him as he walked towards the rue de Belgique. A phrase his father had used echoed in his head: *City of Perfidy . . . City of Perfidy*. He rubbed the ink from his fingertips and hailed a *petit taxi*.

'*Vous allez où, monsieur?*'

Spike checked the time. Through the taxi windscreen, the lights of Europe looked that little bit further away.

'*Monsieur?*'

PART THREE

Zagora Zween

47

Spike woke on his side, vibrations jolting through his body. He had slept on his left arm, which felt numb through lack of blood. He tried to roll over but a wooden board blocked his way. Opening his eyes, he made out a shape beneath the blanket on the opposite bunk: Zahra, her hair thick and loose. He felt a small pang as he saw the dark strands dampened to her forehead as on a sleeping child.

The window of the couchette was covered by a blind marked 'Office National des Chemins de Fer'. Sunlight lanced through it into Spike's eyes. He rolled out his legs and saw he was still wearing last night's clothes. After feeling beneath the bunk for the reassuring bulk of his bag, he forced the carriage doors apart and stepped out into the corridor.

Rather than coast or scrubland, he saw lush green fields. The train was moving along a ridge, with orchards of pears or apples extending down the slope. He pressed his face to the glass, seeing shaggy sheep driven by a herdsman in a wide-brimmed hat. The herdsman stopped and raised a hand; Spike waved absently back, before realising the man had only been screening his eyes against the glare from the train. Verdant hills rose beyond, mountains in the distance, purple-peaked. In the railway siding, the green fingers of what looked like wild cannabis plants spread from the shingle.

Spike's phone claimed 6.40 a.m. Gibraltar was two hours ahead.

'Dad?'

'Mm?'

'It's Spike.'

'Oh.' He heard a deep sigh. 'Oh.'

'Are you having breakfast?'

'Still in bed.'

'How come?'

'It's . . .' He sighed again. 'Got that thing again. With my chest.'

'Palpitations?'

'Somewhat.'

'That's what the beta blockers are for, Dad. Have you been taking them?'

'They give me diarrhoea.'

'It's better than the palpitations. They're on the list, two a day.'

Rufus's voice sounded distant and small. 'You're coming home soon, aren't you, son?'

'Got to stay in Tangiers for a few more days.'

'Not got ensnared, have you?'

'Just a couple of things to sort out.'

'Don't tell me you're off the wagon?'

'Go to the doctor, Dad. If you go late morning, there's no queue.'

Rufus swallowed at the other end of the line. 'Might just lie here a bit longer. I had a call from Mrs Hassan yesterday. Says you deserve a medal. Got her boy out of trouble.'

'He stands trial in Gibraltar not Morocco. That's it.'

'No better place to be. The levanter's finally shifted. We've a nice dry southerly. I can hear the gulls outside.'

'You'll get up soon, won't you, Dad?'

There was a sudden shriek as the train switched tracks. Spike put a hand out smartly to the carriage wall.

'Where are you, son? Sounds like a tramp steamer.'

'Better go, Dad. Bye.'

The sun changed angle, exposing Spike's reflection like a ghost in the window. He called a different number.

'All hail the conquering hero,' Galliano said. 'What time did you get in?'

'I didn't.'

'Delayed?'

'There's been a complication.'

Spike told Galliano how he had discovered Abdallah's body. 'I can't leave the country now until they've established cause of death.'

'*Ten cuidado*, Spike.'

'I'm just going to lie low for a few days.' Spike heard a door open at the end of the corridor. A man appeared; he wore a prayer cap and a full beard with a clean-shaven upper lip. He withdrew abruptly, giving Spike a glimpse of red rucksack as the door slammed behind him.

'Spike?'

'I need you to do something for me, Peter.'

'You name it.'

'Dunetech, Solomon's company. I think it's time to shine a bit of light on proceedings.'

Spike heard a pen and paper readied.

'It's a clean technology business, right? Backing from sovereign investors. Renewable energy funds. Philanthropists with an eye on the buck. They're using Ruggles & Mistry to sort out their tax liabilities in Gibraltar.'

'So?'

'This is a sensitive time. Chequebooks readied. New offices built. I think Esperanza may have stumbled onto something at a crucial moment.'

'Such as?'

'Just see what you can dig up on the founders, Nadeer Ziyad and Ángel Castillo. And an ex-British Army officer called Tobias Riddell.' Spike heard Galliano chuck away one pen to pick up another. 'Maybe you could talk to Belinda Napier at Ruggles. Ask her for the skinny on Dunetech.'

'Think I'm still *persona non grata* with Napier.'

'Take her to a vodka bar. And can you drop in on my dad? Check he's OK?'

'Will do. So when are you back?'

'Looking like Friday.'

'Sorry?'

Spike checked his phone screen: half a bar of reception. 'What kind of thing,' he heard Galliano say as he put the handset back to his ear, 'might –'

The line went dead. Outside, the landscape had lost its verdure: pebbly ground, rocky outcrops. Hearing footsteps, Spike turned to find Zahra in the corridor. She wore baggy drawstring trousers and a long-sleeved black T-shirt. Her headscarf was off and her hair free; she was older than Spike had thought, early thirties probably. As she rubbed her eyes, he saw faint frown lines on her forehead.

'What time is it?' she yawned.

'Coming up to seven.'

She turned and gazed out of the window. 'Hopefully we'll make the next bus.'

'How long's the journey?'

'Couple of hours, if it doesn't break down first. *Tired*,' she added in an elongated voice. When she yawned again, Spike caught her eyes dart his way. The pupils were cold and alert.

48

The bus had been driving for two hours and there was still no sign of the desert. The road followed a gorge with a river below and steep, crumbly walls of orange rock above. They were travelling downhill, but only just; the watercourse was deep and sluggish, content to creep along the base of this narrow fissure, spreading its goodness to the limited flat space on either side, where belts of almond groves grew interspersed with the occasional cuboid mud hut.

Spike stared out of the bus window, sunshine slanting through onto his forearms. He wondered not for the first time if a person could get burnt through glass. Zahra sat beside him, hair still loose, waving intermittently at a small, silent boy who kept peeking from between the foam-spilling seat backs.

The brakes mewled plaintively as the bus slowed into a corner. Outside, Spike saw three grey apes sitting on an outcrop of rock, two adults and an infant. 'Barbary macaques,' he said, looking back round. 'Same as in Gibraltar.'

'You have monkeys in Gibraltar?' Zahra said, craning her neck to see.

'We call them apes, because they don't have much of a tail. Only place in Europe where they're wild.'

'How did they get there?'

'In reality, pets for the British garrison. But according to legend, they crossed over from the Atlas Mountains in a secret tunnel beneath the Straits.'

'Maybe this is the start of that tunnel. The old caravan route from the desert.'

Spike stared up at the vertical walls of orange rock.

'You know,' Zahra said, 'I think that's the first time I've seen you smile.'

He ran a hand through his short dark hair and looked ahead.

Zahra waved again at the child, who was encouraged back round by its mother and presented with something sticky to eat from a rolled-up handkerchief. Spike cleared his throat. 'So you slept OK?'

'Yes.' She breathed out. 'Thanks for coming, Spike.'

'I can't leave the country anyway.'

'I suppose not.'

Another rickety single-decker came tearing round the corner. Spike saw the bright polka dots of headscarves leaning on the windows. 'There's a bus every day,' Zahra said. 'You can be back in Tangiers by tomorrow night.'

'Is there phone reception in your village?'

'Not sure. These days.' She reached into a woven handbag for a bottle of water and offered it to Spike.

'You first.' As she drank, he watched her larynx glide up and down her tanned, glistening throat. When the bottle came to him, he was careful not to finish it. The water had a hot saline taste, filled from the tap at Meknes station. Zahra's bag shifted forward as a wooden toy rolled from under the seat in front.

'I've never seen a dead body before,' she said, putting a foot down on her bag.

Spike turned. 'Are you sure he was only asking for his mother?'

'*Sakarat al mowt.*'

'Sorry?'

'Death noise.'

'Death rattle?'

The mother stood to retrieve her child's toy.

'Yes,' Zahra said. 'Death rattle.'

49

The river broadened out and the gorge on either side of the road reduced to friable, horizontal shelves of rock. Spike saw a man in a turquoise turban leaning against a dead tree, smoking a roll-up as the bus sped by. The driver changed up a gear, heedless of potholes and boulders.

Spike felt a tap on the shoulder. Zahra was mouthing at him; he plucked out his headphones.

'What are you listening to?' she said.

He showed her the iPod screen with its image of an emaciated man in black, hair tied back in a ponytail, violin at his chin. 'Niccolò Paganini,' she read aloud, putting the stresses in the right places. He reached over to tuck a plug into her neat little ear. She screwed up her face at once. 'Is a string broken?' she shouted.

He lowered the volume. 'Paganini was the greatest violin virtuoso of his era.'

'I'll take your word for it,' Zahra replied.

He unlinked them, then plugged himself back in. Outside, the road emerged into a wasteland of stones and shrunken shrubs. The river was just a trickle now, a green ribbon vanishing into the hazy brown horizon. From the corner of his eye, he saw Zahra slip a mobile phone out of her bag. He turned down the music; she spoke in a strange kind of Arabic, quick and low. She flashed him a look, then put the phone away.

A range of hills rose in the distance, the parched, cracked earth before them like a dried-out seabed. Shimmering at their base was a Legionnaire-type settlement: fortified terracotta walls, minarets poking above. 'Is that your village?' Spike asked, switching off his music altogether.

'It's where I went to school. Erg Makeem.'

'Is it near your village?'

'An hour's walk. Then a bus.'

'Every day?'

'Twice.'

Spike steered a finger along the soused sponge of an eyebrow. The sun seemed low in the sky.

'My cousins are going to pick us up,' Zahra said.

'Is that who you were phoning?'

'I was just updating them.'

'So they do have signal.'

'Landline.'

'What did you tell them about me?'

She pursed her lips. 'They know I want to move to Europe. That's why I learned English. When I said I was bringing you, they just . . . assumed.'

'Assumed what?'

'That you would be helping me.'

Spike reached automatically for his pocket, checking for the sweaty rectangle of his passport against his thigh.

'I had to tell them something,' Zahra protested. 'They're very traditional.'

A billboard flashed by the roadside. 'DUNETECH,' it read. '*Powering a Greener Future.*'

50

The bus pulled over at a crossroads as Spike, Zahra and three men in turquoise turbans got out. The driver's assistant clambered up a ladder to the roof and unfastened the guy ropes holding down their bags. Somehow carrying all of them at once, he bundled back down and dumped them on the stony ground.

Spike's leather bag felt hot to the touch. The sun was directly above yet still seemed low in the sky, as though it had decided to set where it was. A single-storey building with a reinforced door stood back from the road, a camel lying in its shade, chewing on a bridle of chains with long, hairy lips. A small man emerged, overwhelmed by his white robes; Spike caught a glimpse of shelves of canned food behind him. 'Is that your cousin?' he said.

He had to squint to see that Zahra was smiling. 'He's here for the tourists.'

'What tourists?'

'Camel safaris into the desert.'

Zahra spoke to the man in the same rapid language she'd used on the phone. He reached into his robes and took out a coiled black ammonite. When she added something else, he carried the fossil reluctantly back inside.

The bus rumbled away, revealing a dusty lay-by where a white pickup was parked by a minivan. Zahra and the three other passengers set off towards it.

Spike could feel the heat of the sun on his hair. 'Have you got a spare headscarf?' he called out to Zahra, but the wind gusted and she didn't hear.

The strap of Spike's bag kept slipping on his collarbone. He raised his eyes to the sky: the sun seemed even lower, a huge orange saucer docking overhead, pushing downwards.

As the minivan drove away, Spike saw a face pressed to the window. Black beard, shaven moustache ... He seemed to be staring down at Spike with what looked like a patient smile.

The pickup was still parked in the lay-by, white and new-looking. Its doors opened simultaneously and two men got out. Both wore turquoise turbans and button-down beige djellabas. The driver stuck out both arms, letting Zahra walk into the hug. Drawing back, he rubbed his nose three times against hers. His companion did the same, then all three turned to stare at Spike.

The face of the driver was elongated, a thick black moustache curving above a deep, prominent jaw that seemed out of kilter, as though the top half had not been designed to go with the lower. Stopping a few metres shy of Spike, he gave a stage bow, one arm tucked into his stomach, the other sweeping the dusty earth below. Sweat dripped into Spike's eyes as he nodded in response.

The younger man stepped towards him, almost handsome but burdened with a similar jaw. Spike stuck out a hand, but he only wanted the bag.

Zahra came over, touching the sodden back of Spike's T-shirt. The driver glanced round as he walked towards the truck.

'That's Othman,' Zahra said quietly. 'Salem's his kid brother. We'll do the introductions later.'

Both doors slammed as Zahra climbed up over the tailgate and sat down. Once Spike had joined her, they pulled out of the lay-by and onto the road in the direction of the hills they'd seen from the bus. Wedged in by Zahra, Spike stared out at the dust cloud burgeoning behind. The metal had started to burn through the material of his T-shirt; the breeze gave relief, but he knew he was still in full glare, so looked about for a cloth or oilskin. Nothing but a spare tyre with a petrol can inside. He drew his T-shirt over his forehead. The metal seared his back so he held himself away from it, stomach muscles straining.

Zahra turned and smiled. 'Now you are a Bedouin,' she shouted above the engine.

The dust cloud made it hard to see behind, but left and right there stretched nothing but a flat, shimmering void. Spike tucked his forearms beneath the tail of his flapping T-shirt. Zahra had an elbow on the side of the pickup, oblivious to the heat, staring out in silence.

The bumps became less frequent as the dust cloud reduced. Spike peered over the edge: the road looked like a First World dual carriageway, four lanes of dark, puffy tarmac. No other vehicles passed. On the wayside, Spike saw a Dunetech billboard, this time in Arabic.

Zahra moved to her hands and knees, edging around until she stood with her head up above the driver's cabin. Spike did the same. 'Estoy en babia,' he exclaimed.

Rearing above them was a vast, apricot coloured cathedral, smooth-sided and with a peaked, snaking crest along the top. At least a hundred feet high – like the southern tip of the Rock. A similar-sized dune stood adjacent, with a rippled, broader base; smaller dunes continued either side, blending into one another, interlocking like giant orange knuckles.

Zahra's headscarf streamed behind her in the wind as she turned to check Spike's reaction. 'He smiles again,' she shouted.

The road continued on between the dunes. Walls of orange sand blotted out the sun, spatula-smooth. The wind fell and then there was no sound beyond the turning of the engine.

'This is the holy place,' Zahra said quietly. 'The burial land my father would not sell.'

The narrow, shady strip was half filled by road. Outcrops of rock rose on either side, holding in the sand dunes, presumably the reason for the formation of this passageway in the first place.

Spike saw what looked like carvings on their flanks. 'Was the road here before?' he asked.

'Just a track.'

The sun came blazing back as they emerged on the other side. Spike had been expecting a vista of soft rippling sand but instead there stretched the same brown, pebble-strewn crust. As the road curved left, he saw that the rocky outcrop continued all around the base of the sand dune, a few mud huts huddled against it. Beyond, Spike made out the first row of heliopods, glinting in the sun like a silent, waiting army.

51

Still on their feet in the back of the pickup, Spike and Zahra stared out at the village. The first buildings they saw were new-looking single-storey Portakabins. To the rear of each, an identical white picket fence delineated a patch of desert garden – had one picked up the Portakabin, the fence would have come with it. Most seemed unoccupied, the only signs of life stripy woven sheets hammered into the back walls to create makeshift tents.

A pack of beautiful mongrel dogs chased the pickup as it passed a concrete warehouse. Tipper trucks and caterpillar diggers were parked outside. Some kind of open-plan marketplace lay beyond – food stalls, goats, queue of people waiting at a well.

'It's all so different,' Zahra said.

'When were you here last?'

'Six years ago.'

'Imagine how it'll look in another six.'

The plastic-looking minaret of a new-build mosque poked upwards as the track began to rise. Spike stared up the slope. The mud houses were embedded into the rock, their colour the same as the dunes behind. The pickup slowed to a woman in a blue headscarf standing cross-armed outside the entrance to a house. Smoke rose from a hole in the roof behind her. Hens pecked at her feet.

'That's Salwa,' Zahra said as Othman and Salem got out, 'Othman's wife.' Zahra moved her face towards Spike's. 'Don't mention the Sundowner Club. They think I work shelling prawns in a factory in Tangiers.'

'Understood.'

'And don't say you're a lawyer either.'

Spike jumped down. One of the dogs came over, tail rigid as it sniffed Spike's trouser leg. When Salem made to kick it, it bolted off and stood at a distance.

Salwa was joined at the doorway by a drowsy little boy with tangled hair. She stood on her tiptoes to perform the same nose-rubbing ritual with Zahra. Spike heard his name mentioned in a rush of low, coarse sounds. Salwa blinked over, eyes limpid and black, skin as wrinkled as a lost balloon. The child gazed up at him.

Othman and Salem strode past through the open doorway. The entrance was just an antechamber to a deeper, shadier cavern, carved into the rock, its floor covered by a threadbare rug in the centre, various faded cushions around it. Dark, stripy drapes hung on the walls and passageways disappeared into the rock behind. One section was divided off by a curtain fixed to the roof, a waft of smoke and oily food issuing from behind.

Salem barked something, and another woman appeared from behind the screen, brushing down her robes. She wore the same nun-blue headscarf as Salwa, but it framed a younger, sweeter face. When she lowered a hand from her mouth, she revealed a neat cleft palate, the upper lip arching into a pink marquee, tab of dry white tooth below.

Zahra introduced her as Fatiya, wife of Salem. 'Fatiya was at school with me,' Zahra said, voice echoing off the walls. 'She still speaks a bit of Spanish. *Español?*'

Fatiya grinned, then covered her mouth. '*Poquito.*'

The toddler made a dash for Spike, but Salwa stuck out an arm and caught him by the hair. He didn't cry, just sat down on the dirt floor, rubbing his matted head.

'And that's little Rami.'

Salem carried their bags into one of the tunnels. Spike had to hunch down as the temperature cooled. The tunnel curved right into a chamber lit by a brass oil lamp. Salem turned up the flame to reveal a cave of soft cushions and colourful kilim blankets. In one corner sat a broad ceramic bowl with a dented pewter jug of water. Salem said something to Zahra, then backed away like a courtier. She threw Spike an apologetic glance.

'Don't worry about it,' he said, unzipping his leather bag.

Zahra began picking up cushions and dividing them into piles. There was a fetid chill to the air, tomb-like. She ran a finger down the rocky wall, testing for moisture. 'This was where my father slept,' she said.

Spike found what he was looking for in the side pocket of his bag.

52

They sat in a circle on the mud floor of the main chamber. Light shone in through the open doorway, motes of dust spinning like planets in its beam. Spike looked down at his earthenware pot and dipped in some flatbread. The goat stew was spicy but he still regretted adding so much yogurt: it fizzed with a sour, unpasteurised rawness. Due to Ramadan, he was the only one eating – he'd tried to refuse but Zahra had insisted. Bedouin hospitality. The others watched him as he chewed, analysing the size and constitution of each mouthful.

Conversation comprised Othman talking to Zahra, who would then translate to Spike. A tune played over in Spike's head as he sipped his sage tea. 'Tea in the Sahara . . .'

'Othman wants to know what you do.'

'Tell him I'm a teacher. *Profesor*. I teach history and English in Gibraltar.'

Fatiya peered from behind the curtain to check Spike's bowl. As she seemed to be head chef, Spike had made the gift of the bag of saffron to her. Since then, she hadn't stopped staring. Salwa hissed at her unseen, and she retreated back behind the curtain.

'They want to know if you earn well as a teacher.'

'Fabulously well. Can you ask them if they both work for Dunetech?'

At the sound of the name, Othman and Salem swivelled their heads like owls.

'Dunetech?' Spike repeated, looking at each in turn.

Othman shielded his mouth and whispered something to his younger brother. They'd both removed their turbans, their cropped black hair displaying the same dainty ears as Zahra.

'They want to know where you heard about Dunetech,' she said.

'Tell them I saw it on the billboard. Is it possible to visit the site?' Spike focused on Othman as he spoke.

Zahra translated again; Spike thought he caught the word 'al-Manajah' in the reply.

'Othman says we can drive down there this afternoon.'

Spike nodded his thanks, and Othman and Salem rose to their feet, the sound immediately drawing Salwa from behind the curtain. Fatiya followed with another earthenware pot; Spike shook his head regretfully. '*No más, gracias.*'

Fatiya moved behind him, hitching up her robes as she sat. Spike glanced over at Zahra, who smiled.

'*Muy calor-o,*' Fatiya said in her faltering Spanish.

He heard a cork stopper removed, then felt a cool sensation on his forehead as Fatiya leaned forward to rub in some unguent. Despite himself, he shut his eyes in relief. When she reached the back of his neck, her fingertips began describing circles, working the fatty paste into his tanned skin as she murmured, '*Duna, duna . . .*'

In the corner of the room, Spike made out a small dark shape. The little boy, Rami, watching on in silence.

53

Salem had stayed at home so Spike and Zahra were sitting up front with Othman. As they raced along the tarmac road, Spike made out the first line of heliopods glinting in the distance, a tall white tower looming over them like a sentinel.

To the left of the road, a patch of green stood out from the hazy emptiness. Spike thought he saw tents erected amid the palm and acacia trees. Zahra was jammed against him, right thigh pressed forcibly to his; she pointed through the open passenger window and said something to which Othman grunted a reply.

'What was that?' Spike said.

'Othman says the older generation doesn't want to settle in the village. They're still camping at the oasis.'

'Does the river resurface there?' Spike said.

'Yes, but it's salty.'

'How come?'

'This part of the Sahara used to be an inland sea. There's still salt in the sand and rocks. It seeps into waterholes.'

'How do you get drinking water?'

'You have to dig down deep.'

Spike saw a plume of smoke rising from the oasis. 'Did you say "al-Manajah" just then?' he asked.

Othman peered round and grinned, eyes away from the road. 'Al-Manajah,' he repeated.

'The al-Manajah are the main tribe,' Zahra said. 'In winter they roam with their livestock, then come back here in summer.'

Othman was still grinning across at Spike; fortunately the road was straight.

'Just thirty thousand Bedouin left in this part of Morocco,' Zahra said. 'Tuareg in the desert, Berbers in the mountains. We're a bit like you, clinging to your piece of rock.'

'Clinging to your sand dune.'

Another off-road vehicle was coming the other way. Spike caught a glimpse of a bearded driver with something red beside him on the passenger seat. 'Did you see that?' he said as he clambered back round.

'What?'

'That was the man from the train. And the bus.'

'Sorry?'

'You were with him in the Café des Étoiles.'

Zahra gave Spike a concerned look, as though the heat were getting to him. He shut his eyes and rubbed his forehead, still sticky with Fatiya's unguent.

Othman slowed the pickup. The lines of heliopods extended on either side of the road, twenty or so in a row, each unit five metres apart. The concrete tower above them was fifteen metres high, black cables snaking up its edges, a hollow diamond shape at the base and an upper ledge lined with similar small black cameras to those in Nadeer Ziyad's garage. In front of the tower spread an open-ended hangar. Othman parked beside it. The bonnet ticked. Othman got out and Spike followed.

As soon as Othman reached the nearest heliopod, he stuck out a sandal and slapped it down on the circular concrete base. '*Sssswww,*' he said, waving a hand. He picked up a handful of dust, which scattered at once in the breeze.

Zahra followed Spike and Othman into the hangar. A heap of orange sand was piled at one end beside an industrial cement mixer and a fleet of wheelbarrows.

'This is where they make –'

'The concrete for the bases?'

'I see you've picked up Bedouin dialect.'

'Ask him how many more units they're going to put in.'

Zahra translated, then listened to the answer. 'He doesn't know the exact number. But they start the day after Ramadan.'

'How many workers?'

She asked again. 'Hundreds. Half from the village and half on their way back from the desert. The Bedouins can work in the heat.'

Othman was beckoning to Spike to admire the cement mixer, but he went back outside. A clicking came from overhead: he looked up and saw a heliopod's mirrored panel rotating. Dust trickled down. There were more clicks as the rest of the row followed.

Spike squinted into the distance. The sand dunes blocked off the route to the foothills of the mountain range they'd crossed on the bus. 'Is there a back road that leads to the site?' he asked Zahra when she came out.

'Don't think so.'

'Could you ask?'

Zahra called back to Othman, who was marching out of the hangar, gait stiff. 'No,' she replied, 'nothing but desert between here and Algeria.'

'Can you move the sand dunes? Dynamite them?'

'They're protected by law. Anyway, the wind would blow them back.'

'Rendering your burial ground rather a valuable point of entry,' Spike said.

Othman began climbing into the pickup, clench-jawed. From behind came more clicking as the next row of heliopods followed the movement of the sun.

54

The intervening hours had not improved the goat stew. The front door was closed – the wind was getting up – and the room eye-wateringly smoky, illuminated by oil lamps which gave off waxy, aromatic fumes.

Othman had taken to staring at Spike as he spoke, using Zahra as an unacknowledged interpreter. Spike kept hearing the word '*Visa*', the 'V' pronounced as a 'W'. 'Just tell him I'll sort every-thing out,' Spike said, getting to his feet.

Salem sat up at once on his cushions. Both he and Othman followed Spike with their eyes, moustaches gleaming with oil from their hastily eaten meal. Salwa and Fatiya were on stools by the stove, bowls on their laps like air hostesses in the galley. They started in surprise, then bowed their heads.

'*Disculpe*,' Spike said.

'*De nada*,' Fatiya murmured in Spanish, hand over her pink cleft.

'It's the other way,' Zahra called from the opposite side of the curtain. Spike re-emerged and walked into the tunnel at the far end of the chamber, unlatching the back door and entering the desert night. An outhouse stood in an open yard; he navigated through the darkness, stumbling in a foxhole. Those heliopods were not doing their job yet – at least not in Zagora Zween.

The lavatory was just a drop into the earth; Spike smelled faeces disturbed as his urine spattered. He threw down a scut-tle of sawdust, then set off back for the house. The wind had started to gust, warm as a hairdryer. A nice Saharan southerly . . . Spike wondered how long it would take to reach Gibraltar and his father.

A hatchway off the corridor was ajar, light filtering from within. Spike eased it open and saw a handmade wooden crib inside, presumably containing little Rami. Propped on two nails above the crib rested a heavy-looking rifle. Spike listened for a child's breathing, then returned to the main chamber.

The crockery had been cleared and a shisha pipe lit. Spike settled back onto his cushions as Othman bubbled smoke through cloudy water. The odour was of apples and cloves; Salem inhaled, then passed the tube to Spike. It didn't taste like cannabis; didn't taste like tobacco either. Coals glowed; Spike offered some to Zahra, sensing the gaze of Othman and Salem as she accepted, sucking in and coughing.

Salwa appeared with coffee. She pursed her lips in disapproval as she gave a glass to Zahra. When the pipe came back, Spike drew in more smoke. This time when he passed it to Zahra, he wasn't sure who was watching.

The coffee was granular: pungent and strong. Salem lit some incense in a chalice lined with mother-of-pearl. Outside, the wind swept through the desert. Spike caught Zahra's eye and they both smiled.

Othman was speaking; Zahra kept her gaze on Spike. 'He wants to know what your father does.'

'Retired.'

'From?'

'Guess.'

'Teacher?'

'Correct.'

Othman spoke again.

'He wants to know –' Zahra began.

'What?'

'If your mother is respectful.'

Spike forced a smile. 'Was respectful . . . Not especially, which was one of her most endearing qualities.'

Othman started to stand, grunting at the curtain as Salwa appeared, headscarf off, black hair halfway down her back. Fatiya followed, hair also loose, a strand gripped in her cleft mouth.

Othman grabbed Spike's hand. '*Yalla ruh*,' he said, shoving it into Zahra's.

Fatiya giggled as Spike and Zahra entered the tunnel in the rock.

55

Zahra sat down on a cushion at the edge of the chamber. Spike turned up the oil lamp, catching his fisheye reflection in its tarnished amber: cheeks dark-stubbled, forehead still shiny with unguent. He sat down heavily beside her, their shoulders touching momentarily as the waxy smell of burning carbon crept through the room. One of the women had tidied away Spike's bag: his clothes were folded carefully by the wall.

'Embarrassing,' Zahra sighed.

'Don't worry about it.'

They stared ahead, chests sinking and rising in time.

'I'm sorry about your mother,' Zahra said.

Spike altered his position on the cushions.

'What happened?'

'Why do you want to know?' There was a pause. 'She killed herself.'

He sensed Zahra's gaze but refused to meet it. He knew how earnest her look would be. They always were. Lying back, he stared up at the dirty, red-draped ceiling. 'She was a musician,' he said, 'Maltese, originally. Twenty years younger than my father. They worked together at the same school in Gibraltar. After I was born, she changed to giving violin lessons at home. Bit by bit, she stopped practising altogether. She used to like a gin and tonic in the evenings; after a while she'd be drunk by lunch. One afternoon, she cancelled a lesson and took the car out. Drove off the edge of a cliff.' Spike made a sharp whistling between his teeth, indicating the sound of the wind rushing over the bonnet. 'My father always said it was an accident. Banned alcohol from the house. Bought a dog and that was the end of it.' He glanced over at Zahra, who'd drawn up her knees beneath her kaftan. 'Everybody has their tale of woe, Zahra. How about you? Where's your *mamma*?'

'Dead.'

'How?'

'Giving birth to me.'

He softened his tone. 'So it was just you and your father here?'

'It was different then. Everyone knew everyone. In the mornings we used to climb the sand dune behind the house. You can bathe in sand before it gets too hot.'

'And now your cousins have taken over the house?'

An echo came, a groan of sexual activity – Spike thought back to his room at the Continental. Zahra waited for the noise to fade. 'When my father went away, yes.'

'What do they think happened to him?'

'They don't want to know. They're both illiterate anyway.' She undid her headscarf and her inky hair came free. 'Tell me,' she said. 'How does a Gibraltar lawyer end up in Chinatown? That was a strange thing to do.'

'Blame my father.'

'The teacher?'

'Last year he was diagnosed with a rare illness. He needs special medication so I have to go to the Spanish pharmacy each month in La Línea de la Concepción.'

'La Línea de la Concepción,' Zahra repeated.

'It's a town just over the Spanish border. It's dirt poor so they hate Gibraltarians. They wake up every morning and see the Rock with all its expensive new buildings. They see a car with Gibraltar plates, they scratch it. They find a Gibraltarian alone, they shout abuse.'

'I thought Gibraltarians were basically Spanish.'

'We've been cut off from Spain for so long that there's not much Spanish blood. Italian and Portuguese, Maltese and Jewish. A bit of British, with all the soldiers who've been there.'

'Is that where you get your blue eyes?'

Spike gave her a quizzical look. 'So one evening I was taking a short cut home. A gang of Spaniards followed me. I saw one flash a switchblade and thought, Run. But they knew the streets better than me. So I walked right up to them. Offered them a cigarette. And nothing happened. People always expect you to run. So I do the opposite.'

'Luck can run out,' Zahra said. 'And we had to run, didn't we?' The grunts became more urgent. 'What do you think happened to Abdallah?' she asked after a moment.

'We'll find out when the post-mortem comes in.'

'You put a lot of faith in the Tangiers police.'

Spike turned to look at her. 'I think I found that jeep,' he said.

She propped herself up on one elbow. The oil lamp projected long, wavy shadows onto the stone walls, intermingling with Spike's own.

'It belongs to a man called Nadeer Ziyad,' he said. 'Heard of him?'

Zahra shook her head.

'Co-founder of Dunetech.'

'You think he was driving?'

'Not personally.'

'Then what. . . ?'

Spike propped himself up too. 'I've got a couple of theories.'

Their eyes met.

'The first is the obvious one. Esperanza dislikes her stepfather. You bump into her at the Sundowner Club and make her even more suspicious. She goes and talks to an ex-employee, Abdallah al-Manajah, trying to dig the dirt. Abdallah is crazy – you saw his flat. He's so thrown by this pretty girl coming to see him, he kills her then himself a few days later.'

'And the other?'

'The other is more . . . complicated.'

Their eyes locked.

'That burial site between the sand dunes,' Spike said. 'It's in a strategic position. Dunetech would have needed it to build their road. Otherwise they couldn't get in construction supplies. I don't know your father but . . . let's just say they did pay him off. That's an illegal bribe. Maybe Esperanza found out about it. Contacted Abdallah to learn more. That's why they ended up dead.'

'You think Dunetech would kill them for that?'

'They're about to sign a massive deal. They can't afford for anything to surface about the company. Especially as they're pitching themselves as such a socially responsible business.'

Zahra moistened her lower lip as she thought. 'But why go after us?'

'After you, I'm afraid. They knew you'd met Esperanza. They were worried Esperanza might have told you about the bribe.'

'How did they know I'd met Esperanza?'

'Maybe they were following her. Or they spoke to Marouane, found out about your argument. Anyway, yesterday afternoon I mention Abdallah's name to Nadeer. Three hours later, Abdallah is dead. There's a pattern emerging.'

'How about your client?'

'Solomon? He just happened to be the last person seen with Esperanza.'

'You don't think he's involved?'

'No.'

'How can you be sure?'

'I know him.'

'You're very confident about people.'

'We were at school together. Twelve years.'

'So he's your friend.'

Spike's mind drifted back. 'He used to get a hard time in the playground. I helped him once – got punched a few times, punched a few people back. After that he wouldn't leave me alone.'

A louder moan rang out, as though the two brothers were competing.

'How long will you stay here?' Spike said.

'A week or so. See if I can get any answers about Ibrahim.'

'Ibrahim?'

'My father.'

'And then?'

'Back to Tangiers to apply for another visa.'

'You've tried before?'

'Five times.'

'No luck?'

'You think they want some Bedouin girl in Europe?'

'But your English –'

'Means nothing.'

'Well, I probably ought to get back tomorrow.'

'Don't worry,' Zahra said tersely. 'I've spoken to Othman. He'll drive you to the bus stop in the morning.'

Spike reached for the oil lamp. 'Mind if I turn this down?'

'Off is better.'

Spike extinguished the flame. In the darkness he heard a swish as Zahra removed her kaftan. He caught a waft of citrus perfume, then rolled over to face the wall.

56

Spike woke after dreaming of a thunderstorm. His bladder felt taut, his lungs shrunken and dry, reminding him of why he'd given up smoking. After a minute of trying to go back to sleep, he pushed himself up, cursing under his breath.

A faint glow was coming from the tunnel; Spike used it to locate his trousers, espadrilles and a fresh white T-shirt, glancing, as he dressed, at the heap of blankets on the far side of the room. He was impressed by how silently Zahra slept, until he realised she was gone.

He walked through to the main chamber. The open doorway spread a runner of lemony light over the mud-packed ground. The stove was still smouldering as a man lay on the central cushions, arms splayed, cotton nightdress revealing hairy ankles. Spike heard a loud, moist snore: Salem, flat on his back, unmarked bottle by an outstretched hand.

Spike strode carefully past him to the corridor, catching a whiff of yeasty hooch. The back door was double-bolted; Spike turned round, poking his head through the hatch to check the peaceful shape of Rami, still sleeping in his cot.

Outside, the light was pale and washed-out, the sun concealed, the stillness of the air oppressive. Desert mornings were not as chilly as he had been led to believe. Moving to one side, he saw a plastic tub soaking last night's crockery. He unzipped his flies in a corner by a thorn bush. A cockerel crowed. Dew clung to prickly foliage. The rich orange sand dune formed a sharp contrast to the brilliant blue sky.

From the corner of his eye, he saw a tall, shawled figure emerge onto the dirt track. He zipped up. The sun rose over the top of the dune, and he saw a headscarf sparkle: Zahra. She was walking quickly, glancing occasionally behind.

Spike stepped out onto the track. Two stray dogs were lying opposite one another, touching paws, enjoying this tranquil, human-free moment. Zahra was about forty metres ahead, skirting the village along the line of the dunes. Spike thought about calling out, but didn't.

Approaching the rock face at the base of a dune, he caught the sweet-sour tang of sun-warmed rubbish: the village midden heap, carved into an indentation. A small fox with bat ears watched from amid the rubbish bags and oil drums. Hens pecked on the path. The fox followed Spike with its yellow eyes.

Zahra had passed the prefabricated houses and was climbing the rocky mound that marked the end of the village. Spike saw her glance left and right; he readied himself to raise a hand in greeting, but she disappeared down the other side.

A breeze tickled the nape of Spike's neck as he reached the top of the mound. To his right ran the wide road that led to the heliopods – Zahra was walking parallel to it over arid, featureless scrub. A hundred metres ahead of her lay the green oasis.

A single needle of light fired from the solar-power site. One became two, until an entire pincushion was gleaming back, bright as magnesium. The sun had mounted the dune behind and caught Spike up.

He descended the slope, keeping his espadrilles square-on to avoid slipping. Once on flat ground, he felt solid slabs of bedrock beneath the sand. Three-inch thorns grew between; a pale, translucent scorpion fled Spike's foot, tail curved like a cracked finger as it plunged into a bolt-hole.

Spike walked on, feeling the hot roughness rise through his rope soles as the sun teased a first bead of sweat from his brow. Zahra was fifty metres ahead now. He checked behind: the hillock he'd just climbed obscured the village, and for a moment all he could see was the crumbly orange rock and the smooth sand of the dune. This absence of human habitation caused a brief, seasick feeling before he turned back round, taking comfort in the distant tents pegged out around the oasis.

He increased his pace. The sun troubled him less as the breeze picked up. It gave a sudden blast, like a blow from bellows, prickling his neck with grit. Then the air went still.

Ahead, Zahra was almost at the oasis. She was jogging now, keen to escape the sun. Spike wondered if he should shout out; instead he looked back round to check his location.

Head turned, he stared into the distance. The sand dune behind the village appeared to have changed position. It was as though it had stepped forward from the other dunes in order to move up the line. Spike's eye muscles relaxed and he looked out more clearly. The momentary pleasure at being able to see without squinting ebbed when he realised that the sun had gone in. He glanced up at the sky. A cloud of dust was blotting it out.

He swivelled back round and started running. The shadows grew darker. 'Zahra!' he called, and saw her glance over one shoulder before the dust cloud blurred her to brown.

Visibility faded further until Spike could see no more than a metre ahead. He slowed down. Was he even going in the right direction? He tried to look around but the sand was too painful. The whistling grew shrill, like a train conductor's signal. His damp, prickly T-shirt puffed out in front; the ankles of his cargo trousers billowed as he jumped in the air and felt himself carried a metre. The smell was of hot sawdust.

He could barely see his shoes now. He shouted and felt sharp salty powder coat his throat and nose. An image flashed into his mind of the concrete bases of those heliopods: he crouched into a ball as the sand squalled on his neck and scalp. What if he were buried here? Shielding his eyes, he caught a glimpse of the dune ahead. That meant the road was in the other direction. If he could find the road, it would lead him back to the village.

He shunted back round until he was facing the opposite way. Still crouching, he placed one espadrille in front of the other and fought to make progress forward. A plastic bag flew by, inflated like a toy parachute. The noise was all around, increasing in strength like a jumbo preparing for take-off.

Heart thumping, Spike wrinkled his nose to breathe. His head felt light, but like a tightrope walker he managed to construct a forward line with his espadrilles, one step at a time. His clothes were clinging to his chest and thighs; the skin on his head felt like it was being rubbed with sandpaper.

In front stretched a perpendicular line. He half straightened up and was nearly blown over; hunching again, he shuffled forward until he felt the soft spring of tarmac beneath his feet.

Grit gouged at the corners of his eyes. Slowly he manoeuvred himself round into the direction he hoped was the village. The prickling on his face was unbearable. He turned back – better to head for the site, find shelter in the concrete hangar. If that was locked, he could use the walls as a break.

The wind was on his back now, propelling him on. After a few steps, he heard a noise. Distant and hollow, like a foghorn in the Straits. He forced his head round and saw the muffled glow of headlights. The vehicle was moving almost as slowly as he was. It drew up beside him. A white pickup.

'Hey!' Spike called, and more dust flew into his mouth.

The passenger door opened a fraction, then slammed closed. Straining against the wind, it started to reopen. Spike edged towards it, hands over ears. He looked up to see Othman hunching on the road, headscarf flailing behind him like a ship's pennant.

Othman's jaw was clenched. His arm began to rotate as though he were bowling a cricket ball. Something hard hit the top of Spike's head. The wailing of the wind grew still.

57

Spike tried to swallow but his mouth was too dry. He gave a cough and felt a salty bolus of sand scrape down the back of his throat. Breathing through his nose, he opened his eyes. His chin lolled forward; he started to raise it but felt a pain in his head, as though someone were grinding a finger down on the skull.

Blinking crust from his eyes, he stared lazily ahead. He was slumped in a chair at the edge of a room paved in concrete. He heard a voice and saw a man in a blue turban sitting cross-legged in front of him, heating something on a Campingaz stove. Othman. The hangar. The pickup truck . . . Spike snorted and felt a plug of sand pop from one nostril. What an idiot he'd been venturing out like that.

He pressed down with his feet. Nothing happened. He tried to move his arms: still nothing. A first squirt of adrenalin washed through him. 'Othman?' he managed to say, voice coming out as a croak.

He heard a sudden clatter of cooking utensils as Othman shot to his feet. Salem appeared beside him, overbite clamped shut as though he had grave news to impart.

Spike felt his head pulse as he flicked his eyes to the doorway. A woman was standing beside it: Fatiya.

'*Dónde Zahra?*' Spike mumbled.

Fatiya gave a giggle, covering her mouth with one hand. Othman called out and she came and stood in front of Spike.

'*Bisha'a,*' she said with a coy grin.

He tried to stand again but something was restricting his ankles. Looking down, he saw his feet strapped to the front two chair legs. He tried to move his hands: they were bound to the top of the back legs.

He raised his eyes to Fatiya's face. Her small white tooth rose like a tusk. Salem passed her a square of paper. Spike recognised his business card.

'*Abogado?*' Fatiya said with a smile. Lawyer.

Spike snorted again; they must have been through the wallet he'd left in his chamber.

'*Abogado, no profesor,*' Fatiya continued, as Salem passed her a larger piece of card, face as serious as a court official. '"Dunetech",' Fatiya read aloud. She held up the invitation to the Investor Roadshow. '*Abogado para Dunetech,*' she concluded.

Spike half shook his head. '*Abogado, sí,*' he groaned. '*Para Dunetech, no.*'

Fatiya translated this to Salem; he moved towards Othman, who was cross-legged again in front of the stove. In one hand Othman held a large serrated knife with a blue plastic handle. He turned the flat of the blade in the roaring flame.

Spike looked more urgently at Fatiya. He tried to move his legs but succeeded only in shuffling the chair. He strained outwards with his hands; the rope seemed less tight on his left wrist. He started to rotate the joint.

Othman called something to Fatiya, which she mangled into harsh, accented Spanish. '*Tú es abogado para Dunetech. Sí o no?*'

'*No,*' Spike said.

'*No?*'

'*No, no, no.*'

Salem hove back into view, a small wooden box in his hands. Keeping his distance, he circled Spike like a matador. A moment later Spike felt hands clasp his forehead from behind. The skin stung; he struggled but Salem's grip was too firm. The wooden box dipped before his eyes, open-sided like an insect inspection chamber without the glass.

Spike struggled again as he felt the box pressed into his mouth. Shutting his lips and teeth, he heaved in air through his nose. Salem had managed to hook Spike's forehead in the crook of his elbow, lowering his free hand to his mouth, fingers working open the lips. Spicy-tasting nails slid beneath Spike's teeth; he opened his jaw, then snapped it closed.

'*Neik!*' he heard as the box and the hand disappeared. Spike's breath rasped again as another blow hit the top of his head.

58

Spike's neck was tilted backwards. His jaw ached. He flopped down his chin, feeling drool spill from cracked lips. Fatiya was standing in front of him, still holding his business card in one hand and the Dunetech invitation in the other. Her expression now was more intrigued than amused.

When Spike tried to close his mouth, he found an object wedged between his teeth. He probed with his tongue and felt the rough grain of wood. A splinter came off and he drew his tongue back in, breathing through his nose.

The raised voice of Othman echoed from ahead. Fatiya glanced round and nodded, smile returning. '*Bisha'a,*' she said. '*Verdadero o falso. Si ambollaz, falso. Si no ambollaz, verdadero.*'

Spike couldn't speak with the box in his mouth. *Ambollaz . . .* what the hell did that mean? Steps now on the concrete floor; Othman above him, brandishing the knife.

Now Spike struggled properly, twisting his wrists back and forth, feeling the rope scrape against the cut he'd got in China-town. Kicking with both legs, he slid the chair backwards as Salem appeared at Othman's side, left hand bandaged in tissue paper, right holding a pair of cooking tongs.

Spike gave a grunt, flailing forward with his legs. For a moment he was free, but then his shoulder slammed down onto the concrete floor as the chair toppled over.

Salem yanked him back up, muttering disapproval. Spike felt queasy as the room twisted then straightened. Othman returned to the Campingaz, blade in the blue flame. Spike continued to swivel his wrists but his strength was failing.

Salem had vanished. Spike felt him make another grab at his forehead, then lose his grip on the slippery skin. He came back round to the front, kneeling as he cradled Spike's jaw from below. Now Spike could only shift his head from side to side like a fish trying to dislodge a hook.

Head cocked in concentration, Salem inched the tongs towards Spike's mouth. He tried to spit out the box, but his jaws were clamped around it. He felt the chilly metal slip through the side of the box to explore the cavity of his mouth. It nuzzled at his tongue then pinched down hard on the tip.

Slowly, Salem began to draw Spike's tongue out through the open sides of the box. Othman reappeared; Spike's eyes flitted between the two of them. The blade of the knife glowed red as Othman leaned in close, Spike trying to withdraw his tongue, but the grip of the tongs was too firm. He spat but nothing came. When he coughed, droplets of saliva crackled and slid on the fiery knife blade.

Spike closed his eyes, breathing in deeply. The image of the red-hot metal glowed beneath his eyelids like the sun. He tried to detach himself, send himself floating over the Rock, looking down at the levanter cloud, at the moat-like Straits, at his father, shuffling alone through the backstreets . . .

The scream seemed to issue from elsewhere, a bestial shriek, a stuck pig or a lamb at the point of slaughter. Spike inhaled desperately as the pain spread through his lips, his throat, the deep-set nerves of his teeth. He smelled sweet burnt flesh, then felt a wad of something soft come away as the blade was withdrawn. He sucked in his tongue, tucking it beneath his dry lower lip.

'Bisha'a,' he heard in Fatiya's giggly voice. 'Bisha'a.'

59

When Spike next opened his eyes, his tongue was throbbing in concert with his heart. He tried to close his mouth but the box was still there. Othman, Salem and Fatiya surrounded him in a circle. Salem held the tongs, stepping forward to Spike's face. Rather than suffer the sharp indignity of the metal, he lolled his tongue out through the gap in the box. It felt as fat and raw as marinated meat.

Othman and Salem both tilted their heads, staring down like a pair of fastidious dentists. '*Shouf*,' Othman said. '*Shwíya*.' They withdrew to the Campingaz.

'*Ambollaz*,' Fatiya grinned, wagging a finger. '*Falso*.'

Ambollaz . . . *ampollas*: blisters. Silence until Spike felt a tap on the shoulder.

'*Tú*,' Fatiya said. '*Por qué estás aquí?*'

Spike let his eyes close as the fingers worked out the saliva-soaked box from his mouth. His jawbone gaped, giving a sweet moment of respite before the throbbing restarted.

'*Por qué estás aquí?*'

His head dropped. Strings of white saliva hung from his mouth. *Why are you here?*

'*Duna?*'

'Mmm.'

'*Qué?*'

'No.' The word came out as a cough. He felt his jaw gripped again, fingers pinching his nose. The attempt to resist was mental only. He opened his mouth to breathe, and the box slotted back into place. The roar of the Campingaz cranked up.

The tongs again; Spike felt the heat of the blade as it hovered over his upper lip. He shut his eyes, trying to remove himself once more, when a shout came from up ahead: '*Ey!*'

The heat reduced; Spike opened his eyes and saw Zahra standing in the doorway.

'*Iryaa!*' she shouted, and everyone stopped moving. Spike had time to wonder why her arrival signalled such authority. Then he saw that she was holding in her arms the rusty hunter's rifle he'd seen hanging above Rami's crib.

'*Iryaa!*' she shouted again, advancing past the threshold.

Slowly, Othman placed the knife down on the floor. Zahra jabbed forward with the rifle and Othman, Salem and Fatiya all moved backwards.

As Zahra edged closer to Spike, Othman stepped away from the group. The rifle wavered in Zahra's hands. Then she shut her eyes and squeezed the trigger.

The kick caused the barrel to wheel up violently. There was a smack like the flick of a towel, then a deep gonging as the bullet collided with one of the wheelbarrows. Spike heard something fizz not far from his face, then a neat rustle as the bullet ricocheted into the heap of orange sand on the other side of the hangar.

Othman, Salem and Fatiya crouched down, hands on heads. Zahra yelled again, and they dropped to their knees.

She continued towards Spike. He widened his eyes in greeting. A warm stream of saliva spilled down one side of his chin.

'*Wakafy!*' she cried. A sharp smell of cordite hung in the air. She transferred the rifle to her left arm; now it pointed directly at the concrete floor. With her right hand, she reached for the box in Spike's mouth. The rough-grained wood tore at the wound on his tongue, making him twist his neck in pain. She glanced over, nostrils flaring, then gently drew the box out.

The relief was even sweeter than before. His head fell forward and more saliva spilled. Just letting his jaw hang was the most exquisite feeling. He came back to attention as Zahra made a grab for the rifle.

Othman was up on his feet. Spike saw Zahra squeezing the trigger again. 'Reload,' he tried to say, but only a tired exhalation emerged.

Othman's jaw was clenched so hard that rivets seemed to extend from its sides. His eyes were black. Two metres ahead of him lay the knife. He stepped towards it.

'Lever,' Spike grunted. 'Got to reload.'

Zahra lowered her gaze, then slid her hand up from the stock to draw back the bolt. A thin metallic chink broke the silence, like a triangle at the end of a symphony. Spike saw the empty shell come to rest by his feet. Othman saw it too and stopped moving.

Zahra bent down, eyes on Othman as she stuck out an arm for the knife. Rifle barrel scraping over concrete, she backed towards Spike, knife in her left hand. When she reached his chair, she shouted again, and Othman returned to his knees. He lowered his head, but Spike could see he was still watching.

The barrel of the rifle lay on the floor to Spike's right. He felt a shaky pressure as Zahra began sawing at the ropes binding his hands.

Now it was Salem creeping forward, head down. 'Zahra,' Spike said, hearing the clatter of the knife as she picked up the rifle and stood.

Spike swivelled his wrists, straining them apart, feeling the rope start to fray. With another twist, it gave. The same relief he'd felt in his jaw flooded through his shoulders as he moved his arms forward. He reached for the knife and cut free his ankles. His knees sagged as he got to his feet, forcing him to grip the chair back for support.

Zahra stood by his side. She yelled again and they drew back towards the open doorway. Othman and Salem both raised their heads. As soon as Zahra was at the door, she turned and started to run. Spike lumbered after.

The pickup was parked outside; Spike went to the passenger side as Zahra climbed in behind the wheel, gun pointing down between her legs.

She twisted the key; nothing happened. Othman appeared in the doorway, running towards them. This time, the engine caught and the pickup screeched away. Spike saw Othman sprinting after them in the rear-view mirror before he was lost in a cloud of dust.

Spike put a hand on Zahra's thigh. She jerked the wheel in shock, making the pickup veer right. She straightened up; Spike saw his overnight bag in the footwell below. He leaned his head back against the rest and closed his eyes.

What felt like seconds later, he lurched forward as Zahra braked. She opened her door, took out the rifle and threw it side-on into the desert. The wind had dropped. Ahead shimmered millions of acres of emptiness.

When Zahra got back in, she reached over to Spike's face.

'Water,' he said.

60

The thorns, the sand, the rocks, the dust, the bus, the gorge, the plateau, the train . . .

Spike came to in the half-light, Zahra sitting beside him on the hard mattress of the couchette, rubbing aftersun into his face, neck, ears. She reached down for a bottle of water and tipped some in his mouth. He closed his eyes, letting her rub cream into the lids. Then she lowered her head and kissed him.

She held her lips there, as though afraid to go further, before easing her tongue downwards. Spike's eyes prickled with tears: it felt like he'd just swallowed a sea anenome. He let out a muffled cry, like a scuba diver in distress. Zahra drew back.

'Not on the lips,' Spike managed to say.

She gave an involuntary snort of amusement.

'What?' Spike said. The pain made him laugh as well. Zahra whispered an apology, then kissed his cheek, gently at first, then more passionately, moving her mouth over his, pausing just long enough to see his alarmed expression, before grinning again as she dipped down to his neck.

Once the stinging in his mouth had subsided, he slid his hands beneath the light cotton of her kaftan, running his fingertips up the smooth skin of her stomach until he found the dome of a breast, feeling her hips buck as he touched a small, stiff nipple.

She stopped, sitting up so abruptly that he thought he'd pushed things too far. Swinging one knee over his waist, she straddled him, drawing her kaftan over her outstretched arms and throwing it against the couchette wall.

Spike stared up. Seeing him try to swallow, she bent down for the water bottle, sluicing it into his mouth then over her firm, dark breasts, dripping it warmly from her body to his. He reached forward, undoing his trousers and letting her sit up as he inched them down to his calves. She kissed his bare chest; he wrapped his arms around her back, fingers tracing the half-pipe of her spine. Her skin was as soft as damask. His nose filled with the scent of sweat and suncream.

She moved her face above his, smile replaced by an intense, almost angry, look. He watched her pupils dilate. 'Are you sure you're well enough?' she said.

'Definitely.'

'Do you have any. . . ?'

'In my wallet.'

She reached behind, fingers seeking the small foil square, which she tore in two to work out the shiny pink mollusc inside. With a small, backward shuffle, she hoisted him up. He felt a sharp electric tingle as she pressed the greased cap hard down.

He took her hand and then they were both rolling down the long, ridged condom. Cupping her buttocks, he brushed a thumb over the slick fold between. Breathing more quickly, she reached down and drew aside her knickers.

Spike felt the abrasive cotton edge as she eased herself up and down, head back, one hand on his ribs, the other squeezing her left, then right nipple, almond eyes half closed, long hair coiled over one shoulder. He raised his hands and eased her onto her back. He tried to relax his body, to empty his mind, but now she was grinding back into him, and then there was nothing he could do, the shivers were intensifying, throbbing in time with his tongue, pain mixing with pleasure, everything drawing to a point, like the blood on Abdallah's ceiling, like jagged violins, her moan rising at the same time as his.

The carriage, the seagulls, the hawkers, the *petit taxi*, the sound of her breathing . . . Sleep.

PART FOUR

Tangiers

61

Spike was sure he was home in Gibraltar. He heard the creak of floorboards and assumed his mother was bringing him up a mug of tea. Instead, on opening his eyes, he saw a figure crouching beside the bed. She picked up his trousers, slipping a hand into one pocket and taking out his wallet. After placing it on the dressing table, she reached for another pouch. His passport; now she was creeping towards the door.

'Zahra?' Spike groaned, his voice a full octave lower than normal. He swallowed and felt his throat scrape.

Zahra turned. 'I didn't know you were awake.'

'Mm,' Spike said.

'The receptionist called. He wants a copy of your passport. At least, I think that's what he wants.'

The door closed, leaving just the helicopter whirr of the ceiling fan above. Tentatively, Spike touched his head, feeling a double quail's egg on the crown. Two separate headaches were battling it out in his brain, jockeying for position. He sucked on his tongue: the upper half was swollen with fluid, twice as fat as the lower. The main discomfort, though, was in his throat.

The hotel bedroom at the Continental was either the same as before or of identical layout. The sheets beside him were disturbed. On the dressing table, next to his wallet, lay two mobile phones, his and Esperanza's. He crawled over the bed towards them.

Having retrieved his phone, he lay back. 8 a.m. on Thursday. *Thursday?* He'd lost a day somewhere. He could remember the sandstorm, the knife, Zahra, the rifle. But how he'd got back here he had no idea.

Two voice messages, the first from Inspector Eldrassi, asking him to come by the station, the second from Galliano, asking where the hell he was.

He could see Eldrassi today. That would free him up for the night-boat home, get him back to civilisation, out of this godforsaken country forever. He rolled out of bed and went to the bathroom, stopping as he passed the mirror. His left eye was black, the lid two-thirds closed as a purple sunset blushed through the socket. His forehead and neck were a fuchsia pink; he opened his mouth and saw pale clusters of ulcers crowding his tongue. 'Jesus Christ,' he muttered as he steered a tangerine cord of urine into the lavatory. Water droplets covered the bathtub as though someone had just showered. His stomach rumbled.

Back in the bedroom, he saw Zahra's woven handbag on the floor. Something bulky lay beside it. He stooped down; orange sand shifted from black plastic as he picked the package up. Hearing the door handle turn, he replaced it and rolled back into bed, wincing at the sudden movement.

62

Zahra passed him two veterinary-sized aspirins, which he swallowed painfully with mineral water. The shutters were closed; she sat down at the dressing table beneath them. 'Are you hungry?'

'Beginning to be very.'

'How's the tongue?'

'It only hurts when I breathe.'

She smiled for a moment, then became serious. 'It's called *Bisha'a*.'

The soft sibilants of the word transported Spike back to the hangar.

'It's an ancient Bedouin tradition. Supposed to be illegal but it's still practised in rural areas.'

'I don't see why they bothered. I'd have told them anything.'

'They call it trial by fire. They use it instead of courtrooms.'

Spike kept crackling the plastic water bottle in one hand; he put it down on the floor.

'If the defendant's tongue blisters, it means he's lying. If it doesn't, he's telling the truth. Apparently it's quite accurate. Your mouth gets dry when you lie, so . . .'

'Sounds about as effective as witch ducking.'

Zahra frowned, not understanding the term. 'Do you want me to take you to the hospital?'

'No way.'

'Well, if it's any consolation, I can never go back to my village now.'

'It's no consolation.'

'At least we're even. You rescued me in Chinatown. I rescued you in Zagora Zween.'

An uncomfortable silence passed. 'Thank you,' Spike said eventually.

Zahra undid her headscarf and shook back her still-damp hair. Something in the motion made Spike's groin stir, as though it knew something his mind didn't. 'What time did we get in?' he asked.

'About 10 a.m. You kept repeating "Hotel Continental" so we came here. You've been asleep. You had a fever.' She smiled, as though waiting for something more. He felt as though he were missing a detail. 'What were you doing,' he asked, 'in the desert?'

She lowered her eyes. 'I went to find something.'

'What?'

'A secret.'

'Abdallah's secret?'

'Yes.'

'More than just a death rattle?'

She stood and went over to the plastic-wrapped package. More sand trickled to the floor.

'So what did he say to you?' Spike asked as she brought it over.

'At first I thought he was asking for his mother.'

'But?'

She sat down on the bed. 'He was telling me to *see* his mother. To ask for what was hidden.'

'So you went to her tent by the waterhole ... Did you tell her that her son was dead?'

'She was old; I thought it best not to. She hardly had any possessions. Except this.' Zahra held up the package. 'Buried in the sand outside her tent.'

Spike stared at the layers of faded masking tape around the plastic.

'When the storm died out, I walked home,' Zahra said. 'Salwa told me Othman was angry. I saw he'd been through your stuff.

The pickup was gone and I guessed where he might have taken you.' She pressed a nail through the plastic and tore it open. Another plastic bag inside; she repeated the process, then drew out what looked like a blue hardback book.

Digging her fingers beneath the lid, she bit her lower lip, giving Spike another strangely erotic flashback. The hinge wouldn't come so she passed it over.

Spike's sunburn pulsed as he prised the case apart. Inside lay a videotape; he turned it over in his hands. Twice the size of a normal VHS, a sticker of bleached spidery Arabic on the front. 'What does it say?' Spike asked.

'*Play me.*'

The celluloid band was warped. 'Easier said than done, I suspect.'

From next door came a 20th Century Fox fanfare. Spike smiled as he climbed out of bed.

>

63

Jean-Baptiste's dreadlocks dangled over his face. He flicked them up when he saw Spike. 'Chingongo! I thought you go.'

'Change of plan.'

Jean-Baptiste peered over Spike's shoulder, widening his eyes. '*Bien évidemment, mon frère.* What happened to your face?'

'Beach football. Got out of hand.'

Zahra stepped forward. She still had her hair free. Jean-Baptiste took her hand in greeting, sucking in his small pot belly. '*Enchanté,*' he said, planting a noisy kiss on the back of her hand.

'Jean-Baptiste? Zahra.'

'*Za-rah,*' Jean-Baptiste repeated. 'She speak French?'

'*Mieux en anglais, si possible,*' Zahra replied.

Jean-Baptiste widened his eyes still further. 'She burn you up,' he whispered to Spike as he held open the door.

The room was glowing with its usual bank of monitors. 'Sorry for chaos,' Jean-Baptiste muttered, picking up a pair of Y-fronts, 'sometimes, you know, *pour la créativité . . .*' He turned down the volume, then opened the shutters. 'Now, what is it I can do for Chingongo and his . . .'

Zahra sat down on the bed and drew the tape from her kaftan. Jean-Baptiste frowned as he sat beside her. He examined the tape in his large hands.

'Can you get it to play?' Spike said.

Jean-Baptiste puffed on the celluloid band. 'Not easy like with mobile phone. Model is eight . . . maybe ten year. Where is it from?'

'Home video.'

Jean-Baptiste looked at Zahra. 'You have CCTV in your home?'

'Her father's a judge. Now can you do it?'

Zahra said something in French to which Jean-Baptiste shrugged a response. She added another comment and he laughed.

'What was that?'

'I said it had been in the sand,' Zahra explained.

'And?'

'He told me the damage was from the sun not the sand. I said in the desert you can't tell the difference. He agreed.'

'Is there anything you can do?' Spike said. 'There's money in it.'

Jean-Baptiste clicked his tongue. 'I think impossible. Maybe at the Café des Étoiles . . .'

'What time?'

'I go for usual hour. Five o'clock?'

Zahra reached back for the tape. '*Non*,' Jean-Baptiste said, lifting it away. 'You leave with me. You have the box?'

'It broke,' Spike said. As they made to leave, Jean-Baptiste went to his bedside table and took out the envelope Spike had given him. 'Maybe I talk to your contact soon,' he said. '*La vida española*, uh?'

'Catch you later, Jean-Baptiste.'

64

'Are you sure we can trust him?'

'Yes.'

'The great expert on Morocco,' Zahra muttered as she went over to the landing wall with its framed maps of Tangiers. 'Tourist bullshit,' she said. 'What was in that envelope?'

'Information.'

'What kind of information?'

'I said I could help him get to Spain.'

'You say a lot of things.' She turned away from the wall. The frankness of her glare took Spike back to the sleeper. His memories were still blurred: it was hard to know what was real. 'Look, I'm sorry,' he said, stepping towards her. 'I think I had sunstroke. On the train . . . that actually happened, didn't it?'

'I'm glad it was so memorable.' She walked past him to the hotel-room door. 'Forget it, Spike.'

The door was locked.

'Do you want to grab some breakfast?' Spike said.

'It's Ramadan.'

'Still?'

'The last day.'

'After sundown?'

'I'll be at my friend's house.'

'Which friend?'

'The one I've been staying with since you came to Chinatown.'

'The man with the red rucksack?'

'Not this again. Can I have the key?'

'Why do you need to see him?'

'For my papers.'

'Why do you need those?'

'You don't remember that either?'

He gave her the key and she went inside. As she gathered her bag, he reached out and took her hand. 'I do remember,' he whispered in her ear.

She tried to pull away but he had a hand on her hip. Leaning forward, he kissed the nape of her neck. She turned and faced him. Her lips were swollen, her breath warm. He smelled her sharp scent as she dropped the bag and slid her hands up beneath his T-shirt.

65

Zahra had two little dimples on the small of her back, one each side of her spine. Light, wavy lines traversed her skin, fading into dark treacle. On her right shoulder rose a neat oval bruise where the rifle had recoiled. 'What?' she said as she stepped into a pair of pink knickers.

'Just looking.'

Tutting as though he were a deviant, she pulled on jeans and a tank top. After crouching to her trainers, she held the black kaftan over her head and let it unfurl downwards.

'I think it's depressing.'

She moved to the dressing table beneath the window, using the cracked mirror to tie back her hair. 'What's depressing?'

'The whole covering-up thing.'

'My *foulard*?'

'Your what?'

She gestured at her sequinned headscarf, which she was positioning over her ponytail.

'All of it,' Spike said, lying back. 'The suggestion that if men actually see what you look like, they can't be answerable for their actions.'

'Coming from a man with second-degree sunburn, that sounds a bit naive.' Zahra stood and gave a rich, croaky laugh. 'I find it comforting,' she added, knotting the headscarf beneath her chin. 'I would still wear it in Europe.'

A beat passed. 'I will help you,' Spike said. 'I'll help with your visa. Act as a referee.'

'You don't have to do anything for me.'

'I want to.'

'That's not why I slept with you.'

'Of course.'

She sat down on the side of the bed. 'Show me.'

He stuck out his tongue.

'Better.'

'So I'll meet you at five at the café?'

'Or four? For the application . . .'

'OK.'

'Or five?'

'No, four's fine.'

Zahra took his hand, caressing the palm. 'Look at your long fingers. Like a musician.' She leaned in and kissed him, reaching below the covers, breathing rapidly before drawing away. 'Better not. I have enough praying to do as it is.'

She glanced back from the door and smiled. When she was gone, he slid out of bed and searched through his trousers. His passport was still missing. He checked the dressing table, then heard the bedside phone ring. 'Yes?'

'It's Nadeer. I'm down in reception. Mind if I pop up?'

66

There was a rap at the door. 'Tracked you down at last,' Nadeer said, coming in unasked as Spike stood bare-chested by the bed. 'Christ alive, what happened to your face?'

'Too much sun.'

'I thought you were going home.'

'Got held up.'

Nadeer was back in his suit, a tan leather satchel slung over one shoulder. He looked down at the floor where a 'Rock Hard' condom lay replete and exhausted.

'Have a seat,' Spike said, toeing the condom beneath the bed and sitting up against the headboard.

Nadeer took off his satchel and sat down at the dressing table. 'I was starting to get worried,' he said. 'I called your office and was told you weren't there.'

'I'm touched by your concern.'

'I wanted to check how Solomon was.' As Nadeer reached forward to open the shutters, his reflection caught in the dressing-table mirror. The crack bisected his forehead, warping his face into two distinct parts like a fairground hall of mirrors. 'So what have you been up to, buddy?' he said, sitting back in the shadow.

'Taking some downtime.'

'Here in Tangiers?'

'Yup.'

'That's odd. Because I came by the hotel on Tuesday. They told me you'd checked out.'

Nadeer nudged something along the table with a manicured nail: a hairclip. 'I passed a young lady on the stairs.'

'Oh?'

'A rather pretty young lady. Looked to me like she came from the desert. You know, we have a proverb here in Morocco: "A Bedouin took his revenge after forty years. It was said he was in a hurry." Heard that one?'

'Have you been talking to the receptionist?'

Nadeer stared across. 'Be careful you're not being played, Spike. That's all I'm saying.' He stood. 'Miss Solness was asking after you. You're quite the dark pony. Quite the dark pony.' There was a spot of orange sand on the floor; Nadeer dipped in a finger, checking the colour. Ahead in the corner lay the plastic tape box. 'What's that?' he said, straightening up.

'What's what?'

He walked over and picked up the box, gripping both sides then pressing them together.

'It was here when I checked in.'

From next door came the first notes of a movie soundtrack. Nadeer turned to the wall, then back to Spike. 'I was talking to Professor Castillo. He told me some thug from Gibraltar had been harassing him just when he was at his most fragile.'

'Riddell gave me his address.'

'I wouldn't pay too much heed to Tobes – he's just a donkey I've comfortably stabled.' There was a pause. 'I asked you to my party, Spike. We cut a deal, I seem to remember. It involved you going home to help delay a trial. Call me old-fashioned, but I don't see much evidence of you fulfilling your side of the bargain.'

'Maybe I prefer the long goodbye.'

'There's a ferry to Gibraltar this afternoon. I'd really hate to see all the good work you've done for Solomon go to waste.' He threw the tape box onto the bed, then picked up his satchel and left.

67

'The whole world united cannot harm you as much as you yourself can.'

'Have you got my passport?'

The receptionist opened a drawer and handed it over. 'Shall I
put you down for another night?'

'Why not?'

'May your God go with you, friend.'

'And also with you.'

Spike stepped out into the late Tangiers morning, face immediately throbbing in the heat. Sunscreen and refreshment, his two
main priorities. He passed the guard hut then came out onto the
street. A man was waiting with his back to the whitewashed wall
that ran around the hotel. He was squeezing a squash ball in one
hand.

'I hear you're catching the 3 p.m.,' Riddell said.

'You working on commission now?'

'Comm-iss-ion,' Riddell repeated, aping Spike's accent. 'Is
it Spike or Spick, by the way? I never could tell.' He detached
himself from the wall and followed Spike up a narrow lane at the
edge of the Medina. 'Saw your lady friend back at the hotel,' he
called out.

'Always the voyeur, Riddell.'

'How much she set you back?'

Spike stopped. 'What did you say?'

'Your Bedouin whore. I hear they fuck like bitches in season.
Arseholes even wider than their –'

Spike slammed Riddell back against the wall, one hand on each shoulder. His balding sandy head knocked against the stucco. He looked shocked for a moment, then grinned his stained teeth. With a double sweep of the arms, he pushed Spike's wrists away, using the heel of his hand to jab at the lower part of Spike's stomach. Spike felt his lips open as a pocket of air puffed between them. He tried to breathe in but nothing happened. Riddell kicked his feet away and he fell to his knees. Riddell kicked him again; he slumped to his side.

Men in djellabas bustled by, eyes carefully averted. 'You Gibbos are all the same,' Riddell said as he stood over Spike. 'Piggyback on the garrison for three centuries, then on the banks once the garrison's gone. Inbred camp followers. Leeches.' Spike felt something warm spatter his cheek.

'Now run along and catch your boat, little Gibbo, and go get your kike out of jail.' He walked away, leather soles ticking on the cobbles.

There was spittle on Spike's left cheek. He wiped it off and staggered to his feet, leaning against the wall until he got his breath back.

68

'A mere two days late,' Inspector Hakim Eldrassi said as he stood up from his desk. 'Ouch. I hope that barman didn't catch up with you.'

'May I?' Spike said as he sat down.

Hakim cleared the clutter from his desk, then pushed a sheet of paper towards Spike. 'The translation on the top is my own.'

Spike scanned through. 'Suicide?'

'I was a little surprised myself,' Hakim said, screwing a cigarette between his lips. 'Especially as handwriting samples suggested Mr al-Manajah was left-handed and the knife was found in his right. But there you have it. He was a Bedouin. They go a bit crazy when they leave the desert. Hence all the . . .' Hakim waved his cigarette over the room; seeing the state of his own furniture, he drew it back to his mouth.

Spike read the rest of the statement. 'And the Arabic corresponds to the English?'

'No doubt you will extricate yourself on a technicality if there are any problems.'

Spike signed, then handed it back. 'Any chance of a copy?'

'In . . . theory.' Hakim turned to lift two styrofoam cups from the antique photocopier. 'I'll telephone the port authorities and have your name removed from the list,' he said. 'You should be pleased. Passage home. Trial in Gibraltar. No extradition for your client.' He dropped the blurred copy onto Spike's lap.

'So what happens now?'

'I celebrate the Eid ul-Fitr with my wife and daughters,' Hakim replied as he sat down. 'Watch the fireworks. Come back on Monday to deal with a tourist mugging.' He turned up the corner of a piece of paper. 'Round up a few of the more persistent *sans-papiers*.' He turned up another. 'It's most odd. All the big crimes seem to have disappeared.'

'Have you heard of a man called Nadeer Ziyad?'

Hakim grinned through his fug of smoke. 'Do you remember the advice I gave you when we first met?'

'Remind me.'

'There's a catamaran to Gibraltar at 3 p.m.' Hakim reached into the bin for a scrap of paper. 'I'll need to liaise with your friend, Sergeant Navarro,' he said. 'The Hassan file will have to be conveyed to Gibraltar. This is my mobile number. Tell her to call me.'

Hakim clipped the scrap of paper to the photocopied statement. Spike read it as he came out onto the street. Beneath the digits were the words 'CATCH THAT BOAT'.

69

A bandstand and bunting-clad Bedouin tent were being erected on the beach below the police station. Spike walked away up the coast road, pausing as a lorry rumbled by, its rear compartment stacked with crates of wide-eyed lambs. He passed a travel agent on the Place de la Marche Verte, where a poster advertised twice-weekly ferries from Genoa to Tangiers. He wondered how things might have turned out had his forebears made that journey across the Mediterranean instead of to Gibraltar.

As he climbed the winding alleys of the Medina, the hawkers recognised him, steering their approaches elsewhere. '*Uzbek*,' one of them said. '*Ma ka'in mushkil.*'

There was a charge in the air, the streets even busier than usual, shopkeepers swabbing foamy terraces, trailer mopeds making deliveries. Spike took out his phone; Galliano picked up at once. 'Spike! *Cacarruca.* Where have you –'

'Out of reception.'

'Are you home?'

'Almost.'

'All OK?'

Ahead, a man with a lank ponytail was queuing at a butcher's shop. His flaccid double chin quivered as he haggled over price . . . Spike wheeled into a back alley.

'Spike?'

'Did Nadeer Ziyad call the office?'

'Don't think so.'

'Didn't leave a message?'

'Not that I know of. Listen, Spike, I've been looking into Dunetech. I even winkled some info out of Napier. It's not millions we're talking about. It's billions.'

'Dirhams?'

'Euros.'

'How many?'

'A brace, and that's just the first round of investment.'

Threads of silk wound down the alleyway, taut against the tiled walls; Spike followed them until they disappeared through the doorway of a fabric shop.

'How's the fund structured?'

'From what I could tell this is Nadeer's chance to persuade Daddy he can run the show on his own. I went down to Companies House, and you're right, the holding vehicle is registered in Gib. Forty-nine per cent held by third-party outside investors. Thirty per cent by the Ziyad Family Settlement – that's Nadeer and his old man. Ten per cent by Ángel Castillo. Six in a charitable trust called the Ziyad Foundation. And the remaining five has been siphoned into a separate vehicle called "Interzone Holdings".'

'Who's behind Interzone Holdings?'

'Couldn't penetrate it. Senior management, perhaps.'

'Or the governor of Tangiers. Any mention of Toby Riddell?'

'Checked Google, Lexis. Nothing.'

Spike jumped at a whip-crack: a woman emptying a bucket.

'Spike?'

'Yes.'

'I think you should come home.'

'You're in good company. Did you check on my dad?'

'Alive and well. Bit bolshie.'

'Taking his medication?'

'So he says. Look, Spike, you've done what you set out to do. There's talk of getting Solomon bail.'

'I'll give you a call when my boat gets in.'

From the terrace of the Café Central, Spike watched as a chef took receipt of a lamb and led it bleating by a string through the kitchen back door. The Petit Socco hummed and bustled, shoeshine boys doing a brisk trade, elderly fish seller completing a sale. Spike turned up his iPod.

The last caprice, No. 24 in A minor. Spike listened to the crazed pizzicato, thinking about how Paganini's sun had started to set from this point on. His life as a travelling virtuoso had taken him to Paris, where he'd poured his earnings into setting up the Casino Paganini. The venture had been such a disaster that he'd had to auction off his musical instruments to pay the debts. With failing health he'd returned south, refusing the last rites of a priest and dying alone aged fifty-seven, spindly arms draped over his last remaining violin, before being buried – toothless and emaciated – in unconsecrated ground.

Spike checked the time, wondering what aphorism the receptionist might have for this career arc. The boat for Gibraltar left in an hour. He didn't even have Zahra's phone number. Another girl cut adrift.

He switched off the music; the bustle of the Petit Socco refilled his ears. After paying up, he set off towards the Kasbah.

The maid jabbed upwards with her broom as Spike climbed the spiral staircase. When he reached the door, he slid the small brass key out of the lock. The sun dazzled his eyes as he stepped out onto the terrace. Closing the door, he locked it and slipped the key into his pocket.

The hot tub burbled, murkier than before, a decomposing lump bobbing in the surface scum. Ángel Castillo was slumped in the same wooden chair.

'*Profesor Castillo?*' Spike called out.

Ángel's polo shirt was streaked with sweat and whisky. His beard had grown thicker and his deeply tanned cheeks drooped beneath the rose-coloured blotches under his eyes. At his feet lay a half-empty bottle of J&B and a round cardboard box of Moroccan sweets and pastries.

Spike touched his shoulder and he gave a groan. He shook him and there was a sudden intake of breath, followed by a hacking clearance of the throat. Then he smacked his lips and lowered his head again.

Spike slapped him hard across the chops; this time his head shot upright, bloodshot eyes blinking as they took in Spike's backlit presence.

'Aren't you going to offer me a drink?' Spike said.

A smile spread across his cracked lips. For a moment Spike saw he must once have been very handsome. 'It got to you too,' he said.

'What did?'

'This city. It got to you in the end.'

Spike moistened his blistered tongue. 'I suppose it did.'

Ángel began to laugh; Spike picked up his glass and sloshed it full of whisky. The smile died. 'I told you not to come back, *Heebralta*.'

'Today's different. I've got the tape.'

Ángel squinted upwards.

'The tape from Zagora Zween.'

His sunburnt knuckles whitened as he clenched his glass.

'So I'll ask you one last time: who killed your stepdaughter?'

'You,' Ángel sighed, whisky dripping down his stubble. 'Me. Everyone.'

Spike took out his mobile phone. 'Just one call,' he said, holding it up. 'One call and the tape goes to the police in Gibraltar.'

'What *tape*?'

'Abdallah al-Manajah's tape.'

Ángel clumsily put down his glass, wiping his mouth with his sleeve.

'Tell me the truth,' Spike said, 'and you get the tape. Lie, and I make the call.' He stepped forward. 'You raped her, didn't you? You raped your own stepdaughter, then murdered her.'

Ángel made a sideways chop with one hand, sweeping the tumbler off the table where it skidded unbroken into the hot tub. He made a grab for the whisky bottle but Spike got to him in time, digging a forearm beneath his throat and pressing a knee into his thigh. He spoke quietly: 'When I send that tape to the police everything you've worked for will end. Your Dunetech legacy will die. No more Sun King, just a common criminal.' The hot tub came back on. 'Nod if you understand.'

Ángel's throat made a rattling like Abdallah al-Manajah's.

'Nod . . .'

Ángel nodded and Spike withdrew, hearing him gulp in air then cough it back out. He held up a hand as though asking for time; Spike walked back to the bar, returning with a fresh tumbler which he filled to the brim.

Like a priest giving communion, Spike held the whisky to Ángel's mouth. He gulped it down as easily as apple juice, then shivered his head, spitting twice onto the decking. '*Vale*,' he said. 'We went to meet the Bedouin ourselves.' He coughed. 'At Zagora Zween.'

Spike held up his mobile phone as if to remind Ángel of the threat. Feeling for the recording function on the side, he slid the button forward with a thumb. 'Who's we?'

'Me and Nadeer. And the site manager, Abdallah. We assumed he wanted more money. Drove him down to the land, told him we would only widen the road, a road that was already there. But that stupid peasant *cabrón* wouldn't listen.'

'Then?'

'We took him to the site. I showed him a heliopod, explained how much larger the power field could become if only we had the proper access. But still he refused. We had the cash ready, thousands in US dollars. When I opened the briefcase, he shoved it back in my face. Cut my lip. Banknotes everywhere, blowing in the wind. He slipped, hit his head on the base of one of the units. At first we thought he'd just knocked himself out, but then I saw the blood.' Ángel's hands were steady enough now for him to feed himself.

'Go on,' Spike said.

'We panicked. This was Ibrahim al-Mahmoud, the Bedouin elder. The leader of his people. Abdallah told us he knew where the concrete was still wet. We threw the body into the foundations of the hangar, waited until it sank. Abdallah gathered up most of the cash. We told him he could have it if he kept quiet. Then we drove back to Tangiers.'

'But he didn't keep quiet.'

'There was a video – CCTV from the storage tower. Abdallah said he wanted a monthly stipend or he would take the tape to the villagers. He didn't ask for much. We paid up and that was the end of it.'

'Until now.'

Ángel grinned. 'Abdallah heard about our expansion plans. He got greedy. Came to my office; came here, we argued. Then he saw Esperanza.'

Spike paused. 'So Abdallah killed Esperanza because you wouldn't pay him more money?'

'No,' Ángel said forcefully. 'I think Abdallah told the Bedouins in the village. The relatives of Ibrahim. He told them what we had done, and they killed my stepdaughter to avenge the death of their leader. And to punish me.' Ángel poured himself another glass, eyes starting to glaze. 'So you are right, *Heebralta*. Maybe I did kill her.' He gazed through the trellising. 'They will come for me next. They are down there, waiting. I have always known it. *Los beduinos*.' The hot tub stopped bubbling, exposing a clatter from the doorway. Ángel finished his drink and lowered his head.

Spike was still on his feet, phone held out. 'I've just come back from Zagora Zween. The Bedouins couldn't give a fuck about Ibrahim's disappearance. They only want to keep their jobs. Abdallah didn't avenge himself by telling *them* what you did to Ibrahim. It was Esperanza he told. After that, Esperanza threatened to go to the police, so you cut her throat before she could.'

Ángel's neck began to sag.

'You killed your own stepdaughter, then had Abdallah killed as well.'

'No,' Ángel murmured. '*La quería.*' I loved her.

The terrace door shook. Spike switched off the record button and returned to the bar, placing the last two bottles of J&B beside Ángel's chair leg. As he unlocked the door, he found the maid huddled behind it. He passed her the key then went downstairs, Ángel still repeating in the background, '*La quería . . . la quería . . .*'

230

72

Spike strode up the rue de Belgique. He'd listened to the recording twice but all that was audible were his own questions and the steady burble of the hot tub. Too much ambient noise. He swore under his breath as he inputted a number.

'I was about to call you,' Hakim said. 'We need you to come back to the station. There's been a problem with your statement.'

'Forget my statement,' Spike said. 'I've got a body for you.'

'I'm sorry?'

'In Zagora Zween. Sunk into the concrete beneath a hangar at the Dunetech site.'

'I don't understand.'

'A Bedouin elder called Ibrahim al-Mahmoud. Killed by either Ángel Castillo or Nadeer Ziyad. They may be responsible for the murder of Esperanza too. Do you understand me?' Grilles were rattling up from shop windows. People kept staring.

'There is a witness,' Hakim resumed, 'who says she saw you and a girl enter Abdallah al-Manajah's flat. You never mentioned any girl. You told me you were alone.'

'I'm giving you the solution to a murder and you're quibbling over witness statements? If you've got all this time on your hands, why not drive down to Zagora Zween with a pickaxe and smash up some concrete?'

'Are you at the Hotel Continental, Mr Sanguinetti?'

Spike stopped. 'How did you know I wasn't on the boat?'

Silence at the other end.

'You asked me to catch the 3 p.m. boat,' Spike went on. 'Who told you I wasn't on it?'

'Where are you, please, Mr Sanguinetti?'

Spike switched off his phone and continued up the rue de Belgique, hearing the distant wail of a police siren as he neared the Café des Étoiles.

73

The café was empty save for the same white-haired barman wash-ing glasses. Spike checked the time: 3.50 p.m. Zahra was due at four, Jean-Baptiste at five. He ordered a Coke and sat at a stool, looking ahead at the door through which Jean-Baptiste had disap-peared the last time they were here. Moving his drink to one of the low round tables, he waited until the barman had his back turned.

After knocking on the door, Spike heard the sound of chains being removed as a young Moroccan with severe acne appeared in the gap. Behind him, Spike sensed the familiar glow of moni-tors. '*Jean-Baptiste, por favor?*'

The boy shook his head, then closed the door. Spike looked back at the barman, who was staring at him. '*Mon ami*,' Spike called over.

The chain jangled to reveal Jean-Baptiste, tall and stern in his white prayer robes. 'We say 5 p.m., no?'

'Have you seen Zahra?'

'*Qui ça?*'

'The girl. Zahra.'

Jean-Baptiste shook his head.

'Does the tape work?'

'I do not try. Later.'

'Can you try now?'

Someone called from behind him in Arabic. 'I go,' Jean-Baptiste said. 'I find *you*, uh?'

The door closed and Spike returned to the table. Another police siren droned outside. The barman continued to stare.

Spike pressed in his solar plexus, bruised from where Riddell had hit him. It was after four . . . maybe he should just hide out here until the night boat. He drank some more Coke. His phone rang. 'Zahra?'

'It's Nadeer.'

Spike put down his bottle.

'I've heard about the videotape,' Nadeer said. 'You still there?'

'Yes.'

'It's a fake, of course, but an irritant. You have it with you?'

'What if I do?'

'I understand you and your Bedouin sweetheart have been rubbing the police up the wrong way. Something about a false witness statement? We could probably make that disappear.'

'I've got a different idea,' Spike said. 'You get Ángel Castillo to give a full confession to Esperanza's murder and I'll consider not posting the tape to Gibraltar.'

'Now you're being silly.'

'If you say so.'

'Your girlfriend's rather keen for you to bring the tape here. Isn't that right, Tobes?'

Spike heard a muffled scream in the background. 'Bullshit,' he said.

'Well, she's not with you, is she? What colour are her panties, Tobes?'

'Pink,' Spike heard shouted in the background.

'Pink,' Nadeer repeated. 'So bring the tape with you in half an hour. You remember the villa. Send the taxi away then ring the bell on the gatepost.' There was a pause. 'Half an hour, Spike. Don't make her wait.'

The line went dead. Spike felt his heart banging against his ribs like a prisoner in a cell. He stood and walked to the café entrance, glancing left and right up the street. Four thirty. His head felt dizzy; he waited for his breathing to regulate then returned inside, hammering on the back door.

Spike barged in as soon as the teenaged boy opened up. Rather than TV monitors, the glow was from laptops. The room smelled of weeks of stale perspiration.

Jean-Baptiste and a crew-cut Moroccan sat staring at a fold-up screen. Displayed was a black-and-white image of heliopods, filmed from above. Numbers ticked along the base.

Jean-Baptiste turned his slack face. 'That tape,' he said.

'Have you made a copy?'

Jean-Baptiste said something to the Moroccan, who hit a key on the computer. 'We burning DVD now,' Jean-Baptiste said.

'I need the original.'

He spoke again to his colleague. 'Is it . . . real?'

'Yes. Can I have the original?'

'Not finished.'

'I need it right away.'

'You want help, Chingongo?'

'Just the tape. The tape and a pen and paper . . .' Spike scoured the cluttered room and saw a printed sheet on a table. 'Pen, pen . . .'

The boy gave Spike a chewed biro and he wrote out the home addresses of Peter Galliano and Jessica Navarro on the back of the sheet. On the screen, the black-and-white image was forward winding. Nothing changed but the numbers at the base.

'*Beaucoup* bad shit,' Jean-Baptiste said as he ejected the tape and handed it over.

'Listen,' Spike said, 'I've got to meet someone. If I don't come back, you're to post DVD copies of the tape to Gibraltar. I've got money . . .' He laid out a two-hundred-dirham note.

'What you mean, don't come back?'

Spike moved to the door, then turned. 'The El Minzah Hotel. How good are your contacts?'

Jean-Baptiste stuck up a thumb.

'One more favour, Jean-Baptiste, and I'll buy you a first-class ticket to Madrid.'

74

Spike held down the buzzer as soon as the taxi pulled away. There was no one in the sentry box, just the same stone lions eyeballing the road. A small black CCTV camera peered down from the gatepost.

'Yes?' came a voice.

'It's Sanguinetti.'

The mechanism began to whirr, and Spike slipped at once between the gap. Cicadas pulsed in the palm trees lining the driveway. Strips of late sun shone between their trunks, heating Spike's skin as he passed through them. In his right hand, in lieu of the tape box, he held a plastic carrier bag.

The dizziness returned as he remembered Zahra's smile as she'd left the hotel room. He'd let her go, failed to protect her . . . He stopped, wiping a sleeve across his forehead. He needed to concentrate. He continued up the curved section of driveway into the turning circle.

No cars, no liveried butler to welcome him. He crunched over gravel to the gatehouse tunnel. Another CCTV camera tracked his paces.

The swimming pool glowed in the last rays of the sun. Squatting like a silver toad at its rim was the heliopod.

Spike walked up the right-hand edge of the pool. The doors to the main house began sliding apart, and Toby Riddell stepped outside, frowning at the sun, a smile on his freckled face. He wore a navy, brass-buttoned blazer and high-waisted chinos. His sandy hair was combed back, as though he were ready to go out for the evening. His black shoes glinted.

'You've got the tape then,' he called out.

Spike held up the plastic bag.

'Great,' Riddell shouted. 'Bring it over, then you can take the girl.'

Spike took a step towards the heliopod, then stopped. 'No,' he said. 'Zahra first. Then the tape.'

Riddell glanced over Spike's shoulder at the doorway which led down to the underground garage. 'Uh-uh, sunshine,' he replied. 'Other way round.'

As Spike started to turn back towards the gatehouse, he saw Riddell's right hand dip beneath his blazer. Spike would have thought that the pistol was fake, but for the long black silencer screwed to its muzzle.

'Hands nice and visible,' Riddell called out.

Spike raised the plastic bag up above his head. Riddell was coming towards him over the terrace.

'Higher. Where I can see them.'

Using his fingertips, Spike felt for the handles of the plastic bag and knotted them together. Riddell was almost at the heliopod now, skirting towards him along the edge of the pool. Spike could see his yellow teeth as he smiled, piggy eyes squinting at the sun.

Breathing out slowly, Spike transferred the plastic bag to his left hand. It dangled down. He swayed it back and forth. Then he looped it into the air so that it landed with a plop in the middle of the pool.

Riddell's smile disappeared. He steered his gaze to the pool, where the tape was floating, buoyed by the air in the bag. 'That was stupid,' he said, looking back at Spike.

'You'd better get it before it sinks,' Spike replied. 'Or you'll never know if it's genuine.'

Riddell twisted both hands, angling the pistol, as though aiming up beneath Spike's chin.

'And if it's not genuine,' Spike called out, 'then I'm the only person who can tell you where the original is.'

Riddell glanced again at the plastic bag. 'Not one fucking muscle,' he said, as he backed along the edge of the pool.

The water darkened Riddell's chinos as he splashed down the steps. The plastic bag was creeping towards the deep end, drawn by the cleaning current. Riddell was up to his waist, still pointing the pistol at Spike. His blazer tails swirled. The bag was just three metres in front. When he turned his eyes to check its position, Spike sprinted towards the heliopod and crouched down behind it.

There was no bang from the gun, just a cymbal-like reverberation as the bullet hit the side of the heliopod. A higher-pitched clang followed, as Spike crouched down lower, protected by the metal shaft. In front, he could hear Riddell thrashing about in the water, trying to get an angle for the shot.

Grimacing, Spike placed his hands on the shaft of the heliopod and shoved outwards. The current prickled his palms as though he were gripping the stem of a rose. The heliopod started to rock as the metal clanged again, right by Spike's ear. Directing all his strength into his arms, he heaved again until it tipped on its stand, landing with a heavy splash in the water.

Sharp droplets sprayed up onto Spike's face; he was teetering on the flagstone edge, hands clawing at the air, trying to switch his momentum backwards. Elbows by his ears, he held himself there, looking down and seeing Riddell frozen in the middle of the pool, plastic bag beside him, one hand still on the pistol, the other clutching back and forth, sinews on the side of his neck like ropes as his face angled upwards to the setting sun.

A crackle came from the water: the heliopod was sinking, drawing its forked tail of wires behind it. Now Riddell's entire body was convulsing. As Spike finally fell back onto the terrace, he heard Riddell give out a long falsetto scream. Then there was nothing but the rhythmic saw of cicadas and the slow, steady chug of the filtration system.

75

Spike glided like an automaton, a torso on mechanical legs. The lights were on in the gatehouse; he descended to the garage, taking the steps three at a time. Then he saw her. Sitting on a metal chair in the middle of the concrete floor, motionless, brown hessian sack over her head. 'Zahra!'

Her shoulders began to twist; he pulled off the sack and saw her eyes wide, hair lank and sweaty, electrical tape over her mouth. She kept glancing beyond him, blinking as though in warning.

'It's OK,' Spike said, 'you're safe now.' He moved behind her; her wrists and ankles were taped behind the chair.

With unsteady fingers, he set about unpeeling the tape. Her hands came free first; he knelt to her ankles and untied them too. She stood shakily and threw her arms around him. The strip of tape on her mouth had been softened by saliva; Spike eased it off and pressed his lips to hers. As they kissed, he stroked the damp hair back from her face.

Above them stretched the bank of CCTV units. One monitor showed the driveway, one the pool terrace. Spike reached up and pressed eject: a large black cassette slid out, the same make as the one he'd just thrown into the pool. He ejected the others and slung them in the hessian sack.

Zahra was still tearing off the last of the dangling strands of tape. 'They grabbed me outside the hotel,' she said, 'they wanted the tape –'

'Are you hurt?'

She shook her head. 'One of them kept touching me. I've seen him before at the Sundowner, he was –' She stopped. 'He had a gun.'

'Not any more.'

'How did . . . ?'

'Shh,' Spike said. 'We can talk later.'

He steered her up the vehicle ramp. The lever drew no response so they turned and ran up the garage stairs to the terrace.

'*Ya Allah*,' Zahra said, covering her mouth with a hand.

Riddell was floating face down in the water. His legs dangled and his wrists hung limply by his ears. On the tiled base of the pool, the heliopod lay side-on like a space-age shipwreck. The plastic bag containing the tape had caught on a mirrored petal; it flapped in the current beside the set-square shape of the pistol. Above, in the filtration system, bobbed a dark, oily squash ball.

'Let's get back to the road,' Spike said, and they turned and ran down the tunnel.

76

They pushed through the shadowy shrubs of the El Minzah gardens. A street band was playing, the music blending with the cheers of a crowd. A police siren shrieked behind; they waited until the blue flashing lights had passed, then carried on through the foliage.

Empty wooden sunloungers surrounded the hotel pool. The underwater lights were on, the sight of the shimmering water giving Spike a queasy feeling in his stomach. He blinked away a flashback of Riddell's floating body.

They continued towards the glass doors. The first two were draped by velvet; through the next two along Spike made out the same trestle tables he had seen at the Roadshow. He turned back to Zahra, who kept tightening and loosening the knot on her headscarf. 'You surviving?' he said. Taking her hand, he led her to the darkest spot by the windows. 'I've got to find Jean-Baptiste. Will you wait here?'

She sat down on a sunlounger; he leaned in and kissed her.

The first glass doors were locked. Spike tried the next, flattening his palms to the glass. The panes came apart; he glanced back at Zahra, then slipped quietly inside.

The buffet was even more lavish than before, skewers of rare lamb, samovars of mint tea, flaky Moroccan pastries, soft cloying nougat oozing with fondant. The curtains at the far end were closed. Indistinct voices came from behind.

Spike crept forward, seeking the midpoint of the curtains. Parting them with his thumbs, he peered through. Nadeer Ziyad was standing at the lectern. Among the Americans, Chinese, Japanese and Europeans in the audience, Spike saw more Moroccans than before, some in traditional dress, most in suits. The blonde bob of Regina Solness leaned towards the governor's shaven head.

'The festival of Eid ul-Fitr is a time for thanks,' Nadeer was saying, 'a time for universal gratitude. What better day, then, to . . .'

Spike widened the curtains further. The DVD trolley lay ahead in the aisle; beside it, in the same seat that Spike had taken at the Roadshow, Spike saw the lofty, proud head of Jean-Baptiste, dreadlocks tied back in a ponytail.

The screen behind Nadeer was down but it didn't look as though there were plans to use it. Two porters in fezzes flanked the door. They seemed as transfixed by Nadeer as everyone else.

'After this long period of hardship,' Nadeer continued, 'it is only natural to look forward to something bright, to a chance to make good the . . .'

A black cable snaked up the aisle towards the DVD player. Spike crouched down, feeling under the velvet until he had it in his hand. Looking again through the gap, he gave the cord a tug. There was a click of plastic on wood; he yanked again and saw Jean-Baptiste's head turn.

'A truly *global* initiative,' Nadeer was saying, 'which the rest of the world will look upon as . . .'

Jean-Baptiste stepped into the aisle and moved behind the DVD trolley. A constellation of red and green lights twinkled on the unit.

'. . . the *genuine* sense that history – Actually,' Nadeer broke off, 'we didn't book any VT for tonight, so –' The screen behind him lit up. The porters, not understanding Nadeer's English, reached for the switches by the door and turned off the lights.

'*Ama nas aghbiaa*,' Nadeer hissed in Arabic, but all eyes were on the screen now, making Nadeer himself turn.

The footage was silent. In grainy black and white, two men were arguing. Only one of their faces was visible, a tall handsome man in a turban. His indignant expression was one Spike had come to know well. The tall man raised his hands as though making an emphatic point. Suddenly his turban unravelled like a ribbon, arms falling limply by his sides as he sank to the ground out of shot, as quickly as if someone had flicked an 'off' switch. The man he had been arguing with leapt back in panic: Spike caught a glimpse of the thick salt-and-pepper hair of Ángel Castillo. A third man appeared in shot, face to the camera. His dark wavy hair was shorter but the glinting eyes and hawk's nose were unmistakable. Nadeer held a pistol with a silencer in one hand. He pointed it downwards; it kicked back and a cone of light flashed from the muzzle.

There was an intake of breath from the audience. A woman screamed. Nadeer looked round from the screen. 'I don't know what kind of prank this –'

The sequence restarted: Jean-Baptiste had edited it into a loop. A murmur rose as the turbaned man fell again from shot. 'This is outrageous . . .' Nadeer said as he stepped down from the lectern. He shouted in Arabic, then began striding down the aisle towards Jean-Baptiste.

The *danse macabre* was on its third showing; Spike heard a low sobbing from behind. He spun round to see Zahra watching the screen from over his shoulder.

Nadeer was running now towards the DVD unit as Jean-Baptiste backed up the aisle.

'*Oho*,' Spike heard behind. '*Oho, oho . . .*'

Most of the audience were on their feet. Heads turned as Zahra lurched for the gap between the curtains, flailing her arms at Nadeer, who stopped now, staring at her, face transformed for a

243

moment into the small, scared boy Spike had seen captured in a school photograph.

The DVD was still playing as Jean-Baptiste came marching through the curtains and helped Spike drag Zahra, shrieking and clawing, back through the glass doors.

77

They sat together in the darkness beneath the Medina walls. 'I've just spoken to my friend,' Spike said to Jean-Baptiste. 'He'll get you into Spain by tomorrow night. From then on, you're on your own.'

Spike turned to Zahra. Her arms were clasped around her knees, forehead leaning against them. Her shoulders shook. 'Zahra?'

She looked up, eyes brimming.

'We should get going. The man said we have to be there in half an hour.'

Zahra swallowed then gave a weak nod.

The three of them looked up as a firework exploded above, fired from the festival celebration on the beach, arcs of red glittering streamers embracing the night sky. Spike got to his feet, Jean-Baptiste following.

Zahra was still sitting; Spike reached down and took her hand. She stood, then hugged him, closing her eyes as the unshed tears spilled. 'Feels like my heart has been cut out,' she whispered.

'It's better to know,' Spike said.

Another volley of fireworks; Spike held Zahra's hand as they set off up the coast road. A few metres on, Spike turned. Jean-Baptiste was still standing beneath the walls of the Medina, chin raised defiantly to the burning sky. 'What can I say?' he called out. 'I must like this city.'

Spike smiled and continued hand in hand with Zahra towards the port.

PART FIVE

Gibraltar

78

Spike threw open the French windows. It was a fine day outside, a few wisps of cloud, not too much wind. A new collection of Paganini's chamber music was playing on the iPod dock. Spike detected the gentle, fast-fading notes of a mandolin beneath the violin and bassoon. Altogether a more charming tone than the caprices. He wondered if he shouldn't take a trip to Italy when the weather cooled, see if he couldn't find the run-down quarter of Genoa that had produced this strange, lugubrious man.

The tax books were up on the shelf; open on Spike's desk were Blackstone's *Criminal Statutes* and a copy of the Immigration, Asylum and Refugee Act, the latter coffee-stained with scrutiny.

After switching off the music, and enjoying a brief but necessary burst of the ceiling fan, Spike put on his suit jacket and stuck his head into the adjacent office. 'Making any sense?'

Galliano looked up. He'd trimmed his goatee into a pointy, Lenin-style prong. A pudgy arm was bent protectively around the documents on his desk. 'I'll let you have a butcher's once I'm done.'

Loose sheets of paper littered the floor; billowing from his picture rail was a large white dress shirt. 'See you at the party later?' Spike said.

'*En plan* nice.'

Spike strolled up Main Street towards the Moorish Castle. Two police vans were parked outside; he buzzed himself in and approached the front desk.

'You can't seem to keep away these days,' Alan Gaggero said, looking up from his crossword.

'Got a secret crush on you, Alan.'

'I'll ask Ida to take you down. I-*da*! Long queues today at the border, they tell me.'

'That's the Spanish for you, Alan. *Slopis* and *chiteros* all.'

The stout form of Ida Milby-Low materialised to escort Spike past the scanner and into the dank, lower reaches of the castle.

79

Spike stood beneath the CCTV camera and planted a flake of tissue on the lens. He stepped away from the wall just as the door opened. 'Quarter of an hour do you?' asked Ida.

'Better make it half.'

'*Vale vishi.*'

The moment the bolt closed, Spike pulled the detainee towards him. They kissed for a full minute, each holding the other close. Spike heard Arabic words rustle in his ear like palm fronds in the levanter.

'What does that mean?' he asked as he sat down at the table.

'I'll give you a full demonstration once I'm out of here,' Zahra replied.

Spike bent down to remove a stack of papers from his briefcase. 'The good news is we've been able to fast-track your application,' he said. 'The hearing's set for Wednesday. I just need you to initial this.'

Zahra took the pen then signed.

'Aren't you going to read it first?'

'I trust you.'

Spike reached over and turned the page. 'We're going for "Asylum from Persecution". Given the latest events in Tangiers, I can't see there being a problem.'

Zahra initialled the other document, then sat back, slim arms folded across her kaftan. Her face was drawn but her eyes were bright. 'Tell me,' she said.

She knew the first part already. After the unexpected screening at the El Minzah Hotel, all foreign investors had withdrawn from the Dunetech deal. In an investigation led personally by the governor of

Tangiers, the hangar at the Dunetech site had been dug up and the concrete-embalmed body of Ibrahim al-Mahmoud discovered. Nadeer Ziyad had been arrested on suspicion of murder and his alibi for the night of the death of Esperanza Castillo re-examined – he had indeed been in Rabat, yet flight records revealed he had returned by helicopter and could therefore have been back in Tangiers by late afternoon. Solomon Hassan had since been released, all charges dropped.

'Now they're reinvestigating Abdallah's death too,' Spike said. 'Basically, whatever the Moroccan authorities can throw at Nadeer, they will. A modern-day Icarus, my father keeps saying. Anything to keep soaring higher.'

'He's a coward and a murderer. And Ángel Castillo?'

Spike reached for his briefcase and took out a Moroccan newspaper. 'Jumped off his roof last week. Landed on a shack made of shopping trolleys.'

'And you think this will help my application?'

'Nadeer still has a lot of influence in Morocco. Two Bedouins dead. Not safe for you to go back.'

Zahra shut her eyes. 'They buried my father yesterday. In the sacred place. I spoke to Othman on the phone.'

The sound of that name caused Spike's tongue to throb. He put the documents back in his briefcase.

'How about the other man?' Zahra said.

'What other man?'

'In the swimming pool.'

'Oh, him,' Spike said. 'Inspector Eldrassi concluded he must have accidentally brushed against the heliopod, received an electric shock, and ended up pushing it and himself into the water. Funny that, as it was almost impossible to tip over.'

Zahra gave Spike an ironic look. 'How about the gun?'

'Oddly enough, that didn't seem to come up.'

A heavy steel clank cut the air.

'Two more days,' Spike said, making a 'V' for victory. 'Just two more.'

80

Spike, Rufus and General Ironside walked side by side beneath Southport Gate, where the faded coat of arms of Charles V of Spain still showed on the pink stucco. Rufus's short-sleeved shirt revealed scrawny, liver-spotted wrists. A canvas tote bag was hooked over one shoulder, which he had refused to let Spike carry.

Spike encouraged General Ironside's lead away from a lamp post. As they passed the entrance to the Trafalgar Cemetery, Spike glanced in at the neat gravestones, thinking of the disordered chanting of the Marshan. A Coke can had been jammed on one of the spikes of the metal railings, like some dire medieval warning to soft-drink fans.

'And you think Margo Hassan will be there?' Rufus said.

'She wouldn't miss it.'

'Good-oh,' said Rufus, brushing back his mane of silver hair, 'there's one waiting.'

They crossed the forecourt to the ticket hut. Spike took out a ten-pound note but the pretty salesgirl shook her head. 'You with the Hassan party?'

'That's right.'

'All taken care of. *Pish pine.*'

Rufus batted away Spike's hand as he tried to help him into the cable car. By degrees, Rufus rocked himself inside before lowering himself painfully down onto the furthest bench. Spike gathered the General in his arms and climbed in too. The cogs began to crunch as the car soared into the void.

Spike stared out. The unadorned facade of the Great Synagogue appeared to the right, the first to be built on the Iberian peninsula after Spain had expelled the Sephardic Jews in the fifteenth century. A Hindu temple stood alongside, while on the far left rose the mosque and minaret of Europa Point, with the Catholic and Anglican cathedrals emerging slowly into view in front.

'Had a letter from Malta this morning,' Rufus said.

Spike looked round. Rufus's narrow, sockless ankles were exposed where his trousers had ridden up. 'From your uncle and aunt. They want us to come over in May.'

'Why the sudden olive branch?'

'It would have been your mother's sixtieth birthday.' Rufus turned and gazed out as another no-frills jumbo banked round to land on Gib's tiny, aircraft-carrier-sized runway.

'Want to go?' Spike said.

Rufus jutted a non-committal lip.

'We could stop off at Genoa. Make a holiday of it.'

'Maybe, son. Maybe.'

Spike craned his neck as they passed beneath the final pylon. The Upper Rock was closed to tourists at this hour but the cable-car terrace was swarming with people. 'Looks like he's hired out the whole place.'

'Man of means,' Rufus said, reaching down to tickle General Ironside's ribs.

81

As soon as they were up the steps, Rufus tottered away towards Margo Hassan, who broke off a conversation to kiss him hello. Over by the bar, Peter Galliano was puffing on a Silk Cut Ultra as he relayed a lengthy anecdote to two bearded men wearing yarmulkes.

A Spanish waitress passed with a tray of tumblers; Spike took two. 'Told you we'd have that drink,' he said as he gave one to Jessica Navarro.

'It doesn't count if it's free.'

They stepped out of the bar area onto the rear terrace, a semi-circular platform protruding from the flank of the Rock. The sun was setting, pinking up the water that surrounded on three sides, Mediterranean to the east, Atlantic to the west, Straits interlinking. Ahead, the thin sandy isthmus that connected Gibraltar to Spain pointed at La Línea like an accusation. In contrast to the marshy flatlands of the *campo* beyond, the Rock rose as dramatically and mysteriously as a sphinx.

'I hear she's very beautiful,' Jessica said.

'Who's that?'

'Oh, don't be coy with me, Spike Sanguinetti. Just your type, too. Ripe for the rescuing.' Above her white capri pants, Jessica wore a silver satin top that reminded Spike of Regina Solness. Her chestnut hair was loose from its bun, thick and glossy. 'Know what they're calling you at the station now?'

'Surprise me.'

'The Devil's Advocate.'

'Bit harsh.'

'One week in Tangiers and everyone ends up dead.'

Spike switched his empty glass for a full one from a passing tray.

'Prison looks like it's done him good,' Jessica said, gesturing across the terrace to where Solomon Hassan was working the crowd, clean-shaven in an oxford shirt, pressed chinos and navy docksider shoes. His pouchy cheeks had been levelled off and he seemed taller somehow, shoulders back, barrel chest out. Comb grooves remained in the slicked, dark hair and his little round spectacles had been replaced by designer tortoiseshell frames.

'You scrub up pretty well yourself,' Spike said. 'Your hair looks good down.'

Jessica gave a grimace. 'Please, Spike.'

Feeling a tap on the shoulder, Spike turned to see Margo Hassan, head bowed, palms out. 'What you've done,' she said, voice quaking, 'it's beyond . . . just *beyond* . . .'

Jessica mouthed 'I'll leave you to it' and headed back inside to the bar. Mrs Hassan thrust out both arms, drawing Spike into the same low-cut green top she'd worn in his office. Her perfume was excessive.

'He'll reward you, of course,' she said as she reached up to dab her lipstick from Spike's face. 'He told me so himself.'

'He's already paid my fees and expenses.'

'I mean personally. He'll be a rich man soon.'

'Will he?'

'Well, someone has to resurrect Dunetech. It's a good company. Millions of lives to be saved.'

'I think Solomon may be some way down the pecking order.'

Mrs Hassan looked askance. 'My Solly? I wouldn't be so sure.'

Inside, Rufus was sitting by the picture window, watercolour pad on lap, General Ironside dozing beneath his chair. He beckoned to Margo Hassan, who squeezed Spike's hand before walking over.

On the far side of the terrace, Solomon was listening to the chat of a rival lawyer. He lowered his gaze as Jessica passed him, clamping his eyes onto the tight fit of her trousers, scanning from her bare calves to her neat behind. Seeing Spike watching, he returned to his conversation.

Spike felt his face grow hot as he sipped his drink. From the corner of his eye he saw Solomon coming over. 'My friend and saviour,' Solomon said, arms cruciform, mineral water in hand.

'I hear you're off back to Tangiers,' Spike said.

Solomon lowered his hands. He had two skin-coloured plasters around the thumbnails. 'Be a shame for a few bad apples to spoil the barrel.'

'Thought you'd have had enough of that place.'

'Got a meeting with the governor. See what we can salvage from the wreckage.'

'No catamaran till Friday.'

'I chartered a Sunseeker. Wanted to return in more style than I left.'

'Leaving tonight?'

'At nine. But feel free to stay on. The bar's open late.'

Spike felt the blood start to thump in his ears like a drum.

'You OK, *picha*?' Solomon said. 'You look a little flushed.'

'Must be the punch.'

'Tequila sunrise,' Solomon corrected. 'Seemed . . . appropriate.' He raised a hand to his ear in a 'call me' gesture as a suit left the party.

'What's Interzone Holdings?'

Solomon's bull neck swivelled Spike's way.

'How much is it worth to you? Thirty million? Forty?'

Solomon's new spectacles were of a clearer glass, the large empty pupils behind them reminding Spike of something he couldn't quite place. 'Let's imagine a scenario,' Spike said quietly. 'A young man in a hurry is promised a chunk of a company that's about to become very valuable. A girl is threatening to reveal something that will compromise that value. The girl is stubborn and won't be persuaded. A man like that might take . . . desperate measures.'

Solomon shrugged. 'That man is Nadeer Ziyad.'

'What if Nadeer were just mopping up your mess?' Spike hissed. 'If Nadeer committed his crime years ago, then was forced to keep yours hidden from investors when you lashed out at Esperanza?'

Solomon stared back blankly until his face selected a smile. He threw a heavy arm over Spike's shoulder, exposing a dark oval of perspiration on his shirt. 'I know your games by now, Mr Sanguinetti,' he grinned. 'They're what make you such a formidable advocate.'

Disco music started in the bar. More tequila sunrises circulated. Spike freed himself from Solomon's grip and took out his mobile phone. 'There's still an hour till your boat goes,' he said. 'Let's get some air.'

Spike pushed through the crowd, sensing Jessica and Galliano's enquiring stares. Solomon remained behind, dead-eyed, an amused smile still playing on his lips.

82

Spike walked away from the cable-car station up the footpath that ran along the top of the Rock. The ground above was screened off by the barbed-wire fence of an MI6 listening post, one of the last remaining British military installations – a giant golf ball on a tee, rows of satellite dishes, a barred roadway leading down to a secret network of caves and tunnels inside the Rock.

A musty, damp-dog smell came from up ahead. Three grey apes were lounging in the dust, circles of bluebottles orbiting their heads. Fruit and vegetables were provided in the Apes' Den, but they were always greedy for that extra stolen snack. Spike made a lunge at them with his arms; they consented to hop lazily onto a limestone outcrop.

At the point where the music from the party had dulled to a distant throb, Spike stopped on the path. A crumbling stone platform extended outwards, with a low parapet wall protecting from the drop down the Rock, part of the eighteenth-century fortifications built to provide flanking fire on besieging Spanish troops. A thousand feet below looped the coast road; Spike recognised the spot where his mother's Sunbeam Alpine had smashed over the cliffs all those years ago. A herring gull displayed its broad, off-white wingspan in the nothingness. Beyond, the last rays of the sun bloodstained the Straits.

A noise came from behind: Spike spun round to see Solomon Hassan striding up the path. The apes watched on from their crag. The limestone of the Rock glowed a soft red.

'You intrigue me, *compa*,' Solomon called out as he joined Spike on the platform. His smile remained in place but moisture beaded his upper lip.

Spike still had his phone in his hand; he held it out and snapped a photo, hearing the camera give its ersatz click. As he checked the picture, he realised what Solomon's empty pupils reminded him of – the stained, wooden masks hanging on the walls of Ángel Castillo's house. He swivelled the screen to Solomon, now just a foot away. 'Look at yourself.'

Solomon tilted his head. Shoulder muscles rippled his sweaty shirt.

'That fat, feeble face.'

Solomon frowned, then turned to glance out to sea. Spike followed his gaze to where a sleek Sunseeker motor yacht was heading for Marina Bay, cruising effortlessly over the hidden currents.

'At the party just now,' Spike said, still holding out the photo, 'I remembered something Jessica Navarro told me. That you had a smell about you. One of life's fall guys. A born loser.'

Solomon looked back at his own image, then took a step forward, forcing Spike closer to the parapet. 'And suddenly it made sense,' Spike said, edging away from a gap in the wall. 'Nadeer hung you out to dry, didn't he? He asked you to get close to Esperanza, to persuade her not to tell the police about the Bedouin's murder. So you befriended her. Slept with her. But still she wouldn't budge. So back you went to Nadeer, explained the situation until he sweetened the deal, set up Interzone Holdings, a slice of the action if you could shut her up for good. You knew Dunetech had the police in their pocket – all you needed to do was pluck up the courage, buy a knife, then choose a discreet location. But Nadeer double-crossed you.'

Solomon looked above the handset into Spike's face, his irises swallowed up by pupils as dark and deep as tunnels. 'Nadeer behaved exactly as I thought he would,' he said. 'As did you, my friend.'

It was Spike's turn to frown. 'I don't follow.'

'Of course not, Spike. Because you're always one step ahead.'

Spike edged further along the wall. 'You mean you *knew* the police would come after you?'

'I suspected they might.'

'Then why risk killing her? I don't . . .'

Spike watched Solomon turn and glance up at the satellite dishes which crowned the peak of the Rock.

'You always knew about the videotape,' Spike said.

'Who do you think paid that fat fuck his hush money?'

'You were drip-feeding me information . . . just enough to help me to find the tape.'

'I knew you'd get there eventually. You never could resist a damsel in distress.'

'And once the tape was found,' Spike went on, 'you knew it was inevitable that the crime you committed would be pinned on Nadeer.'

'Or Castillo. Let's not forget he was in the video too. Joint enterprise murder, if my legal research is up to scratch.'

'Leaving you in full control of Dunetech.'

Solomon's thick lips formed a smirk.

'How about Toby Riddell? How could you know that –'

'Riddell would just have followed the pay cheque,' Solomon said. 'A mere foot soldier, Spike, same as you. Same as most people.' He removed a BlackBerry from the pocket of his chinos. 'It's hardly a fucking war crime, anyway,' he muttered as he twisted the cog. 'Christ. Get over it.'

With a slide of the thumb, Spike clicked off the record button on his phone and walked back up to the path. A cluster of stone-pine saplings had seeded themselves in the scrub; Spike drew their resinous, Mediterranean perfume deep into his lungs as he found play on the handset and put it to his ear. Solomon's voice returned unencumbered by ambient noise: '*You're always one step ahead . . .*'

Switching off the recording, Spike dialled Jessica Navarro's number. As he waited for her to pick up, he stared out from the Rock. The sun had finally gone and the Straits were cast in shadow. Spike looked away and continued up the path.

A NOTE ON THE AUTHOR

Thomas Mogford read Modern Languages at Oxford University and holds a Postgraduate Diploma in Law from City University, London. He works for ITV Sport as a translator and reporter on the UEFA Champions League. His short fiction has been published in *The Field* magazine, *Litro* and *Notes from the Underground*. He is married and lives in London.